THIRTEEN UNCANNY TALES

[*See page 159*

He beheld his own reflection . . . and recoiled in positive terror

THIRTEEN UNCANNY TALES

CHOSEN AND EDITED BY

ROGER LANCELYN GREEN

Between the moonlight and the fire
In winter twilights long ago,
What ghosts we raised for your desire
To make your merry blood run slow!
Andrew Lang

With colour frontispiece
and line drawings in the text by

RAY OGDEN

LONDON: J. M. DENT & SONS LTD
NEW YORK: E. P. DUTTON & CO. INC.

ROGER LANCELYN GREEN was born on 2nd November 1918 at Norwich, but has spent most of his life at Poulton-Lancelyn in Cheshire, where his ancestors have been Lords of the Manor for thirty generations. He spent most of his childhood at home, owing to ill health, but in 1937 entered Merton College, Oxford, where he took an honours degree in English Language and Literature, followed by the post-graduate degree of Bachelor of Letters, and later was Deputy Librarian of the college for five years. He has also been a professional actor, an antiquarian bookseller, a schoolmaster and a Research Fellow at Liverpool University for short periods. Since 1950 he has lived at Poulton-Lancelyn and devoted most of his time to writing.

Besides scholarly works on Andrew Lang, Lewis Carroll, A. E. W. Mason, J. M. Barrie and others, he has written many books for young readers. These include adventure stories such as 'The Theft of the Golden Cat' (1955), fairy-tale fantasies such as 'The Land of the Lord High Tiger' (1958), and romances set in Greece of the legendary period such as 'Mystery at Mycenae' (1957) and 'The Luck of Troy' (1961). But he is best known for his retelling of the old myths and legends, from 'King Arthur' (1953) and 'Robin Hood' (1956) to 'Heroes of Greece and Troy' (1960) and 'Myths of the Norsemen' (1962). He has visited Egypt once and Greece many times, and has written about them for young readers, telling of their history as well as of their legends—his own favourites being 'Old Greek Fairy Tales' (1958), his adventure story set in ancient Greece, Scandinavia and Britain 'The Land Beyond the North' (1958), 'Ancient Egypt' (1963), and 'A Book of Myths' (1965).

Made in Great Britain at the Aldine Press, Letchworth, Herts, for J. M. Dent & Sons Ltd, Aldine House, Bedford Street, London. First published in this edition 1970.

SBN: 460 05085 0

ACKNOWLEDGMENTS

The compiler and publishers are grateful to the following for permission to include copyright material:

The Bodley Head Ltd and Henry Z. Walck Inc. for 'The Book of Thoth' from *Tales of Ancient Egypt*, © Roger Lancelyn Green, 1967; the Trustees of the Estate of Sir Arthur Conan Doyle, John Murray (publishers) Ltd and Mary Yost Associates for 'The Striped Chest' from *The Conan Doyle Stories* by Sir Arthur Conan Doyle; Messrs J. M. Dent and Sons Ltd for 'A Pair of Hands' from *Old Fires and Profitable Ghosts* by Sir Arthur Quiller-Couch; John Murray (Publishers) Ltd for 'The Lights of Spencer Primmett's Eyes' from *Salted Almonds* by F. Anstey; John Farquharson Ltd for 'Man-Size in Marble' from *Grim Tales* by E. Nesbit; the Owner of the Copyright of H. G. Wells for 'The Door in the Wall' from *Collected Short Stories* by H. G. Wells; Edward Arnold (Publishers) Ltd for 'The Haunted Doll's House' from *A Warning to the Curious* by M. R. James; Geoffrey Bles (Publishers) Ltd and Harcourt, Brace & World Inc. for 'Forms of Things Unknown' from *Of Other Worlds* by C. S. Lewis, copyright © 1966 by the Executors of the estate of C. S. Lewis.

CONTENTS

ILLUSTRATIONS

COLOUR

BLACK AND WHITE

INTRODUCTION

'I WANTS to make your flesh creep!' as Joe, the Fat Boy, said to old Mrs Wardle in *Pickwick Papers*—and this is an ambition as old as story-telling.

Doubtless the cavemen told ghost stories as they sat round their fires, and certainly the primitive savages of Australia and New Zealand were telling them—and believing them—when the first explorers and traders and missionaries from the western world settled in their countries and learnt their languages.

Most of the fairy-tales began, before the invention of writing, as stories 'all true, or just as good as true' told and handed down orally from generation to generation. We do not know the age of the fairy-tales, nor can we tell when different incidents were added or various changes made. Only when stories were written down and have survived in literary form can we say anything certain about the earliest uncanny tales.

The first one in this collection is about the oldest that can be found. The ancient Egyptians seem to have accepted ghosts and other such marvels without question. Everyone was believed to have his ghostly double, or *Ka*; so it was natural to expect that occasionally a *Ka* might leave its living body for a little while and appear as a wraith, or leave the tomb in which its dead body lay awaiting the final day of judgment and return to earth as a ghost. Setna's uncanny adventures with the magic Book of Thoth exist in a manuscript written about 3000 years ago, though this may be a copy of a much older manuscript, and Setna himself is described as the son of Rameses II, who reigned from 1290 to 1224 B.C.

At about the same time the Mycenaeans, the ancestors of the ancient Greeks, were telling ghost stories and including them in the minstrels' lays and songs which Homer used as the basis of the *Iliad* and the *Odyssey* a few hundred years later, and which also supplied most of the myths and legends preserved for us in Greek and Latin literature.

Many of these old stories tell of ghosts or other uncanny creatures. It was, after all, only the ghost of Eurydice who followed Orpheus up from the Underworld, and was snatched back again when he disobeyed the command and lost her by looking behind him to see if she was following. And it was certainly the ghost of Achilles which appeared on his funeral mound after the fall of Troy and demanded that Polyxena, the Trojan princess whom he had loved when he was alive, should be sacrificed to him as his share of the spoils of Troy, so that her ghost might come to join him in the land of the dead.

Although not properly ghosts, many creatures even more uncanny haunted the world in the heroic age of ancient Greece. What could be more gruesome than the Gorgons? These three monstrous women had snakes growing out of their heads instead of hair, they had great tusks like wild boars, brazen hands and golden wings with which they flew. Anyone who looked at them was immediately turned to stone; but Perseus, by looking only at her reflection in a polished shield, managed to cut off the head of Medusa, the only one of the Gorgons who was mortal. Her sisters, Stheno and Euryale, were immortal; not only could no one kill them, but presumably, if one follows the legend to its logical conclusion as C. S. Lewis did, they would remain alive under any circumstances, even without air and in the extremes of heat and cold that they would encounter if either of them found herself outside the Earth's atmosphere.

Almost as gruesome were the Furies who pursued Orestes after he had killed his mother Clytemnestra. Indeed, in *The Eumenides*, the play by Æschylus which is based on this legend, the ghost of Clytemnestra appears on the stage to rouse the Furies, who form the Chorus, to continue in their pursuit of Orestes.

Other ghosts appeared in other Greek tragedies, such as that of her murdered son Polydorus in *Hecuba* by Euripides, and the dead King Darius in Æschylus's *Persians*. Indeed several of the ancient Greek theatres have underground passages from behind the stage to the middle of the orchestra so that a ghost could appear suddenly out of the ground.

While we usually think of ghosts appearing of their own accord —and definitely unwanted by those whom they haunt—there are many old tales of how they were called up from the Land of the Dead, as Odysseus summoned many famous heroes and heroines when he 'came to the limits of the world, to the deep-flowing Oceanus' and made a sacrifice of the blood of sheep on the waste shore in the groves of Persephone, as Circe the Witch had instructed him.

Odysseus called up the dead, and in particular the blind Theban seer Tiresias, to learn of the future; and for the same reason Saul, King of Israel, sought the Witch of Endor who brought before him the ghost of the Prophet Samuel—'an old man cometh up, and he is covered with a mantle. . . . And Samuel said to Saul: "Why hast thou disquieted me, to bring me up?" And Saul answered: "I am sore distressed, for the Philistines make war against me . . . therefore I have called thee, that thou mayest make known unto me what I shall do."'

In Scandinavian mythology also we find Odin, the King of the gods of Asgard, calling out of her grave the ghost of the dead witch Volva to learn the doom that was hanging over his beloved son Baldur the Beautiful: 'He sang there spells of the dead to dead Volva; needs must she rise, a ghost, and answer.' But in another Scandinavian story the ghostly Glam comes to haunt an Icelandic homestead, and has to be laid by the hero Grettir the Strong—just as in our own Anglo-Saxon epic Beowulf fights with the Mere-dwellers, Grendel and Grendel's mother, though these are evil monsters 'of the kin of Cain' and not ghosts.

On a much lighter note the Greek writer Lucian about A.D. 150 collected a number of ghost stories and tales of magic and enchantment which Tychiades the Doubter chances to hear at a gathering where such tales are being told—rather as at the house party in Andrew Lang's 'House of Strange Stories'.

The tales which Tychiades found so impossible to believe included several about charms and cures and oracles which I have left out. One of the three which I have retold, that of the haunted house in Corinth, is rather like another story told about fifty years earlier in a letter from the Roman author Pliny about a haunted house in Athens:

'There was a house at Athens large and capacious, but forsaken and of a very ill name. In the depth of night, a noise was heard in it, and if you listened closer the rattling of chains, first at a distance, then very near you. Presently appeared a spectre in the shape of an old man, worn out with age, meagre, and dejected, with a long beard and bristled hair; he wore fetters on his legs and chains on his hands, and shook them. On this, the inhabitants of the house passed several uneasy and melancholy nights; want of sleep brought a distemper upon them, and this, redoubling their terror, was followed by death. For in the day time, though the phantasm was absent, the memory of the appearance was still before their eyes, and their past fear produced a longer.

'Upon that, the house was quitted, and left entire to the phantasm. Yet an advertisement was put upon it, for the selling or letting it, if any stranger was inclined to the bargain.

'Athenodorus the philosopher came to Athens, he read the inscription; hearing the price and suspecting the lowness of the terms, he enquires, and is informed of every circumstance, and yet takes it, indeed the more readily upon that account.

'About evening he orders a bed in the fore-part of the house, calls for his writing-tables, his pencil, and a light. He dismisses all his family to the inner part of it, then he applies himself closely to writing, that his mind should not be vacant and form to itself imaginary fears and appearances. At first a profound silence reigned throughout the house as at other times; then the shaking of irons and the clink of chains began. He did not raise his eyes or lay down his pencil, but confirmed his resolution and was content only to listen.

'Then the noise increased and approached nearer, and sometimes was heard as at the entrance of the door, and sometimes within it. He looks back, sees it, and owns the shape as it was described to him. It stood still and beckoned with the finger as if it called him. He made a sign with his hand that it should stay a little and again set himself to his writing. The spectre renewed the noise of his chains and rattled them about the ears of the philosopher. He looked back, it beckoned again as before. So, without more delay, he takes up the light and follows it. It stalked along with a slow pace, as if it were over laden with the chains, turned into a court belonging to the house, and vanished.

'When he was left alone Athenodorus laid some weeds and leaves, which he pulled off for the purpose, for a mark upon the place. The next day he went to the magistrates and advised them to give an order for digging up the spot. Several bones were found in it, bound up and entangled with chains which the body, putrefied by the length of time and lying in the ground, had left behind it, bare: for the flesh had been eaten off by the irons.

'They were gathered up and buried publicly, and the house afterwards was free from the apparition, after this last duty was paid to it by a solemn interment.'

[Pliny's *Epistles*, Book VII, number xxvi. Translated by John Henley, 1724.]

This, the first and basic ghost story of its kind, I have given complete in the suitable gravity of its early eighteenth-century translation, so that all subsequent attempts to 'make your flesh creep' may be compared with it.

But of course this is not the only kind of uncanny tale—and indeed tales do not need ghosts to qualify for inclusion in the Fat Boy's repertoire—as the rest of the stories in this volume will show.

There is no ghost in 'The Bottle Imp', for example, though it is one of the most brilliantly uncomfortable tales to be found —and Stevenson was an enthusiast for what he called 'crawlers' and an expert at their construction, as readers of *Dr Jekyll and Mr Hyde* and more orthodox ghost stories such as 'The Body Snatcher' and 'Thrawn Janet' will agree.

The haunting is more traditional, though almost as exciting, in Washington Irving's 'Legend of Sleepy Hollow', and much more traditional in 'The House of Strange Stories' described by Andrew Lang, who was an expert on all the ghost stories of folk-lore and history, as he was on all the old fairy tales of the world.

Many unexpected authors tried their hand at making the flesh creep in various ways. Conan Doyle produced a whole volume of *Tales of Twilight and the Unseen* and another of *Tales of Terror and Mystery*. 'The Striped Chest' is one of the most exciting and unexpected, though not one of the most gruesome. It is certainly a story of mystery and the unseen, and when read for the first time offers excellent material for the amateur detective: 'You know my methods, Watson. Apply them!'

A yet more unexpected writer of 'crawlers' is E. Nesbit (but even Mrs Molesworth wrote two volumes of ghost stories!). Although there is none of her usual kind of magic in it, there is certainly all the suspense she knew so well how to create—and a very disturbing glimpse of the supernatural to make this perhaps the creepiest crawler in the present collection.

Quiller-Couch haunts more gently in a country cottage in his Delectable Duchy: a charming variation of Pliny's basic haunted house theme. M. R. James supplies an even more unusual haunted house, more creepy than Quiller-Couch's, though by no means as gruesome as he could be.

But, as I said before, ghosts are not necessary to make a story uncanny. There is a most unusual touch of the supernatural in 'The Door in the Wall' through which H. G. Wells managed once to wander most unexpectedly, away from his usual macabre, insect-haunted other-world and jocular fantasies.

This selection is rounded off with the humorously creepy in which F. Anstey, of *Vice Versa* fame, excelled, and the most unexpected bit of uncanniness in the book — C. S. Lewis's last 'science fiction' story.

But this is not the end—as one would expect with ghost stories. This is only the beginning for those who are not easily frightened and want to grope further into the haunted darkness of the imagination. Those brave enough may continue with Conan Doyle's more horrific tales like 'The Brown Hand' and 'The Case of Lady Sannox'; may read further among M. R. James's *Ghost Stories of an Antiquary*, and venture among the haunting horrors of Edgar Allan Poe's *Tales of Mystery and Imagination* and Kipling's 'Return of Imray', 'The End of the Passage' and 'The Mark of the Beast'.

I would like to have included some of these which were among the joys and terrors of my own early reading. Why I have not done so is best explained in the words of another Editor of stories for young readers, Andrew Lang, in the Preface to the last of his Fairy Books in 1910:

'It has been suggested to the Editor that children and parents and guardians would like "The Grey True Ghost-Story Book". He *knows* that children would like it well, and he would gladly give it to them; but about the taste of fond anxious mothers and kind aunts he is not quite so certain. Before he was twelve the Editor knew true ghost stories enough to fill a volume. They were a pure joy till bedtime, but then, and later, were not wholly a source of unmixed pleasure. At that time the Editor was not afraid of the dark, for he thought, "If a ghost *is* here, we can't see him." But when older and better informed persons said that ghosts brought their own light with them (which is only too true), then one's emotions were such as parents do not desire the young to endure. . . .' For this reason 'The Grey True Ghost-Story Book' was never edited by Andrew Lang—and 'The Thirteen Most Uncanny Tales I Know' were not included in the present volume by

ROGER LANCELYN GREEN.

Roger Lancelyn Green

THE BOOK OF THOTH

RAMESES the Great, who was Pharaoh of Egypt more than three thousand years ago, had a son called Setna, learned in all the ancient writings, and a magician of note. While the other princes spent their days in hunting or in leading their father's armies to guard the distant parts of his empire, Setna was never so happy as when left alone to study.

Not only could he read even the most ancient hieroglyphic writings on the temple walls, but he was a scribe who could write quickly and easily all the many hundreds of signs that go to the ancient Egyptian language. Also he was a magician whom none could surpass: for he had learnt his art from the most secret of the ancient writings which even the priests of the gods Amen-Ra, Ptah and Thoth could not read.

One day, as he pored over the ancient books written on the two sides of long rolls of papyrus, he came upon the story of another Pharoah's son several hundred years earlier who had been as great a scribe and as wise a magician as he—greater and wiser, indeed, for Nefrekeptah had read the Book of Thoth, by which a man might enchant both heaven and earth, and know the language of the birds and beasts.

When Setna read further that the Book of Thoth had been buried with Nefrekeptah in his royal tomb at Memphis, nothing would content him until he had found it and learnt all his wisdom.

So he sought out his brother Anherru and said to him: 'Help me to find the Book of Thoth. For without it life has no longer any meaning for me.'

'I will go with you and stand by your side through all dangers,' answered Anherru. The two brothers set out for Memphis, and it was not hard for them to find the tomb of Nefrekeptah the son of Amenhotep, the first great Pharaoh of that name, who had reigned three hundred years before their day.

When Setna had made his way into the tomb, to the central chamber where Nefrekeptah was laid to rest, he found the body of the prince lying wrapped in its linen bands, still and awful in death. But beside it on the stone sarcophagus sat two ghostly figures, the *Kas*, or doubles of a beautiful young woman and a boy—and between them, on the dead breast of Nefrepektah, lay the Book of Thoth.

Setna bowed reverently to the two ghosts, and said: 'May Osiris have you in his keeping, dead son of a dead Pharaoh, Nefrekeptah the great scribe; and you also, who ever you be, whose *Kas* sit here beside him. Know that I am Setna, the priest of Ptah, son of Rameses the Greatest Pharaoh of all—and I come for the Book of Thoth which was yours in your days on earth. I beg you to let me take it in peace—for if not, I have power to take it by force or magic.'

Then said the ghost of the woman: 'Do not take the Book of Thoth, Setna son of today's Pharaoh. It will bring you trouble even as it brought trouble upon Nefrekeptah who lies here, and upon me Ahura his wife whose body lies at Koptos on the edge of Eastern Thebes together with that of Merab our son—whose *Kas* you see before you, dwelling with the husband and father whom we loved so dearly. Listen to my tale, and beware!

'Nefrekeptah and I were the children of the Pharaoh Amenhotep and, according to the custom of Egypt, we became husband and wife, and this son Merab was born to us. Nefrekeptah cared above all things for the wisdom of the ancients and for the magic that is to be learned from all that is carved on the temple walls, and within the tombs and pyramids of long-dead kings and priests in Saqqara, the city of the dead that is all about us here on the edge of Memphis.

'One day as he was studying what is carved on the walls in one of the most ancient shrines of the gods, he heard a priest laugh mockingly and say: "All that you read there is but worthless. I could tell you where lies the Book of Thoth, which the god of wisdom wrote with his own hand. When you have read its first page you will be able to enchant the heaven and the earth, the abyss, the mountains and the sea; and you shall know what the birds and the beasts and the reptiles are saying. And when you have read the second page your eyes will behold all the secrets of the gods themselves, and read all that is hidden in the stars.''

'Then said Nefrekeptah to the priest: ''By the life of Pharaoh, tell me what you would have me do for you, and I will do it—if only you will tell me where the Book of Thoth is.'' And the priest answered: ''If you would learn where it lies, you must first give me a hundred bars of silver for my funeral, and issue orders that when I die my body shall be buried like that of a great king.'' Nefrekeptah did all that the priest asked; and when he had received the bars of silver, he said: ''The Book of Thoth lies beneath the middle of the Nile at Koptos, in an iron box. In the iron box is a box of bronze; in the bronze box is a sycamore box; in the sycamore box is an ivory and ebony box; in the ivory and ebony box is a silver box; in the silver box is a golden box—and in that lies the Book of Thoth. All around the iron box are twisted snakes and scorpions, and it is guarded by a serpent who cannot be slain.''

'Nefrekeptah was beside himself with joy. He hastened home from the shrine and told me all that had happened to him and all that he had learned. But I feared lest evil should come of it, and said to him: ''Do not go to Koptos to seek this book, for I know that it will bring great sorrow to you and to those whom you love.'' I tried in vain to hold Nefrekeptah back, but he shook me off him and went to Pharaoh, our royal father, and told him all that he had learnt from the priest.

'Then said Pharaoh: ''What is it that you desire?'' And Nefrekeptah answered: ''Bid your servants make ready the Royal Boat, for I would sail south to Koptos with Ahura my wife and our son Merab to seek this book without delay.''

'All was done as he wished, and we sailed up the Nile until we came to Koptos. And there the priests and priestesses of Isis came to welcome us and led us up to the temple of Isis and Horus.

Nefrekeptah made a great sacrifice of an ox, a goose and some wine, and we feasted with the priests and their wives in a very fine house looking out upon the river.

'But on the morning of the fifth day, leaving me and Merab to watch from the window of the house, Nefrekeptah went down to the river and made a great enchantment.

'First he created a magic cabin that was full of men and tackle. He cast a spell on it, giving life and breath to the men, and he sank the magic cabin into the river. Then he filled the Royal Boat with sand and put out into the middle of the Nile until he came to the place below which the magic cabin lay. And he spoke words of power, and cried: "Workmen, workmen, work for me even where lies the Book of Thoth!" They toiled without ceasing by day and by night, and on the third day they reached the place where the Book lay. Then Nefrekeptah cast out the sand, and they raised the Book on it until it stood upon a shoal above the level of the river.

'And behold all about the iron box, below it and above it, snakes and scorpions twined. And the serpent that could not die was twined about the box itself. Nefrekeptah cried to the snakes and scorpions a loud and terrible cry—and at his words of magic they became still, nor could one of them move.

'Then Nefrekeptah walked unharmed among the snakes and scorpions until he came to where the serpent that could not die lay curled around the box of iron. The serpent reared itself up for battle, since no charm could work on it, and Nefrekeptah drew his sword and, rushing upon it, smote off its head at a single blow. But at once the head and the body sprang together, and the serpent that could not die was whole again and ready for the fray. Once more Nefrekeptah smote off its head, and this time he cast it far away into the river. But at once the head returned to the body, and was joined to the neck, and the serpent that could not die was ready for its next battle.

'Nefrekeptah saw that the serpent that could not die could not be slain, but must be overcome by cunning. So once more he struck off its head. But before head and body could come together he put sand on each part so that when they tried to

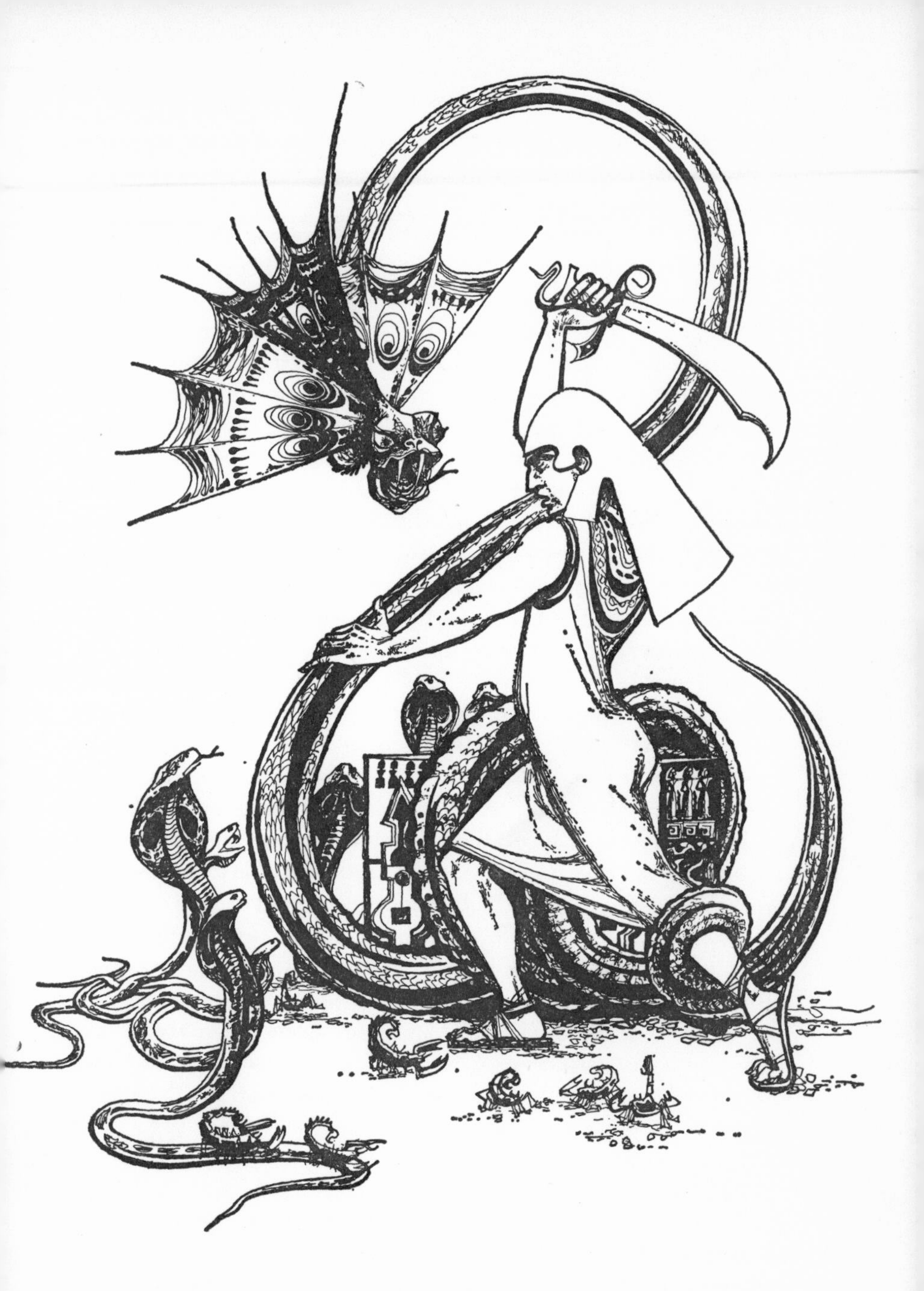

The serpent reared itself up for battle, and Nefrekeptah drew his sword . . .

join they could not do so as there was sand between them—and the serpent that could not die lay helpless in two pieces.

'Then Nefrekeptah went to where the iron box lay on the shoal in the river; and the snakes and scorpions watched him; and the head of the serpent that could not die watched him also: but none of them could harm him.

'He opened the iron box and found in it a bronze box; he opened the bronze box and found in it a box of sycamore wood; he opened that and found a box of ivory and ebony, and in that a box of silver, and at the last a box of gold. And when he had opened the golden box he found in it the Book of Thoth. He opened the Book and read the first page—and at once he had power over the heavens and the earth, the abyss, the mountains and the sea; he knew what the birds and the beasts and the fishes were saying. He read the next page of spells, and saw the sun shining in the sky, the moon and the stars, and knew their secrets—and he saw also the gods themselves who are hidden from mortal sight.

'Then, rejoicing that the priest's words had proved true, and the Book of Thoth was his, he cast a spell upon the magic men, saying: "Workmen, workmen, work for me and take me back to the place from which I came!" And they toiled day and night until they brought him back to Koptos where I sat waiting for him, taking neither food nor drink in my anxiety, but sitting stark and still like one who is gone to the grave.

'When Nefrekeptah came to me, he held out the Book of Thoth and I took it in my hands. And when I read the first page I also had power over the heavens and the earth, the abyss, the mountains and the sea; and I also knew what the birds, the beasts and the fishes were saying. And when I read the second page I saw the sun, the moon and the stars with all the gods, and knew their secrets even as he did.

'Then Nefrekeptah took a clean piece of papyrus and wrote on it all the spells from the Book of Thoth. He took a cup of beer and washed off the words into it and drank it so that the knowledge of the spells entered into his being. But I, who cannot write, do not remember all that is written in the Book of Thoth—for the spells which I had read in it were many and hard.

'After this we entered the Royal Boat and set sail for Memphis. But scarcely had we begun to move, when a sudden power seemed to seize our little boy Merab so that he was drawn into the river and sank out of sight. Seizing the Book of Thoth, Nefrekeptah read from it the necessary spell, and at once the body of Merab rose to the surface of the river and we lifted it on board. Not all the magic in the Book, nor that of any magician in Egypt, could bring Merab back to life; but nonetheless Nefrekeptah was able to make his *Ka* speak to us and tell us what had caused his death. And the *Ka* of Merab said: "Thoth the great god found that his Book had been taken, and he hastened before Amen-Ra, saying: 'Nefrekeptah, son of Pharaoh Amenhotep, has found my magic box and slain its guards and taken my Book with all the magic that is in it.' And Ra replied to him: 'Deal with Nefrekeptah and all that is his as it seems good to you: I send out my power to work sorrow and bring a punishment upon him and upon his wife and child.' And that power from Ra, passing through the will of Thoth, drew me into the river and drowned me."'

'Then we made great lamentation, for our hearts were well nigh broken at the death of Merab. We put back to shore at Koptos, and there his body was embalmed and laid in a tomb as befitted him.

'When the rites of burial and the lamentations for the dead were ended, Nefrekeptah said to me: "Let us now sail with all haste down to Memphis to tell our father the Pharaoh what has chanced. For his heart will be heavy at the death of Merab. Yet he will rejoice that I have the Book of Thoth."

'So we set sail once more in the Royal Boat. But when it came to the place where Merab had fallen into the water, the power of Ra came upon me also and I walked out of the cabin and fell into the river and was drowned. And when Nefrekeptah by his magic arts had raised my body out of the river, and my *Ka* had told him all, he turned back to Koptos and had my body embalmed and laid in the tomb beside Merab.

'Then he set out once more in bitter sorrow for Memphis.

But when it reached that city, and Pharaoh came aboard the Royal Boat, it was to find Nefrekeptah lying dead in the cabin with the Book of Thoth bound upon his breast. So there was mourning throughout all the land of Egypt, and Nefrekeptah was buried with all the rites and honours due to the son of Pharaoh in this tomb where he now lies, and where my *Ka* and the *Ka* of Merab come to watch over him.

'And now I have told you all the woe that has befallen us because we took and read the Book of Thoth—the book which you ask us to give up. It is not yours, you have no claim to it, indeed for the sake of it we gave up our lives on earth.'

When Setna had listened to all the tale told by the *Ka* of Ahura, he was filled with awe. But nevertheless the desire to have the Book of Thoth was so strong upon him that he said:

'Give me that which lies upon the dead breast of Nefrekeptah, or I will take it by force.'

Then the *Kas* of Ahura and Merab drew away as if in fear of Setna the great magician. But the *Ka* of Nefrekeptah arose from out his body and stepped towards him, saying:

'Setna, if after hearing all the tale which Ahura my wife has told you, yet you will take no warning, then the Book of Thoth must be yours. But first you must win it from me, if your skill is great enough, by playing a game of draughts with me—a game of fifty-two points. Dare you do this?'

And Setna answered: 'I am ready to play.'

So the board was set between them, and the game began. And Nefrekeptah won the first game from Setna, and put his spell upon him so that he sank into the ground to above the ankles. And when he won the second game, Setna sank to his waist in the ground. Once more they played, and when Nefrekeptah won, Setna sank in the ground until only his head was visible. But he cried out to his brother who stood outside the tomb:

'Anherru! Make haste! Run to Pharaoh and beg of him the great Amulet of Ptah, for by it only can I be saved, if you set it upon my head before the last game is played and lost.'

So Anherru sped down the steep road from Saqqara to where Pharaoh sat in his palace at Memphis. And when he heard all, he hastened into the temple of Ptah, took the great Amulet from its place in the sanctuary, and gave it to Anherru, saying:

'Go with all speed, my son, and rescue your brother Setna from this evil contest with the dead.' Back to the tomb sped Anherru, and down through the passages to the tomb-chamber where the ghost of Nefrekeptah still played at draughts with Setna. And as he entered, Setna made his last move, and Nefrekeptah reached out his hand with a cry of triumph to make the final move that should win the game and sink Setna out of sight beneath the ground for ever. But before Nefrekeptah could move the piece, Anherru leapt forward and placed the Amulet of Ptah on Setna's head. And at its touch Setna sprang out of the ground, snatched the Book of Thoth from Nefrekeptah's body and fled with Anherru from the tomb. As they went they heard the *Ka* of Ahura cry: 'Alas, all power is gone from him who lies in this tomb.' But Nefrekeptah answered: 'Be not sad: I will make Setna bring back the Book of Thoth, and come as a suppliant to my tomb with a forked stick in his hand and a fire-pan on his head.'

Then Setna and Anherru were outside, and at once the tomb closed behind them and seemed as if it had never been opened.

When Setna stood before his father the great Pharaoh and told him all that had happened, and gave him the Amulet of Ptah, Rameses said: 'My son, I counsel you to take back the Book of Thoth to the tomb of Nefrekeptah like a wise and prudent man. For otherwise be sure that he will bring sorrow and evil upon you, and at the last you will be forced to carry it back as a suppliant with a forked stick in your hand and a fire-pan on your head.'

But Setna would not listen to such advice. Instead, he returned to his own dwelling and spent all his time reading the Book of Thoth and studying all the spells contained in it. And often he would carry it into the temple of Ptah and read from it to those who sought his wisdom.

One day as he sat in a shady colonnade of the temple he saw a maiden, more beautiful than any he had ever seen, entering the temple with fifty-two girls in attendance on her. Setna gazed fascinated at this lovely creature with her golden girdle and headdress of gold and coloured jewels who knelt to make her offerings before the statue of Ptah. Soon he learnt that she was called Tabubua, and was the daughter of the high priest of the cat-goddess Bastet of the city of Bubastis to the north of Memphis —Bastet who was the bride of the god Ptah of Memphis.

As soon as Setna beheld Tabubua it seemed as if Hathor the goddess of love had cast a spell over him. He forgot all else, even the Book of Thoth, and desired only to win her. And it did not seem as if his suit would be in vain, for when he sent a message to her, she replied that if he wished to seek her he was free to do so—provided he came secretly to her palace in the desert outside Bubastis.

Setna made his way thither in haste, and found a pylon tower in a great garden with a high wall round about it. There Tabuba welcomed him with sweet words and looks, led him to her chamber in the pylon and served him with wine out of a golden cup.

When he spoke to her of his love, she answered: 'Be joyful, my sweet lord, for I am destined to be your bride. But remember that I am no common woman but the child of Bastet the beautiful —and I cannot endure a rival. So before we are wed write me a scroll of divorcement against your present wife; and write also that you give your children to me to be slain and thrown down to the cats of Bastet—for I cannot endure that they shall live and perhaps plot evil against our children.'

'Be it as you wish!' cried Setna. And straightway he took his brush and wrote that Tabubua might cast his wife out to starve and slay his children to feed the sacred cats of Bastet. And when he had done this, she handed him the cup once more and stood before him in all her loveliness, singing a bridal hymn. Presently terrible cries came floating up to the high window of the pylon— the dying cries of his children, for he recognized each voice as it called to him in agony and was then still.

But Setna drained the golden cup and turned to Tabubua, saying: 'My wife is a beggar and my children lie dead at the pylon foot. I have nothing left in the world but you—and I would give all again for you. Come to me, my love!'

Then Tabubua came towards him with outstretched arms, more lovely and desirable than Hathor herself. With a cry of ecstasy Setna caught her to him—and as he did so, on a sudden she changed and faded until his arms held a hideous, withered corpse. Setna cried aloud in terror, and as he did so the darkness swirled around him, the pylon seemed to crumble away, and when he regained his senses he found himself lying naked in the desert beside the road that led from Bubastis to Memphis.

The passers-by on the road mocked at Setna. But one kinder than the rest threw him an old cloak, and with this about him he came back to Memphis like a beggar.

When he reached his own dwelling place and found his wife and children there alive and well, he had but one thought and that was to return the Book of Thoth to Nefrekeptah.

'If Tabubua and all her sorceries were but a dream,' he exclaimed, 'they show me in what terrible danger I stand. For if such another spell is cast upon me, next time it will prove to be no dream.'

So, with the Book of Thoth in his hands, he went before Pharaoh his father and told him all that had happened. And Rameses the Great said to him: 'Setna, what I warned you of has come to pass. You would have done better to obey my wishes sooner. Nefrekeptah will certainly kill you if you do not take back the Book of Thoth to where you found it. Therefore go to the tomb as a suppliant, carrying a forked stick in your hand and a fire-pan on your head.'

Setna did as Pharaoh advised. When he came to the tomb and spoke the spell, it opened to him as before, and he went down to the tomb-chamber and found Nefrekeptah lying in his sarcophagus with the *Kas* of Ahura and Merab sitting on either side. And the *Ka* of Ahura said: 'Truly it is Ptah, the great god, who has saved you and made it possible for you to return here as a suppliant.'

Then the *Ka* of Nefrekeptah rose from the body and laughed, saying: 'I told you that you would return as a suppliant, bringing the Book of Thoth. Place it now upon my body where it lay these many years. Yet do not think that you are yet free of my vengeance: unless you perform that which I bid you, the dream of Tabubua will be turned into reality.'

Then said Setna, bowing low: 'Nefrekeptah, master of magic, tell me what I may do to turn away your just vengeance. If it be such as a man may perform, I will do it for you.'

'I ask only a little thing,' answered the *Ka* of Nefrekeptah. 'You know that while my body lies here for you to see, the bodies of Ahura and Merab rest in their tomb at Koptos. Bring their bodies here to rest with mine until the Day of Awakening when Osiris returns to earth—for we love one another and would not be parted.'

Then Setna went in haste to Pharaoh and begged for the use of the Royal Boat. And Pharaoh was pleased to give command that it sail with Setna where he would. So Setna voyaged up the Nile to Koptos. And there he made a great sacrifice to Isis and Horus, and begged the priests of the temple to tell him where Ahura and Merab lay buried. But, though they searched the ancient writings in the temple, they could find no record.

Setna was in despair. But he offered a great reward to any who could help him, and presently a very old man came tottering up to the temple and said:

'If you are Setna the great scribe, come with me. For when I was a little child my grandfather's father who was as old as I am now told me that when he was even as I was then his grandfather's father had shown him where Ahura and Merab lay buried—for as a young man in the days of Pharaoh Amenhotep the First he had helped to lay them in the tomb.'

Setna followed eagerly where the old man led him, and came to a house on the edge of Koptos.

'You must pull down this house and dig beneath it,' said the old man. And when Setna had bought the house for a great sum from the scribe who lived in it, he bade the soldiers whom Pharaoh had sent with him level the house with the ground and dig beneath where it had stood.

They did as he bade them, and presently came to a tomb buried beneath the sand and cut from the rock. And in it lay the bodies of Ahura and Merab. When he saw them, the old man raised his arms and cried aloud; and as he cried he faded from sight, and Setna knew that it was the ghost of Nefrekeptah which had taken on that shape to lead him to the tomb.

So he took up the mummies of Ahura and Merab and conveyed them with all honour, as if they had been the bodies of a queen and prince of Egypt, down the Nile in the Royal Boat to Memphis.

And there Pharaoh himself led the funeral procession to Saqqara, and Setna placed the bodies of Ahura and Merab beside that of Nefrekeptah in the secret tomb where lay the Book of Thoth.

When the funeral procession had left the tomb, Setna spoke a charm and the wall closed behind him leaving no trace of a door. Then at Pharaoh's command they heaped sand over the low stone shrine where the entrance to the tomb was hidden; and before long a sandstorm turned it into a great mound, and then levelled it out so that never again could anyone find a trace of the tomb where Nefrekeptah lay with Ahura and Merab and the Book of Thoth, waiting for the Day of Awakening when Osiris shall return to rule over the Earth.

Roger Lancelyn Green

THE DOUBTER

BY LUCIAN OF SAMOSATA (*c.* A.D. 150)

TYCHIADES did not believe in ghosts, nor in magic—nor in anything which he had not seen with his own eyes, or felt had been proved to the satisfaction of his own powers of reasoning.

Therefore he found himself very much out of place when he called on his elderly and learned acquaintance Eucrates, and found him laid up with gout and surrounded by a group of friends all of whom were suggesting cures.

For, very soon, Tychiades realized that each cure proposed was more preposterous than the last, varying from sympathetic magic to spells, charms and words of power.

'Surely you learned men do not believe in these cures which are so contrary to the scientific discoveries of the great doctors of Kos?' he exclaimed at last. 'What earthly good can a dead weasel picked up with the left hand and wrapped in a piece of newly-flayed lionskin—or deerskin as one of you suggests—do to a man with gout? And how can his health be affected either way by mere words such as those which charlatans and showmen use at a carnival?'

Indignantly the sick man's friends began trying to prove how right they were and how wrong Tychiades was to doubt their words. For each seemed able to produce a remarkable example of a supernatural experience—and each story seemed to be taller than the last.

One told of a miraculous cure for snake-bite effected by a single word; another of a charm which drew all the snakes out of a great wood; and a third of an even more magical way of turning serpents to dust once they were gathered together.

When Tychiades still doubted their words, they went on to tell of terrible midnight meetings with Hecate the Goddess of Witches; of the pack of Hell-hounds which followed her, and of chasms opening in the earth down which the Land of the Dead could be glimpsed by living eyes.

'Surely you do not doubt the very gods?' asked several of the indignant friends of Eucrates. 'Hades, the ruler of the dead, and his queen Persephone? The terrible punishments of the wicked in Tartarus, and the happiness of the good in the Elysian Fields where the meadows of asphodel bloom for ever, and the incense tree sweetens the air?'

'All this I take on trust,' answered Tychiades. 'Though except for the tales the poets tell—of how Orpheus went down to the Realm of Hades to bring back Eurydice; of the adventures there of Heracles and Theseus; of Odysseus seeking counsel from the ghosts of the dead—we have no proof even of these things.'

'No proof?' exclaimed Eucrates, sitting up suddenly on his couch. 'Listen, and I will give you such a proof that you will never doubt again!'

All his friends, Tychiades among them, gathered closer round the old man, and he went on:

'You all remember my beloved wife and how dear she was to me? Well, when she died I made it plain for all to see that my love did not end with her death, but endured as strongly as ever. For I gave her a truly magnificent funeral, and I took care to burn on the pyre with her all the ornaments and clothing which she had loved so much during her life. Yes, for her sake I even burned her valuable jewellery and garments that I could have sold for large sums of money.

'Well, seven days after her death, as I was lying here on this very couch, just as I am now, trying to console myself in my grief at her loss by reading Plato's book on the immortality of the soul, she suddenly appeared before me. Yes, my beloved Demaenete herself, looking just as she had done in her lifetime, appeared sitting at the end of my couch.

'I could hardly believe my eyes at first. But in a little while I caught her in my arms and burst into tears.

'"'Do not weep, beloved husband,'' she said in the gentle voice which I never thought to hear again in this world. ''It is I who should be crying, not you. For in the land of the dead everyone is making fun of me because I have only one sandal. Yes, when you burnt all my things with me on my funeral pyre you forgot one of my golden sandals, which had fallen to the ground and got kicked under that chest without anyone noticing it. I have come back to ask you to send it after me so that I may no longer be a thing of scorn——'' She would have said more, but at this moment the Maltese lapdog began to bark with terror, and at the sound she faded away and my arms clasped only the empty air.

'We found the golden sandal under the chest, just where she had said it was. We burnt it with all due ceremony—and she has rested in peace ever since.'

Tychiades was a bit staggered by this story, and, while he was wondering what to say, Arignotos the philosopher strode into the room.

'Here's a man who will stand up for me!' Tychiades exclaimed with a sigh of relief.

'You seemed to be discussing something very serious when I came in,' said Arignotos, taking a seat at the end of the table and helping himself to wine. 'What opinion is Tychiades putting forward that he wants me to defend for him?'

'We have been trying to persuade him to believe in ghosts and magic,' explained Eucrates. 'But he does not seem able to believe anyone's evidence except his own.'

'What!' cried Arignotos, 'not believe in ghosts, in spite of all the evidence for their existence? Eye-witnesses' evidence at that?'

'You can at least sympathize with my reasons for doubting,' said Tychaides. 'All these may have seen ghosts or had uncanny experiences, but I have never done so. If I saw a ghost I should of course believe in ghosts just as they do.'

'I can at least help to convince you by an experience of my own,' said Arignotos. 'If ever you go to Corinth, ask for the house of Eubatides near the grove of cornel trees and get the doorkeeper, Tibios, to show you the place where I laid the ghost which once haunted it.'

'Tell us about it,' exclaimed Eucrates eagerly.

'The house was so haunted as to be quite uninhabitable,' answered Arignotos. 'A hideous ghost prowled through it night after night, scaring everyone away. By the time I was called in to help, the place was already almost a ruin.'

'What did you do?' asked Tychiades.

'When I had heard all about it,' answered Arignotos, 'I moved into the house one evening armed with a number of Egyptian books on the subject of ghosts. The owner tried to dissuade me, fearing for my life, but I knew what I was about. I settled myself in the largest room with a lamp and my books, and was deep in the works of an author of ancient Khem when the ghost appeared. He was a terrifying object: long-haired, filthy, darker in colour than the darkness itself—and he obviously expected that I would turn and run shrieking from the house at the very sight of him, as all other watchers had done. But I sat still, looking him straight in the eyes and commanded him to be gone, using the speech of the ancient priests of Egypt, and the words of Thrice-mighty Hermes whom they call Thoth.

'At first he towered over me, his form seeming to vary hideously while he strove to overcome me. But as I spoke he shrank away and retreated into a corner. At last, as I uttered the greatest Word of Power that I knew, he sank out of sight into the floor of the room and troubled me no more.

'Having marked the place where I had laid the ghost, I went quietly off to sleep. But next morning, when Eubatides, the owner of the house, and his friends came timorously along to give decent burial to what was left of me, I met them smiling, led them to the place, and said simply: "Dig here!"

'They did as I bade them, and six feet down they came upon the mouldering body of a man who had obviously died an ill death. At my command they took him up and burned him on a fine funeral pyre. From that day on no ghost has troubled the house of Eubatides in Corinth.'

There was silence after Arignotos had finished his story, and Tychiades felt almost convinced by it.

Presently, however, he remarked: 'I wish that Democritos the learned man from Abdera in Thrace was here. Like me, he refused to believe in ghosts and all such marvels, and to prove his point went and lived in a tomb outside the city gates. There he dwelt for many months quite untroubled by anything uncanny, working away at his books as if the tomb were a room in the library of Alexandria. Several young men of Abdera, wishing to frighten him, dressed themselves up in shrouds, with masks painted to resemble skulls, and came to haunt him one night. But he took no notice of them, beyond remarking: "Do stop being such idiots," and at last they gave up and went home to bed.'

'That only showed his good sense,' answered Arignotos. 'He at least knew a fake ghost from a true one. But it does not prove that true ones do not exist, nor indeed is it anything to the point. He was simply lucky that the tomb in which he dwelt was not haunted, and that no magician or other learned man came along with powers which to unbelievers like him and you would seem impossible, and convince him of his mistake.'

'I must admit that when I was a young man I was almost as sceptical as you, Tychiades, still seem to be,' said Eucrates. 'But after I had finished at the University I went on a journey to Egypt to increase my knowledge—and there met with a man so learned that he soon convinced me that all one can learn at Athens, or Alexandria, or here at Samosata is no more than the first lessons a child learns at home when compared with the real wisdom still preserved by the priests of Memphis and Egyptian Thebes. He was said to have lived underground for twenty-three years in the Serapium, learning all the mysteries of Isis and Thoth and the rest.'

'You mean Pancrates,' said Arignotos. 'He was my master too, and one more learned does not tread the earth today. Where did you find him?'

'Near Thebes,' answered Eucrates, 'where I had been to listen to the wonderful statue of Memnon which sings each day at sunrise. Very soon, from being simply his pupil I became his disciple, and at length set out with him on his way down the Nile to Memphis and Alexandria.

'Before we started he persuaded me to dismiss all my servants, assuring me that we would be better waited on by those whom he could summon to serve us than by any ordinary dependants.

'Sure enough, whenever we stopped for the night he would take some common wooden object—the bar of the door, a broom or even a large wooden pestle—put a cloak round it, speak a spell over it, and tell it to do his bidding and appear to everyone else like an ordinary man. It would go off and draw water for us; it would buy provisions in the markets; it would cook our meals and then wait on us more skilfully than the best trained butler I have ever seen. Then, when he had finished with its services, he would mutter another spell and turn it back into an ordinary doorbar or broom or pestle.

'I was naturally eager to learn these spells from him. But he was jealous and secretive, and refused to teach them to me. One day, however, I hid behind the door while he was setting one of these uncanny servants to work, and heard the spell. It was an easy one to remember, consisting of only three words, so I readily committed them to memory.

'I was eager to try them out. So a few days later when Pancrates was lecturing in the market place, I went into our house, shut the door, took up the wooden pestle, wrapped it in a cloak as I had seen him do, and spoke the spell over it. At once it came to life and stood waiting for my orders. "Fetch water!" I commanded. Instantly it seized the water-jar and set off at top speed to the canal which was just behind the house. It returned in a moment, filled all our utensils, and hastened out to fetch more water. "That's enough!" I cried. "Stop bringing water!" But my words made no difference. It went on carrying in jar after jar of water and pouring it into the already full pots, until the house itself was half full.

'In a panic lest Pancrates should return and find what I had done, I snatched up an axe and split the pestle down the middle. But what was my horror when each half of the pestle seized a

'It went on carrying in water . . . until the house itself was half full'

huge water jar and began bringing water into the house twice as fast as before! In vain I cursed myself for my folly in trying the spell which turned the pestle into a servant before learning that which turned it back into a piece of wood. I should certainly have been drowned and the whole city flooded if Pancrates had not come in at that moment and seen what was going on.

'Swiftly he muttered words which I could not hear, and at once the two halves of the pestle were no more than pieces of wood. Then, without so much as a glance at me, he turned and strode out of the house. Nor have I seen him again from that day to this.'

'And can you still turn a pestle into a servant?' asked Arignotos eagerly.

'Quite easily,' answered Eucrates. 'But I dare not do so, for if I did I could not turn him back again into a pestle, and if he began carrying water, Deucalion's Flood would come again and we should all be drowned.'

Tychiades had been more than half convinced by the story Arignotos told about the haunted house in Corinth. But this last tale of Eucrates as a sorcerer's apprentice, which everyone in the room seemed to accept as solemn fact, convinced him that one story was no truer than another.

'I hope you will soon be cured of your gout—by whatever means,' he said to Eucrates as he rose to leave the room. At the door he turned and added: 'But I am never likely to be cured of being a doubter—any more than the rest of you seem likely to be cured from telling the most amazing collection of lies I have ever listened to in all my life! Good night!'

With that he shut the door and went away in a hurry.

W. A. Craigie

THE STORY OF GLAM

THERE was a man named Thorhall, who lived at Thorhall-stead in Forsaela-dala, which lies in the north of Iceland. He was a fairly wealthy man, especially in cattle, so that no one round about had so much livestock as he had. He was not a chief, however, but an honest and worthy yeoman.

Now this man's place was greatly haunted, so that he could scarcely get a shepherd to stay with him, and although he asked the opinion of many as to what he ought to do, he could find none to give him advice of any worth.

One summer at the Althing, or yearly assembly of the people, Thorhall went to the booth of Skafti, the law man, who was the wisest of men and gave good counsel when his opinion was asked. He received Thorhall in a friendly way, because he knew he was a man of means, and asked him what news he had.

'I would have some good advice from you,' said Thorhall.

'I am little able to give that,' said Skafti; 'but what is the matter?'

'This is the way of it,' said Thorhall. 'I have had very bad luck with my shepherds of late. Some of them get injured, and others will not serve out their time; and now no one that knows how the case stands will take the place at all.'

'Then there must be some evil spirit there,' said Skafti, 'when men are less willing to herd your sheep than those of others. Now since you have asked my advice, I will get a shepherd for you. Glam is his name, he belongs to Sweden, and came out here last summer. He is big and strong, but not very well liked by most people.'

Thorhall said that he did not mind that, if he looked well after the sheep. Skafti answered that there was no hope of other men doing it, if Glam could not, seeing he was so strong and stout-hearted. Their talk ended there, and Thorhall left the booth.

This took place just at the breaking up of the assembly. Thorhall missed two of his horses, and went to look for them in person, from which it may be seen that he was no proud man. He went up to the mountain ridge, and south along the fell that is called Armann's fell. There he saw a man coming down from the wood, leading a horse laden with bundles of brushwood. They soon met each other and Thorhall asked his name. He said he was called Glam. He was tall of body, and of strange appearance; his eyes were blue and staring, and his hair wolf-grey in colour. Thorhall was a little startled when he saw him, and was certain that this was the man he had been told about.

'What work are you best fitted for?' he asked.

Glam said that he was good at keeping sheep in winter.

'Will you look after *my* sheep?' said Thorhall. 'Skafti has put you into my hands.'

'On this condition only will I take service with you,' said Glam; 'that I have my own free will, for I am ill-tempered if anything does not please me.'

'That will not harm me,' said Thorhall, 'and I should like you to come to me.'

'I will do so,' said Glam; 'but is there any trouble at your place?'

'It is believed to be haunted,' said Thorhall.

'I am not afraid of such bug-bears,' said Glam, 'and think that it will be all the livelier for that.'

'You will need all your boldness,' said Thorhall. 'It is best not to be too frightened for one's self there.'

After this they made a bargain between them, and Glam was to come when the winter nights began. Then they parted, and Thorhall found his horses where he had just newly looked for them, and rode home, after thanking Skafti for his kindness.

The summer passed, and Thorhall heard nothing of the shepherd, nor did any one know the least about him, but at the time appointed he came to Thorhall-stead. The yeoman received him well, but the others did not like him, and the good-wife least of all. He began his work among the sheep, which gave him little trouble, for he had a loud, hoarse voice, and the flock all ran together whenever he shouted. There was a church at Thorhall-stead, but Glam would never go to it nor join in the service. He was unbelieving, surly, and difficult to deal with, and everyone felt a dislike towards him.

So time went on till it came to Christmas eve. On that morning Glam rose early and called for his food. The good-wife answered: 'It is not the custom of Christian people to eat on this day, for to-morrow is the first day of Christmas, and we ought to fast to-day.' Glam replied: 'You have many foolish fashions that I see no good in. I cannot see that men are any better off now than they were when they never troubled themselves about such things. I think it was a far better life when men were heathens; and now I want my food, and no nonsense.' The good-wife answered: 'I am sure you will come to sorrow to-day if you act thus perversely.'

Glam bade her bring his food at once, or it would be the worse for her. She was afraid to refuse, and after he had eaten he went out in a great rage.

'The weather was very bad. It was dark and gloomy all round; snowflakes fluttered about; loud noises were heard in the air, and it grew worse and worse as the day wore on. They heard the shepherd's voice during the forenoon, but less of him as the day passed. Then the snow began to drift, and by evening there was a violent storm. People came to the service in church, and the day wore on to evening, but still Glam did not come home. There was some talk among them of going to look for him, but no search was made on account of the storm and the darkness.

All Christmas eve Glam did not return, and in the morning men went to look for him. They found the sheep scattered in the fens, beaten down by the storm, or up on the hills. Thereafter they came to a place in the valley where the snow was all trampled, as if there had been a terrible struggle there, for stones and frozen earth were torn up all round about. They looked carefully round the place, and found Glam lying a short distance off, quite dead.

He was black in colour, and swollen up as big as an ox. They were horrified at the sight, and shuddered in their hearts. However, they tried to carry him to the church, but could get him no further than to the edge of a cleft, a little lower down; so they left him there and went home and told their master what had happened.

Thorhall asked them what had been the cause of Glam's death. They said that they had traced footprints as large as though the bottom of a cask had been set down in the snow leading from where the trampled place was up to the cliffs at the head of the valley, and all along the track there were huge blood-stains. From this they guessed that the evil spirit which lived there must have killed Glam, but had received so much hurt that it had died, for nothing was ever seen of it after.

The second day of Christmas they tried again to bring Glam to the church. They yoked horses to him, but after they had come down the slope and reached level ground they could drag him no further, and he had to be left there.

On the third day a priest went with them, but Glam was not to be found, although they searched for him all day. The priest refused to go a second time, and the shepherd was found at once when the priest was not present. So they gave over their attempts to take him to the church, and buried him on the spot.

Soon after this they became aware that Glam was not lying quiet, and great damage was done by him, for many that saw him fell into a swoon, or lost their reason. Immediately after Yule men believed that they saw him about the farm itself, and grew terribly frightened, so that many of them ran away. After this Glam began to ride on the house-top by night, and nearly shook it to pieces, and then he walked about almost night and day. Men hardly dared to go up into the valley, even although they had urgent business there, and every one in the district thought great harm of the matter.

In spring, Thorhall got new men, and started the farm again, while Glam's walkings began to grow less frequent as the days grew longer. So time went on, until it was mid-summer. That summer a ship from Norway came into Huna-water (a firth to the

Glam began to ride on the house-top by night, and nearly shook it to pieces

north of Thorhall-stead), and had on board a man called Thorgaut. He was foreign by birth, big of body, and as strong as any two men. He was unhired and unmarried, and was looking for some employment, as he was penniless. Thorhall rode to the ship, and found Thorgaut there. He asked him whether he would enter his service. Thorgaut answered that he might well do so, and that he did not care much what work he did.

'You must know, however,' said Thorhall, 'that it is not good for any faint-hearted man to live at my place, on account of the hauntings that have been of late, and I do not wish to deceive you in any way.'

'I do not think myself utterly lost although I see some wretched ghosts,' said Thorgaut. 'It will be no light matter for others if *I* am scared, and I will not throw up the place on that account.'

Their bargain was quickly made, and Thorgaut was to have charge of the sheep during the winter. The summer went past and Thorgaut began his duties with the winter nights, and was well liked by every one. Glam began to come again, and rode on the house-top, which Thorgaut thought great sport, and said that the thrall would have to come to close quarters before he would be afraid of him. Thorhall bade him not say too much about it. 'It will be better for you,' said he, 'if you have no trial of each other.'

'Your courage has indeed been shaken out of you,' said Thorgaut, 'but I am not going to fall dead for such talk.'

The winter went on till Christmas came again, and on Christmas eve the shepherd went out to his sheep. 'I trust,' said the good-wife, 'that things will not go after the old fashion.'

'Have no fear of that, good-wife,' said Thorgaut; 'there will be something worth talking about if I don't come back.'

The weather was very cold, and a heavy drift blowing. Thorgaut was in the habit of coming home when it was half-dark, but on this occasion he did not return at his usual time. People came to church, and they now began to think that things were not unlikely to fall out as they had done before. Thorhall wished to make search for the shepherd, but the church-goers refused, saying that they would not risk themselves in the hands of evil demons by night, and so no search was made.

After their morning meal on Christmas day they went out to look for the shepherd. They first made their way to Glam's cairn, guessing that he was the cause of the man's disappearance. On coming near to this they saw great tidings, for there they found the shepherd with his neck broken and every bone in his body smashed in pieces. They carried him to the church, and he did no harm to any man thereafter. But Glam began to gather strength anew, and now went so far in his mischief that everyone fled from Thorhall-stead, except the yeoman and his wife.

The same cattleman, however, had been there for a long time, and Thorhall would not let him leave, because he was so faithful and so careful. He was very old, and did not want to go away either, for he saw that everything his master had would go to wreck and ruin, if there was no one to look after it.

One morning after the middle of winter the good-wife went out to the byre to milk the cows. It was broad daylight by this time, for no one ventured to be outside earlier than that, except the cattleman, who always went out when it began to grow clear. She heard a great noise and fearful bellowing in the byre, and ran into the house again, crying out and saying that some awful thing was going on there. Thorhall went out to the cattle and found them goring each other with their horns. To get out of their way, he went through into the barn, and in doing this he saw the cattleman lying on his back with his head in one stall and his feet in another. He went up to him and felt him and soon found that he was dead, with his back broken over the upright stone between two of the stalls.

The yeoman thought it high time to leave the place now, and fled from his farm with all that he could remove. All the live-stock that he left behind was killed by Glam, who then went through the whole glen and laid waste all the farms up from Tongue.

Thorhall spent the rest of the winter with various friends. No one could go up into the glen with horse or dog, for these were killed at once; but when spring came again and the days began to lengthen, Glam's walkings grew less frequent, and Thorhall determined to return to his homestead. He had difficulty in getting servants, but managed to set up his home again at Thor-hall-stead. Things went just as before. When autumn came, the hauntings began again, and now it was the yeoman's daughter who was most assailed, till in the end she died of fright. Many plans were tried, but all to no effect, and it seemed as if all Water-dale would be laid waste unless some remedy could be found.

All this befell in the days of Grettir, the son of Asmund, who was the strongest man of his day in Iceland. He had been abroad at this time, outlawed for three years, and was only eighteen

There was much talk about Glam's walkings

years of age when he returned. He had been at home all through the autumn, but when the winter nights were well advanced, he rode north to Water-dale, and came to Tongue, where lived his uncle Jökull. His uncle received him heartily, and he stayed there for three nights. At this time there was so much talk about Glam's walkings, that nothing was so largely spoken of as these. Grettir inquired closely about all that had happened, and Jökull said that the stories told no more than had indeed taken place; 'but are you intending to go there, kinsman?' said he. Grettir answered that he was. Jökull bade him not do so, 'for it is a dangerous undertaking, and a great risk for your friends to lose you, for in our opinion there is not another like you among the young men, and "ill will come of ill" where Glam is. Far better it is to deal with mortal men than with such evil spirits.'

Grettir, however, said that he had a mind to fare to Thorhall-stead, and see how things had been going on there. Jökull replied:

'I see now that it is of no use to hold you back, but the saying is true that "good luck and good heart are not the same"'. Grettir answered: '"Woe stands at one man's door when it has entered another's house". Think how it may go with yourself before the end.'

'It may be,' said Jökull, 'that both of us see some way into the future, and yet neither of us can do anything to prevent it.'

After this they parted, and neither liked the other's forebodings.

Grettir rode to Thorhall-stead, and the yeoman received him heartily. He asked Grettir where he was going, who said that he wished to stay there all night if he would allow him. Thorhall said that he would be very glad if he would stay, 'but few men count it a gain to be guests here for long. You must have heard how matters stand, and I shall be very unwilling for you to come to any harm on my account. And even although you yourself escape safe and sound, I know for certain that you will lose your horse, for no man that comes here can keep that uninjured.'

Grettir answered that there were horses enough to be got, whatever might happen to this one. Thorhall was delighted that he was willing to stay, and gave him the heartiest reception. The horse was strongly secured in an out-house; then they went to sleep, and that night passed without Glam appearing.

'Your coming here,' said Thorhall, 'has made a happy change, for Glam is in the habit of riding the house every night, or breaking up the doors, as you may see for yourself.'

'Then one of two things will happen,' said Grettir; 'either he will not restrain himself for long, or the hauntings will cease for more than one night. I shall stay for another night, and see how things go.'

After this they went to look at Grettir's horse, and found that he had not been meddled with, so the yeoman thought that everything was going on well. Grettir stayed another night, and still the thrall did not come about them. Thorhall thought that things were looking brighter, but when he went to look to Grettir's horse he found the out-house broken up, the horse dragged outside, and every bone in it broken. He told Grettir what had happened, and advised him to secure his own safety, 'for your death is certain if you wait for Glam'.

Grettir answered: 'The least I can get for my horse is to see the thrall.' Thorhall replied that it would do him no good to see him, 'for he is unlike anything in human shape; but I am fain of every hour that you are willing to stay here'.

The day wore on, and when it was bed-time Grettir would not take off his clothes, but lay down on the floor over against Thorhall's bed-closet. He put a thick cloak above himself, buttoning one end beneath his feet, and doubling the other under his head, while he looked out at the hole for the neck. There was a strong plank in front of the floored space, and against this he pressed his feet. The door-fittings were all broken off from the outer door, but there was a hurdle set up instead, and roughly secured. The wainscot that had once stretched across the hall was all broken down, both above and below the cross-beam. The beds were all pulled out of their places, and everything was in confusion.

A light was left burning in the hall, and when the third part of the night was past Grettir heard loud noises outside. Then something went up on top of the house, and rode above the hall, beating the roof with its heels till every beam cracked. This went on for a long time; then it came down off the house and went to the door. When this was opened Grettir saw the thrall thrust in his head; ghastly big he seemed, and wonderfully huge of feature. Glam came in slowly, and raised himself up when he was inside the doorway, till he loomed up against the roof. Then he turned his face down the hall, laid his arms on the cross-beam, and glared all over the place. Thorhall gave no sign during all this, for he thought it bad enough to hear what was going on outside.

Grettir lay still and never moved. Glam saw that there was a bundle lying on the floor, and moved further up the hall and grasped the cloak firmly. Grettir placed his feet against the plank, and yielded not the least. Glam tugged a second time, much harder than before, but still the cloak did not move. A third time he pulled with both his hands, so hard that he raised Grettir up from the floor, and now they wrenched the cloak asunder between them. Glam stood staring at the piece which he held in his hands, and wondering greatly who could have pulled so hard against him. At that moment Grettir sprang in under the monster's hands, and threw his arms around his waist, intending to make him fall backwards. Glam, however, bore down upon him so strongly that Grettir was forced to give way before him. He then tried to stay himself against the seat-boards, but these gave way with him, and everything that came in their path was broken.

Glam wanted to get him outside, and although Grettir set his feet against everything that he could, yet Glam succeeded in dragging him out into the porch. There they had a fierce struggle, for the thrall meant to have him out of doors, while Grettir saw that bad as it was to deal with Glam inside the house it would be worse outside, and therefore strove with all his might against being carried out. When they came into the porch Glam put forth all his strength, and pulled Grettir close to him. When Grettir saw that he could not stay himself he suddenly changed his plan, and threw himself as hard as he could against the monster's breast, setting both his feet against an earth-fast stone that lay in the doorway. Glam was not prepared for this, being then in the act of pulling Grettir towards him, so he fell backwards and went crashing out through the door, his shoulders catching the lintel as he fell. The roof of the porch was wrenched in two, both rafters and frozen thatch, and backwards out of the house went Glam, with Grettir above him.

Outside there was bright moonshine and broken clouds, which sometimes drifted over the moon and sometimes left it clear. At the moment when Glam fell the cloud passed off the moon, and he cast up his eyes sharply towards it; and Grettir himself said that this was the only sight he ever saw that terrified him. Then Grettir grew so helpless, both by reason of his weariness and at seeing Glam roll his eyes so horribly, that he was unable to draw his dagger, and lay well-nigh between life and death.

But in this was Glam's might more fiendish than that of most other ghosts, that he spoke in this fashion: 'Great eagerness have you shown to meet me, Grettir, and little wonder will it be though you get no great good fortune from me; but this I may tell you, that you have now received only half of the strength and vigour that was destined for you if you had not met with me. I cannot now take from you the strength you have already gained, but this I can see to, that you will never be stronger than you are now, and yet you are strong enough, as many a man shall feel. Hitherto you have been famous for your deeds, but henceforth you shall be a manslayer and an outlaw, and most of your deeds will turn to your own hurt and misfortune. Outlawed you shall be, and ever have a solitary life for your lot; and this, too, I lay upon you, ever to see these eyes of mine before your own, and then you will think it hard to be alone, and that will bring you to your death.'

When Glam had said this the faintness passed off Grettir, and he then drew his dagger, cut off Glam's head, and laid it beside his thigh. Thorhall then came out, having put on his clothes while Glam was talking, but never venturing to come near until he had fallen. He praised God, and thanked Grettir for overcoming the unclean spirit. Then they set to work, and burned Glam to ashes, which they placed in a sack, and buried where cattle were least likely to pasture or men to tread. When this was done they went home again, and it was now near daybreak.

Thorhall sent to the next farm for the men there, and told them what had taken place. All thought highly of the exploit that heard of it, and it was the common talk that in all Iceland there was no man like Grettir Asmundarson for strength and courage and all kinds of bodily feats. Thorhall gave him a good horse when he went away, as well as a fine suit of clothes, for the ones he had been wearing were all torn to pieces. The two then parted with the utmost friendship.

Thence Grettir rode to the Ridge in Water-dale, where his kinsman Thorvald received him heartily, and asked closely concerning his encounter with Glam. Grettir told him how he had fared, and said that his strength was never put to harder proof, so long did the struggle between them last. Thorvald bade him be quiet and gentle in his conduct, and things would go well with him, otherwise his troubles would be many. Grettir answered that his temper was not improved; he was more easily roused than ever, and less able to bear opposition. In this, too, he felt a great change, that he had become so much afraid of the dark that he dared not go anywhere alone after night began to fall, for then he saw phantoms and monsters of every kind. So it has become a saying ever since then, when folk see things very different from what they are, that Glam lends them his eyes, or gives them glam-sight.

This fear of solitude brought Grettir, at last, to his end.

Washington Irving

THE LEGEND OF SLEEPY HOLLOW

FOUND AMONG THE PAPERS OF THE LATE DIEDRICH KNICKERBOCKER

> A pleasing land of drowsy head it was,
> Of dreams that wave before the half-shut eye;
> And of gay castles in the clouds that pass,
> For ever flushing round a summer sky.
>
> 'Castle of Indolence.'

In the bosom of one of those spacious coves which indent the eastern shore of the Hudson, at that broad expansion of the river denominated by the ancient Dutch navigators the Tappan Zee, and where they always prudently shortened sail, and implored the protection of St Nicholas when they crossed, there lies a small market-town or rural port, which by some is called Greensburgh, but which is more generally and properly known by the name of Tarry Town. This name was given, we are told, in former days, by the good housewives of the adjacent country, from the inveterate propensity of their husbands to linger about the village tavern on market days. Be that as it may, I do not vouch for the fact, but merely advert to it, for the sake of being precise and authentic. Not far from this village, perhaps about two miles, there is a little valley, or rather lap of land, among high hills, which is one of the quietest places in the whole world. A small brook glides through it, with just murmur enough to lull one to repose; and the occasional whistle of a quail or tapping of a woodpecker, is almost the only sound that ever breaks in upon the uniform tranquillity.

I recollect that, when a stripling, my first exploit in squirrel-shooting was in a grove of tall walnut-trees that shades one side of the valley. I had wandered into it at noon time, when all nature is peculiarly quiet, and was startled by the roar of my own gun, as it broke the Sabbath stillness around, and was prolonged and reverberated by the angry echoes. If ever I should wish for a retreat, whither I might steal from the world and its distractions, and dream quietly away the remnant of a troubled life, I know of none more promising than this little valley.

From the listless repose of the place, and the peculiar character of its inhabitants, who are descendants from the original Dutch settlers, this sequestered glen has long been known by the name of SLEEPY HOLLOW, and its rustic lads are called the Sleepy Hollow Boys throughout all the neighbouring country. A drowsy dreamy influence seems to hang over the land, and to pervade the very atmosphere. Some say that the place was bewitched by a high German doctor, during the early days of the settlement; others, that an old Indian chief, the prophet or wizard of his tribe, held his powwows there before the country was discovered by Master Hendrick Hudson. Certain it is, the place still continues under the sway of some witching power, that holds a spell over the minds of the good people, causing them to walk in a continual reverie. They are given to all kinds of marvellous beliefs; are subject to trances and visions; and frequently see strange sights, and hear music and voices in the air. The whole neighbourhood abounds with local tales, haunted spots, and twilight superstitions; stars shoot and meteors glare oftener across the valley than in any other part of the country, and the nightmare, with her whole nine fold, seems to make it the favourite scene of her gambols.

The dominant spirit, however, that haunts this enchanted region, and seems to be commander-in-chief of all the powers of the air, is the apparition of a figure on horseback without a head. It is said by some to be the ghost of a Hessian trooper, whose head had been carried away by a cannon-ball, in some nameless battle during the revolutionary war; and who is ever and anon seen by the country folk, hurrying along in the gloom of night, as if on the wings of the wind. His haunts are not confined to the valley, but extend at times to the adjacent roads, and especially to the vicinity of a church at no great distance. Indeed, certain of the most authentic historians of those parts, who have been careful in collecting and collating the floating facts concerning this spectre, allege that the body of the trooper, having been buried in the churchyard, the ghost rides forth to the scene of battle in nightly quest of his head; and that the rushing speed with which he sometimes passes along the Hollow, like a midnight blast, is owing to his being belated, and in a hurry to get back to the churchyard before daybreak.

Such is the general purport of this legendary superstition, which has furnished materials for many a wild story in that region of shadows; and the spectre is known at all the country firesides by the name of the Headless Horseman of Sleepy Hollow.

It is remarkable that the visionary propensity I have mentioned is not confined to the native inhabitants of the valley, but is unconsciously imbibed by every one who resides there for a time. However wide awake they may have been before they entered that sleepy region, they are sure, in a little time, to inhale the witching influence of the air, and begin to grow imaginative—to dream dreams, and see apparitions.

I mention this peaceful spot with all possible laud; for it is in such little retired Dutch valleys, found here and there embosomed in the great state of New York, that population, manners, and customs, remain fixed; while the great torrent of migration and improvement, which is making such incessant changes in other parts of this restless country, sweeps by them unobserved. They are like those little nooks of still water which border a rapid stream; where we may see the straw and bubble riding quietly at anchor, or slowly revolving in their mimic harbour, undisturbed by the rush of the passing current. Though many years have elapsed since I trod the drowsy shades of Sleepy Hollow, yet I question whether I should not still find the same trees and the same families vegetating in its sheltered bosom.

In this by-place of nature there abode, in a remote period of American history, that is to say, some thirty years since, a worthy wight of the name of Ichabod Crane; who sojourned, or, as he expressed it, 'tarried', in Sleepy Hollow, for the purpose of instructing the children of the vicinity. He was a native of

Connecticut; a state which supplies the Union with pioneers for the mind as well as for the forest, and sends forth yearly its legions of frontier woodmen and country schoolmasters. The cognomen of Crane was not inapplicable to his person. He was tall, but exceedingly lank, with narrow shoulders, long arms and legs, hands that dangled a mile out of his sleeves, feet that might have served for shovels, and his whole frame most loosely hung together. His head was small, and flat at top, with huge ears, large green glassy eyes, and a long snipe nose, so that it looked like a weather-cock, perched upon his spindle neck, to tell which way the wind blew. To see him striding along the profile of a hill on a windy day, with his clothes bagging and fluttering about him, one might have mistaken him for the genius of famine descending upon the earth, or some scarecrow eloped from a corn-field.

His school-house was a low building of one large room, rudely constructed of logs; the windows partly glazed, and partly patched with leaves of old copy-books. It was most ingeniously secured at vacant hours, by a withe twisted in the handle of the door, and stakes set against the window-shutters; so that, though a thief might get in with perfect ease, he would find some embarrassment in getting out; an idea most probably borrowed by the architect, Yost Van Houten, from the mystery of an eelpot. The school-house stood in a rather lonely but pleasant situation, just at the foot of a woody hill, with a brook running close by, and a formidable birch-tree growing at one end of it. From hence the low murmur of his pupils' voices, conning over their lessons, might be heard in a drowsy summer's day, like the hum of a bee-hive; interrupted now and then by the authoritative voice of the master, in the tone of menace or command; or, peradventure, by the appalling sound of the birch, as he urged some tardy loiterer along the flowery path of knowledge. Truth to say, he was a conscientious man, and ever bore in mind the golden maxim, 'Spare the rod and spoil the child.' Ichabod Crane's scholars certainly were not spoiled.

I would not have it imagined, however, that he was one of those cruel potentates of the school, who joy in the smart of their subjects; on the contrary, he administered justice with discrimination rather than severity; taking the burthen off the backs of the weak, and laying it on those of the strong. Your mere puny stripling, that winced at the least flourish of the rod, was passed by with indulgence; but the claims of justice were satisfied by inflicting a double portion on some little tough, wrong-headed, broad-skirted Dutch urchin, who sulked and swelled and grew dogged and sullen beneath the birch. All this he called 'doing his duty by their parents'; and he never inflicted a chastisement without following it by the assurance, so consolatory to the smarting urchin, that 'he would remember it and thank him for it the longest day he had to live'.

When school-hours were over, he was even the companion and playmate of the larger boys; and on holiday afternoons would convoy some of the smaller ones home, who happened to have pretty sisters, or good housewives for mothers, noted for the comforts of the cupboard. Indeed, it behoved him to keep on good terms with his pupils. The revenue arising from his school was small, and would have been scarcely sufficient to furnish him with daily bread, for he was a huge feeder, and though lank, had the dilating powers of an anaconda; but to help out his maintenance, he was, according to country custom in those parts, boarded and lodged at the houses of the farmers, whose children he instructed. With these he lived successively a week at a time; thus going the rounds of the neighbourhood, with all his worldly effects tied up in a cotton handkerchief.

That all this might not be too onerous on the purses of his rustic patrons, who are apt to consider the costs of schooling a grievous burden, and schoolmasters as mere drones, he had various ways of rendering himself both useful and agreeable. He assisted the farmers occasionally in the lighter labours of their farms; helped to make hay; mended the fences; took the horses to water; drove the cows from pasture; and cut wood for the winter fire. He laid aside, too, all the dominant dignity and absolute sway with which he lorded it in his little empire, the school, and became wonderfully gentle and ingratiating. He found favour in the eyes of the mothers by petting the children, particularly the youngest; and like the lion bold, which whilom so magnanimously the lamb did hold, he would sit with a child on one knee, and rock a cradle with his foot for whole hours together.

In addition to his other vocations, he was the singing-master of the neighbourhood, and picked up many bright shillings by instructing the young folks in psalmody. It was a matter of no little vanity to him, on Sundays, to take his station in front of the church gallery, with a band of chosen singers; where, in his own mind, he completely carried away the palm from the parson. Certain it is, his voice resounded far above all the rest of the congregation; and there are peculiar quavers still to be heard in that church, and which may even be heard half a mile off, quite to the opposite side of the mill-pond, on a still Sunday morning, which are said to be legitimately descended from the nose of Ichabod Crane. Thus, by divers little make-shifts, in that ingenious way which is commonly denominated 'by hook and by crook,' the worthy pedagogue got on tolerably enough, and was thought, by all who understand nothing of the labour of head-work, to have a wonderfully easy life of it.

The schoolmaster is generally a man of some importance in the female circle of a rural neighbourhood; being considered a kind of idle gentleman-like personage, of vastly superior taste and accomplishments to the rough country swains, and, indeed, inferior in learning only to the parson. His appearance, therefore, is apt to occasion some little stir at the tea-table of a farmhouse and the addition of a supernumerary dish of cakes or sweetmeats, or peradventure, the parade of a silver tea-pot. Our man of letters, therefore, was peculiarly happy in the smiles of all the country damsels. How he would figure among them in the church-yard between services on Sundays! gathering grapes for them from the wild vines that overran the surrounding trees; reciting for their amusement all the epitaphs on the tombstones; or sauntering with a whole bevy of them along the banks of the adjacent mill-pond; while the more bashful country bumpkins hung sheepishly back, envying his superior elegance and address.

From his half itinerant life, also, he was a kind of travelling gazette, carrying the whole budget of local gossip from house to house; so that his appearance was always greeted with satisfaction.

He was, moreover, esteemed by the women as a man of great erudition, for he had read several books quite through, and was a perfect master of Cotton Mather's *History of New England Witchcraft*, in which, by the way, he most firmly and potently believed.

He was, in fact, an odd mixture of small shrewdness and simple credulity. His appetite for the marvellous, and his powers of digesting it, were equally extraordinary; and both had been increased by his residence in this spell-bound region. No tale was too gross or monstrous for his capacious swallow. It was often his delight, after his school was dismissed in the afternoon, to stretch himself on the rich bed of clover, bordering the little brook that whimpered by his school-house, and there con over old Mather's direful tales, until the gathering dusk of the evening made the printed page a mere mist before his eyes. Then, as he wended his way by swamp and stream and awful woodland, to the farmhouse where he happened to be quartered, every sound of nature, at that witching hour, fluttered his excited imagination: the moan of the whip-poor-will [1] from the hill-side; the boding cry of the tree-toad, that harbinger of storm; the dreary hooting of the screech-owl, or the sudden rustling in the thicket of birds frightened from their roost. The fire-flies, too, which sparkled most vividly in the darkest places, now and then startled him, as one of uncommon brightness would stream across his path; and if by chance a huge blackhead of a beetle came winging his blundering flight against him, the poor varlet was ready to give up the ghost, with the idea that he was struck with a witch's token. His only resource on such occasions, either to drown thought or drive away evil spirits, was to sing psalm tunes;—and the good people of Sleepy Hollow, as they sat by their doors of an evening, were often filled with awe at hearing his nasal melody, 'in linked sweetness long drawn out,' floating from the distant hill, or along the dusky road.

Another of his sources of fearful pleasure was to pass long winter evenings with the old Dutch wives, as they sat spinning by the fire, with a row of apples roasting and spluttering along

[1] The whip-poor-will is a bird which is only heard at night. It receives its name from its note, which is thought to resemble those words.

the hearth, and listen to their marvellous tales of ghosts and goblins, and haunted fields, and haunted brooks, and haunted bridges, and haunted houses, and particularly of the headless horseman, or Galloping Hessian of the Hollow, as they sometimes called him. He would delight them equally by his anecdotes of witchcraft, and of the direful omens and portentous sights and sounds in the air, which prevailed in the earlier times of Connecticut; and would frighten them woefully with speculations upon comets and shooing stars; and with the alarming fact that the world did absolutely turn round, and that they were half the time topsy-turvy!

But if there was a pleasure in all this, while snugly cuddling in the chimney-corner of a chamber that was all of a ruddy glow from the crackling wood fire, and where, of course, no spectre dared to show its face, it was dearly purchased by the terrors of his subsequent walk homewards. What fearful shapes and shadows beset his path amidst the dim and ghastly glare of a snowy night!—With what wistful look did he eye every trembling ray of light streaming across the waste fields from some distant window!—How often was he appalled by some shrub covered with snow, which, like a sheeted spectre, beset his very path!—How often did he shrink with curdling awe at the sound of his own steps on the frosty crust beneath his feet! and dread to look over his shoulder, lest he should behold some uncouth being tramping close behind him!—and how often was he thrown into complete dismay by some rushing blast, howling among the trees, in the idea that it was the Galloping Hessian on one of his nightly scourings!

All these, however, were mere terrors of the night, phantoms of the mind that walk in darkness; and though he had seen many spectres in his time, and been more than once beset by Satan in divers shapes, in his lonely perambulations, yet daylight put an end to all these evils; and he would have passed a pleasant life of it, in despite of the devil and all his works, if his path had not been crossed by a being that causes more perplexity to mortal man than ghosts, goblins, and the whole race of witches put together, and that was—a woman.

Among the musical disciples who assembled one evening in each week to receive his instructions in psalmody, was Katrina Van Tassel, the daughter and only child of a substantial Dutch farmer. She was a blooming lass of fresh eighteen; plump as a partridge; ripe and melting and rosy-cheeked as one of her father's peaches, and universally famed, not merely for her beauty, but her vast expectations. She was, withal, a little of a coquette, as might be perceived even in her dress, which was a mixture of ancient and modern fashions, as most suited to set off her charms. She wore the ornaments of pure yellow gold, which her great-great-grandmother had brought over from Saardam; the tempting stomacher of the olden time; and withal a provokingly short petticoat, to display the prettiest foot and ankle in the country round.

Ichabod Crane had a soft and foolish heart towards the sex, and it is not to be wondered at that so tempting a morsel soon found favour in his eyes, more especially after he had visited her in her paternal mansion. Old Baltus Van Tassel was a perfect picture of a thriving, contented, liberal-hearted farmer. He seldom, it is true, sent either his eyes or his thoughts beyond the boundaries of his own farm; but within those, everything was snug, happy, and well-conditioned. He was satisfied with his wealth, but not proud of it; and piqued himself upon the hearty abundance, rather than the style in which he lived. His stronghold was situated on the banks of the Hudson, in one of those green, sheltered, fertile nooks, in which the Dutch farmers are so fond of nestling. A great elm-tree spread its broad branches over it, at the foot of which bubbled up a spring of the softest and sweetest water, in a little well formed of a barrel, and then stole sparkling away through the grass to a neighbouring brook that bubbled along among alders and dwarf willows. Hard by the farmhouse was a vast barn that might have served for a church, every window and crevice of which seemed bursting forth with the treasures of the farm; the flail was busily resounding within it from morning to night; swallows and martins skimmed twittering about the eaves; and rows of pigeons, some with one eye turned up, as if watching the weather, some with their heads under their wings, or buried in their bosoms, and others swelling, and cooing, and bowing about their dames, were enjoying the sunshine on the roof. Sleek unwieldy porkers were grunting in the repose and abundance of their pens, whence sallied forth now and then troops of sucking pigs, as if to snuff the air. A stately squadron of snowy geese were riding in an adjoining pond, convoying whole fleets of ducks; regiments of turkeys were gobbling through the farmyard, and guinea-fowls fretting about it, like ill-tempered housewives, with their peevish, discontented cry. Before the barn door strutted the gallant cock, that pattern of a husband, a warrior, and a fine gentleman, clapping his burnished wings, and crowing in the pride and gladness of his heart—sometimes tearing up the earth with his feet, and then generously calling his ever-hungry family of wives and children to enjoy the rich morsel which he had discovered.

The pedagogue's mouth watered as he looked upon his sumptuous promise of luxurious winter fare. In his devouring mind's eye he pictured to himself every roasting-pig running about with a pudding in his belly, and an apple in his mouth; the pigeons were snugly put to bed in a comfortable pie, and tucked in with a coverlet of crust; the geese were swimming in their own gravy; and the ducks pairing cosily in dishes, like snug married couples, with a decent competency of onion sauce. In the porkers he saw carved out the future sleek side of bacon and juicy relishing ham; not a turkey but he beheld daintily trussed-up, with its gizzard under its wing, and, peradventure, a necklace of savoury sausages; and even bright chanticleer himself lay sprawling on his back in a side dish, with uplifted claws, as if craving that quarter which his chivalrous spirit disdained to ask while living.

As the enraptured Ichabod fancied all this, and as he rolled his great green eyes over the fat meadow-lands, the rich fields of wheat, of rye, of buckwheat, and Indian corn, and the orchards burthened with ruddy fruit, which surrounded the warm tenement of Van Tassel, his heart yearned after the damsel who was to inherit these domains, and his imagination expanded with the idea, how they might be readily turned into cash, and the money invested in immense tracts of wild land, and shingle palaces in the wilderness. Nay, his busy fancy already realised his hopes, and presented to him the blooming Katrina, with a whole family of children, mounted on the top of a waggon loaded with household trumpery, with pots and kettles dangling beneath; and he beheld himself bestriding a pacing mare, with a colt at her heels, setting out for Kentucky, Tennessee, or the Lord knows where.

When he entered the house, the conquest of his heart was complete. It was one of those spacious farmhouses, with high-ridged, but lowly-sloping roofs, built in the style handed down from the first Dutch settlers; the low projecting eaves forming a piazza along the front, capable of being closed up in bad weather. Under this were hung flails, harness, various utensils of husbandry, and nets for fishing in the neighbouring river. Benches were built along the sides for summer use; and a great spinning-wheel at one end, and a churn at the other, showed the various uses to which this important porch might be devoted. From this piazza the wondering Ichabod entered the hall, which formed the centre of the mansion and the place of usual residence. Here rows of resplendent pewter, ranged on a long dresser, dazzled his eyes. In one corner stood a huge bag of wool ready to be spun; in another, a quantity of linsey-woolsey just from the loom; ears of Indian corn, and strings of dried apples and peaches, hung in gay festoons along the wall, mingled with the gaud of red peppers; and a door left ajar gave him a peep into the best parlour, where the claw-footed chairs and dark mahogany tables shone like mirrors; and irons, with their accompanying shovel and tongs, glistened from their covert of asparagus tops; mock oranges and conch-shells decorated the mantel-piece; strings of various coloured birds' eggs were suspended above it; a great ostrich egg was hung from the centre of the room and a corner-cupboard, knowingly left open, displayed immense treasures of old silver and well-mended china.

From the moment Ichabod laid his eyes upon these regions of delight, the peace of his mind was at an end, and his only study was how to gain the affections of the peerless daughter of Van

Tassel. In this enterprise, however, he had more real difficulties than generally fell to the lot of a knight-errant of yore, who seldom had anything but giants, enchanters, fiery dragons, and such like easily conquered adversaries, to contend with; and had to make his way merely through gates of iron and brass, and walls of adamant, to the castle keep, where the lady of his heart was confined; all which he achieved as easily as a man would carve his way to the centre of a Christmas pie, and then the lady gave him her hand as a matter of course. Ichabod, on the contrary, had to win his way to the heart of a country coquette, beset with a labyrinth of whims and caprices, which were for ever presenting new difficulties and impediments; and he had to encounter a host of fearful adversaries of real flesh and blood, the numerous rustic admirers who beset every portal to her heart, keeping a watchful and angry eye upon each other, but ready to fly out in the common cause against any new competitor.

Among these the most formidable was a burly, roaring, roistering blade, of the name of Abraham, or, according to the Dutch abbreviation, Brom Van Brunt, the hero of the country round, which rang with his feats of strength and hardihood. He was broad-shouldered and double-jointed, with short curly black hair, and a bluff but not unpleasant countenance, having a mingled air of fun and arrogance. From his Herculean frame and great powers of limb, he had received the nickname of BROM BONES, by which he was universally known. He was famed for great knowledge and skill in horsemanship, being as dexterous on horseback as a Tartar. He was foremost at all races and cockfights, and, with the ascendancy which bodily strength acquires in rustic life, was the umpire in all disputes, setting his hat on one side, and giving his decisions with an air and tone admitting of no gainsay or appeal. He was always ready for either a fight or frolic, but had more mischief than ill-will in his composition; and, with all his overbearing roughness, there was a strong dash of waggish good humour at bottom. He had three or four boon companions, who regarded him as their model, and at the head of whom he scoured the country, attending every scene of feud or merriment for miles round. In cold weather he was distinguished by a fur cap, surmounted with a flaunting fox's tail; and when the folks at a country gathering descried this well-known crest at a distance, whisking about among a squad of hard riders, they always stood by for a squall. Sometimes his crew would be heard dashing along past the farmhouses at midnight, with hoop and halloo, like a troop of Don Cossacks, and the old dames, startled out of their sleep, would listen for a moment, till the hurry-scurry had clattered by, and then exclaim, 'Ay, there goes BROM BONES and his gang!' The neighbours looked upon him with a mixture of awe, admiration, and good-will; and when any madcap prank or rustic brawl occurred in the vicinity, always shook their heads and warranted Brom Bones was at the bottom of it.

This rantipole hero had for some time singled out the blooming Katrina for the object of his uncouth gallantries, and though his amorous toyings were something like the gentle caresses and endearments of a bear, yet it was whispered that she did not altogether discourage his hopes. Certain it is, his advances were signals for rival candidates to retire, who felt no inclination to cross a lion in his amours; insomuch that when his horse was seen tied to Van Tassel's paling on a Sunday night, a sure sign that his master was courting, or, as it is termed, 'sparking,' within, all other suitors passed by in despair, and carried the war into other quarters.

Such was the formidable rival with whom Ichabod Crane had to contend, and, considering all things, a stouter man than he would have shrank from the competition, and a wiser man would have despaired. He had, however, a happy mixture of pliability and perseverance in his nature; he was in form and spirit like a supple-jack,—yielding, but tough; though he bent, he never broke; and though he bowed beneath the slightest pressure, yet, the moment it was away—jerk! he was as erect, and carried his head as high as ever.

To have taken the field openly against his rival would have been madness; for he was not a man to be thwarted in his amours, any more than that stormy lover, Achilles. Ichabod, therefore, made his advances in a quiet and gently-insinuating manner.

Under cover of his character of singing-master, he made frequent visits at the farmhouse; not that he had anything to apprehend from the meddlesome interference of parents, which is so often a stumbling-block in the path of lovers. Balt Van Tassel was an easy, indulgent soul; he loved his daughter better even than his pipe, and, like a reasonable man and an excellent father, let her have her way in everything. His notable little wife, too, had enough to do to attend to her housekeeping, and manage her poultry; for, as she sagely observed, ducks and geese are foolish things, and must be looked after, but girls can take care of themselves. Thus, while the busy dame bustled about the house, or plied her spinning-wheel at one end of the piazza, honest Balt would sit smoking his evening pipe at the other, watching the achievements of a little wooden warrior, who, armed with a sword in each hand, was most valiantly fighting the wind on the pinnacle of the barn. In the meantime, Ichabod would carry on his suit with the daughter by the side of the spring under the great elm, or sauntering along in the twilight, that hour so favourable to the lover's eloquence.

I profess not to know how women's hearts are wooed and won. To me they have always been matters of riddle and admiration. Some seem to have but one vulnerable point, or door of access; while others have a thousand avenues, and may be captured in a thousand different ways. It is a great triumph of skill to gain the former, but a still greater proof of generalship to maintain possession of the latter, for a man must battle for his fortress at every door and window. He who wins a thousand common hearts is therefore entitled to some renown; but he who keeps undisputed sway over the heart of a coquette, is indeed a hero. Certain it is, this was not the case with the redoubtable Brom Bones; and from the moment Ichabod Crane made his advances, the interests of the former evidently declined; his horse was no longer seen tied at the palings on Sunday nights, and a deadly feud gradually arose between him and the preceptor of Sleepy Hollow.

Brom, who had a degree of rough chivalry in his nature, would fain have carried matters to open warfare, and have settled their pretensions to the lady, according to the mode of those most concise and simple reasoners, the knights-errant of yore—by single combat; but Ichabod was too conscious of the superior might of his adversary to enter the lists against him; he had overheard a boast of Bones, that he 'would double the schoolmaster up, and lay him on a shelf of his own school-house'; and he was too wary to give him an opportunity. There was something extremely provoking in this obstinately pacific system; it left Brom no alternative but to draw upon the funds of rustic waggery in his disposition, and to play off boorish practical jokes upon his rival. Ichabod became the object of whimsical persecution to Bones and his gang of rough riders. They harried his hitherto peaceful domains; smoked out his singing-school, by stopping up the chimney; broke into the school-house at night, in spite of his formidable fastenings of withe and window stakes, and turned everything topsy-turvy; so that the poor schoolmaster began to think all the witches in the country held their meetings there. But what was still more annoying, Brom took all opportunities of turning him into ridicule in presence of his mistress, and had a scoundrel dog whom he taught to whine in the most ludicrous manner, and introduced as a rival of Ichabod's to instruct her in psalmody.

In this way matters went on for some time, without producing any material effect on the relative situation of the contending powers. On a fine autumnal afternoon, Ichabod, in pensive mood, sat enthroned on the lofty stool whence he usually watched all the concerns of his little literary realm. In his hand he swayed a ferule, that sceptre of despotic power; the birch of justice reposed on three nails behind the throne, a constant terror to evil-doers; while on the desk before him might be seen sundry contraband articles and prohibited weapons, detected upon the persons of idle urchins; such as half-munched apples, pop-guns, whirligigs, fly-cages, and whole legions of rampant little paper game-cocks. Apparently there had been some appalling act of justice recently inflicted, for his scholars were all busily intent upon their books, or slyly whispering behind them with one eye kept upon the master; and a kind of buzzing stillness reigned throughout the school-room. It was suddenly interrupted by the appearance of a negro, in tow-cloth jacket and trousers, a round-crowned fragment of a hat, like the cap of Mercury, and mounted on the back of a ragged, wild, half-broken colt, which he managed with a rope by way of halter. He came clattering up to the school door with an invitation to Ichabod to attend a merry-making, or 'quilting frolic,' to be held that evening at Mynheer Van Tassel's; and having delivered his message with that air of importance and effort at fine language which a negro is apt to display on petty embassies of the kind, he dashed over the brook, and was seen scampering away up the hollow, full of the importance and hurry of his mission.

All was now bustle and hubbub in the late quiet school-room. The scholars were hurried through their lessons without stopping at trifles; those who were nimble skipped over half with impunity, and those who were tardy had a smart application now and then in the rear, to quicken their speed, or help them over a tall word. Books were flung aside without being put away on the shelves; inkstands were overturned, benches thrown down, and the whole school was turned loose an hour before the usual time, bursting forth like a legion of young imps, yelping and racketing about the green in joy at their early emancipation.

The gallant Ichabod now spent at least an extra half-hour at his toilet, brushing and furbishing up his best, and indeed only suit of rusty black, and arranging his locks by a bit of broken looking-glass that hung up in the school-house. That he might make his appearance before his mistress in the true style of a cavalier, he borrowed a horse from the farmer with whom he was domiciliated, a choleric old Dutchman, of the name of Hans Van Ripper, and, thus gallantly mounted, issued forth like a knight-errant in quest of adventures. But it is meet I should, in the true spirit of romantic story, give some account of the looks and equipments of my hero and his steed. The animal he bestrode was a broken-down plough-horse that had outlived almost everything but his viciousness. He was gaunt and shagged, with a ewe neck and a head like a hammer; his rusty mane and tail were tangled and knotted with burrs; one eye had lost its pupil, and was glaring and spectral; but the other had the gleam of a genuine devil in it. Still he must have had fire and mettle in his day, if we may judge from the name he bore of Gunpowder. He had, in fact, been a favourite steed of his master's, the choleric Van Ripper, who was a furious rider, and had infused, very probably, some of his own spirit into the animal; for, old and broken-down as he looked, there was more of the lurking devil in him than in any young filly in the country.

Ichabod was a suitable figure for such a steed. He rode with short stirrups, which brought his knees nearly up to the pommel of the saddle; his sharp elbows stuck out like grasshoppers; he carried his whip perpendicularly in his hand, like a sceptre, and, as his horse jogged on, the motion of his arms was not unlike the flapping of a pair of wings. A small wool hat rested on the top of his nose, for so his scanty strip of forehead might be called; and the skirts of his black coat fluttered out almost to the horse's tail. Such was the appearance of Ichabod and his steed, as they shambled out of the gate of Hans Van Ripper, and it was altogether such an apparition as is seldom to be met with in broad daylight.

It was, as I have said, a fine autumnal day, the sky was clear and serene, and nature wore that rich and golden livery which we always associate with the idea of abundance. The forests had put on their sober brown and yellow, while some trees of the tenderer kind had been nipped by the frosts into brilliant dyes of orange, purple, and scarlet. Streaming files of wild ducks began to make their appearance high in the air; the bark of the squirrel might be heard from the groves of beech and hickory nuts, and the pensive whistle of the quail at intervals from the neighbouring stubble field.

The small birds were taking their farewell banquets. In the fulness of their revelry, they fluttered, chirping and frolicking, from bush to bush and tree to tree, capricious from the very profusion and variety around them. There was the honest cock-robin, the favourite game of stripling sportsmen, with its loud, querulous note; and the twittering blackbirds flying in sable clouds; and the golden-winged woodpecker, with his crimson crest, his broad black gorget, and splendid plumage; and the cedar-bird, with its red-tipt wings and yellow-tipt tail, and its little monteiro cap of feathers; and the blue jay, that noisy coxcomb, in his gay light-blue coat and white underclothes; screaming and chattering, nodding and bobbing and bowing, and pretending to be on good terms with every songster of the grove.

As Ichabod jogged slowly on his way, his eye, ever open to every symptom of culinary abundance, ranged with delight over the treasures of jolly autumn. On all sides he beheld vast stores of apples; some hanging in oppressive opulence on the trees; some gathered into baskets and barrels for the market; others heaped up in rich piles for the cider-press. Further on he beheld great fields of Indian corn, with its golden ears peeping from their leafy coverts, and holding out the promise of cakes and hasty-pudding; and the yellow pumpkins lying beneath them, turning up their fair round bellies to the sun, and giving ample prospects of the most luxurious of pies; and anon he passed the fragrant buckwheat fields breathing the odour of the bee-hive, and as he beheld them, soft anticipations stole over his mind of dainty slapjacks, well buttered, and garnished with honey or treacle, by the delicate little dimpled hand of Katrina Van Tassel.

Thus feeding his mind with many sweet thoughts and 'sugared suppositions,' he journeyed along the sides of a range of hills which look out upon some of the goodliest scenes of the mighty Hudson. The sun gradually wheeled his broad disc down into the west. The wide bosom of the Tappan Zee lay motionless and glassy, except that here and there a gentle undulation waved and prolonged the blue shadow of the distant mountain. A few amber clouds floated in the sky, without a breath of air to move them. The horizon was of a fine golden tint, changing gradually into a pure apple-green, and from that into the deep blue of the mid-heaven. A slanting ray lingered on the woody crests of the precipices that overhung some parts of the river, giving greater depth to the dark-gray and purple of their rocky sides. A sloop was loitering in the distance, dropping slowly down with the tide, her sail hanging uselessly against the mast; and as the reflection of the sky gleamed along the still water, it seemed as if the vessel was suspended in the air.

It was toward evening that Ichabod arrived at the castle of the Heer Van Tassel, which he found thronged with the pride and flower of the adjacent country. Old farmers, a spare leathern-faced race, in homespun coats and breeches, blue stockings, huge shoes, and magnificent pewter buckles. Their brisk withered little dames, in close crimped caps, long-waisted short gowns, homespun petticoats, with scissors and pincushions, and gay calico pockets hanging on the outside. Buxom lasses, almost as antiquated as their mothers, excepting where a straw hat, a fine riband, or perhaps a white frock, gave symptoms of city innovation. The sons, in short square-skirted coats with rows of stupendous brass buttons, and their hair generally queued in the fashion of the times, especially if they could procure an eel-skin for the purpose, it being esteemed throughout the country as a potent nourisher and strengthener of the hair.

Brom Bones, however, was the hero of the scene, having come to the gathering on his favourite steed Daredevil, a creature like himself, full of mettle and mischief, and which no one but himself could manage. He was, in fact, noted for preferring vicious animals, given to all kinds of tricks, which kept the rider in constant risk of his neck, for he held a tractable, well-broken horse as unworthy of a lad of spirit.

Fain would I pause to dwell upon the world of charms that burst upon the enraptured gaze of my hero, as he entered the state parlour of Van Tassel's mansion. Not those of the bevy of buxom lasses, with their luxurious display of red and white; but the ample charms of a genuine Dutch country tea-table in the sumptuous time of autumn. Such heaped-up platters of cakes of various and almost indescribable kinds, known only to experienced Dutch housewives! There was the doughty dough-nut, the tenderer oly koek, and the crisp and crumbling cruller; sweet-cakes and short-cakes, ginger-cakes and honey-cakes, and the whole family of cakes. And then there were apple-pies and peach-pies and pumpkin-pies; besides slices of ham and smoked beef; and, moreover, delectable dishes of preserved plums, and peaches, and pears, and quinces; not to mention broiled shad and roasted chickens; together with bowls of milk and cream, all mingled higgledy-piggledy, pretty much as I have enumerated them, with the motherly tea-pot sending up its clouds of vapour from the midst—Heaven bless the mark! I want breath and time to discuss this banquet as it deserves, and am too eager to get on with my story. Happily, Ichabod Crane was not in so great a hurry as his historian, but did ample justice to every dainty.

He was a kind and thankful creature, whose heart dilated in proportion as his skin was filled with good cheer; and whose spirits rose with eating as some men's do with drink. He could not help, too, rolling his large eyes round him as he ate, and chuckling with the possibility that he might one day be lord of all this scene of almost unimaginable luxury and splendour. Then he thought, how soon he'd turn his back upon the old schoolhouse, snap his fingers in the face of Hans Van Ripper and every other niggardly patron, and kick any itinerant pedagogue out of doors that should dare to call him comrade!

Old Baltus Van Tassel moved about among his guests with a face dilated with content and good humour, round and jolly as the harvest moon. His hospitable attentions were brief, but expressive, being confined to a shake of the hand, a slap on the shoulder, a loud laugh, and a pressing invitation to 'fall to, and help themselves.'

And now the sound of the music from the common room or hall summoned to the dance. The musician was an old grayheaded negro, who had been the itinerant orchestra of the neighbourhood for more than half a century. His instrument was as old and battered as himself. The greater part of the time he scraped on two or three strings, accompanying every movement of the bow with a motion of the head; bowing almost to the ground, and stamping with his foot whenever a fresh couple were to start.

Ichabod prided himself upon his dancing as much as upon his vocal powers. Not a limb, not a fibre about him was idle; and to have seen his loosely-hung frame in full motion, and clattering about the room, you would have thought Saint Vitus himself, that blessed patron of the dance, was figuring before you in person. He was the admiration of all the negroes; who, having gathered, of all ages and sizes, from the farm and the neighbourhood, stood forming a pyramid of shining black faces, at every door and window, gazing with delight at the scene, rolling their white eyeballs, and showing grinning rows of ivory from ear to ear. How could the flogger of urchins be otherwise than animated and joyous? the lady of his heart was his partner in the dance, and smiling graciously in reply to all his amorous oglings; while Brom Bones, sorely smitten with love and jealousy, sat brooding by himself in one corner.

When the dance was at an end, Ichabod was attracted to a knot of the sager folks, who, with old Van Tassel, sat smoking at one end of the piazza, gossiping over former times, and drawing out long stories about the war.

This neighbourhood, at the time of which I am speaking, was one of those highly-favoured places which abound with chronicle and great men. The British and American line had run near it during the war; it had, therefore, been the scene of marauding, and infested with refugees, cow-boys, and all kinds of border chivalry. Just sufficient time had elapsed to enable each story teller to dress up his tale with a little becoming fiction, and, in the indistinctness of his recollection, to make himself the hero of every exploit.

There was the story of Doffue Martling, a large blue-bearded Dutchman, who had nearly taken a British frigate with an old iron nine-pounder from a mud breastwork, only that his gun burst at the sixth discharge. And there was an old gentleman who shall be nameless, being too rich a mynheer to be lightly mentioned, who, in the battle of Whiteplains, being an excellent master of defence, parried a musket-ball with a small sword, insomuch that he absolutely felt it whiz round the blade, and glance off at the hilt; in proof of which he was ready at any time to show the sword, with the hilt a little bent. There were several more that had been equally great in the field, not one of whom but was persuaded that he had a considerable hand in bringing the war to a happy termination.

But all these were nothing to the tales of ghosts and apparitions that succeeded. The neighbourhood is rich in legendary treasures of the kind. Local tales and superstitions thrive best in these sheltered long-settled retreats; but are trampled under-foot by the shifting throng that forms the population of most of our country places. Besides, there is no encouragement for ghosts in most of our villages, for they have scarcely had time to finish their first nap, and turn themselves in their graves, before their surviving friends have travelled away from the neighbourhood; so that when they turn out at night to walk their rounds, they have no acquaintance left to call upon. This is perhaps the reason why we so seldom hear of ghosts except in our long-established Dutch communities.

The immediate cause, however, of the prevalence of supernatural stories in these parts, was doubtless owing to the vicinity of Sleepy Hollow. There was a contagion in the very air that blew from that haunted region; it breathed forth an atmosphere of dreams and fancies infecting all the land. Several of the Sleepy Hollow people were present at Van Tassel's, and, as usual, were doling out their wild and wonderful legends. Many dismal tales were told about funeral trains, and mourning cries and wailings heard and seen about the great tree where the unfortunate Major André was taken, and which stood in the neighbourhood. Some mention was made also of the woman in white, that haunted the dark glen at Raven Rock, and was often heard to shriek on winter nights before a storm, having perished there in the snow. The chief part of the stories, however, turned upon the favourite spectre of Sleepy Hollow, the headless horseman, who had been heard several times of late, patrolling the country; and, it was said, tethered his horse nightly among the graves in the churchyard.

The sequestered situation of this church seems always to have made it a favourite haunt of troubled spirits. It stands on a knoll surrounded by locust-trees and lofty elms, from among which its decent whitewashed walls shine modestly forth, like Christian purity, beaming through the shades of retirement. A gentle slope descends from it to a silver sheet of water, bordered by high trees, between which peeps may be caught at the blue hills of the Hudson. To look upon its grass-grown yard, where the sunbeams seem to sleep so quietly, one would think that there at least the dead might rest in peace. On one side of the church extends a wide woody dell, along which raves a large brook among broken rocks and trunks of fallen trees. Over a deep black part of the stream, not far from the church, was formerly thrown a wooden bridge; the road that led to it, and the bridge itself, were thickly shaded by overhanging trees, which cast a gloom about it, even in the daytime; but occasioned a fearful darkness at night. Such was one of the favourite haunts of the headless horseman, and the place where he was most frequently encountered. The tale was told of old Brouwer, a most heretical disbeliever in ghosts, how he met the horseman returning from his foray into Sleepy Hollow, and was obliged to get up behind him; how they galloped over bush and brake, over hill and swamp, until they reached the bridge; when the horseman suddenly turned into a skeleton, threw old Brouwer into the brook, and sprang away over the tree-tops with a clap of thunder.

This story was immediately matched by a thrice marvellous adventure of Brom Bones, who made light of the Galloping Hessian as an arrant jockey. He affirmed that, on returning one night from the neighbouring village of Sing-Sing, he had been overtaken by this midnight trooper; that he had offered to race with him for a bowl of punch, and should have won it too, for Daredevil beat the goblin horse all hollow, but, just as they came to the church bridge, the Hessian bolted, and vanished in a flash of fire.

All these tales, told in that drowsy under-tone with which men talk in the dark, the countenances of the listeners only now and then receiving a casual gleam from the glare of a pipe, sank deep in the mind of Ichabod. He repaid them in kind, with large extracts from his invaluable author, Cotton Mather, and added many marvellous events that had taken place in his native state of Connecticut, and fearful sights which he had seen in his nightly walks about Sleepy Hollow.

The revel now gradually broke up. The old farmers gathered

together their families in their waggons, and were heard for some time rattling along the hollow roads, and over the distant hills. Some of the damsels mounted on pillions behind their favourite swains, and their light-hearted laughter, mingling with the clatter of hoofs, echoed along the silent woodlands, sounding fainter and fainter until they gradually died away—and the late scene of noise and frolic was all silent and deserted. Ichabod only lingered behind, according to the custom of country lovers, to have a *tête-à-tête* with the heiress, fully convinced that he was now on the high road to success. What passed at this interview I will not pretend to say, for in fact I do not know. Something, however, I fear me, must have gone wrong, for he certainly sallied forth, after no very great interval, with an air quite desolate and chop-fallen. Oh these women! these women! Could that girl have been playing off any of her coquettish tricks?—Was her encouragement of the poor pedagogue all a mere sham to secure her conquest of his rival?—Heaven only knows, not I!—Let it suffice to say, Ichabod stole forth with the air of one who had been sacking a hen-roost, rather than a fair lady's heart. Without looking to the right or left to notice the scene of rural wealth on which he had so often gloated, he went straight to the stable, and with several hearty cuffs and kicks, roused his steed most uncourteously from the comfortable quarters in which he was soundly sleeping, dreaming of mountains of corn and oats, and whole valleys of timothy and clover.

It was the very witching time of night that Ichabod, heavy-hearted and crest-fallen, pursued his travels homewards, along the sides of the lofty hills which rise above Tarry Town, and which he had traversed so cheerily in the afternoon. The hour was as dismal as himself. Far below him the Tappan Zee spread its dusky and indistinct waste of waters, with here and there the tall mast of a sloop riding quietly at anchor under the land. In the dead hush of midnight he could even hear the barking of the watch-dog from the opposite shore of the Hudson; but it was so vague and faint as only to give an idea of his distance from this faithful companion of man. Now and then, too, the long-drawn crowing of a cock, accidentally awakened, would sound far, far off, from some farmhouse away among the hills—but it was like a dreaming sound in his ear. No signs of life occurred near him, but occasionally the melancholy chirp of a cricket, or perhaps the guttural twang of a bull-frog, from a neighbouring marsh, as if sleeping uncomfortably, and turning suddenly in his bed.

All the stories of ghosts and goblins that he had heard in the afternoons now came crowding upon his recollection. The night grew darker and darker; the stars seemed to sink deeper in the sky, and driving clouds occasionally hid them from his sight. He had never felt so lonely and dismal. He was, moreover, approaching the very place where many of the scenes of the ghost-stories had been laid. In the centre of the road stood an enormous tulip-tree, which towered like a giant above all the other trees of the neighbourhood, and formed a kind of landmark. Its limbs were gnarled and fantastic, large enough to form trunks for ordinary trees, twisting down almost to the earth, and rising again into the air. It was connected with the tragical story of the unfortunate André, who had been taken prisoner hard by; and was universally known by the name of Major André's tree. The common people regarded it with a mixture of respect and superstition, partly out of sympathy for the fate of its ill-starred namesake and partly from the tales of strange sights and doleful lamentations told concerning it.

As Ichabod approached this fearful tree, he began to whistle; he thought his whistle was answered; it was but a blast sweeping sharply through the dry branches. As he approached a little nearer, he thought he saw something white hanging in the midst of the tree—he paused and ceased whistling; but on looking more narrowly, perceived that it was a place where the tree had been scathed by lightning, and the white wood laid bare. Suddenly he heard a groan—his teeth chattered, and his knees smote against the saddle; it was but the rubbing of one huge bough upon another, as they were swayed about by the breeze. He passed the tree in safety, but new perils lay before him.

About two hundred yards from the tree a small brook crossed the road, and ran into a marshy and thickly-wooded glen, known by the name of Wiley's Swamp. A few rough logs, laid side by side, served for a bridge over this stream. On that side of the road where the brook entered the wood, a group of oaks and chestnuts, matted thick with wild grape-vines, threw a cavernous gloom over it. To pass this bridge was the severest trial. It was at this identical spot that the unfortunate André was captured, and under the covert of those chestnuts and vines were the sturdy yeomen concealed who surprised him. This has ever since been considered a haunted stream, and fearful are the feelings of the schoolboy who has to pass it alone after dark.

As he approached the stream, his heart began to thump; he summoned up, however, all his resolution, gave his horse half a score of kicks in the ribs, and attempted to dash briskly across the bridge; but instead of starting forward, the perverse old animal made a lateral movement, and ran broadside against the fence. Ichabod, whose fears increased with the delay, jerked the reins on the other side, and kicked lustily with the contrary foot: it was all in vain; his steed started, it is true, but it was only to plunge to the opposite side of the road into a thicket of brambles and alder-bushes. The schoolmaster now bestowed both whip and heel upon the starveling ribs of old Gunpowder, who dashed forward, snuffling and snorting, but came to a stand just by the bridge, with a suddenness that had nearly sent his rider sprawling over his head. Just at this moment a plashy tramp by the side of the bridge caught the sensitive ear of Ichabod. In the dark shadow of the grove, on the margin of the brook, he beheld something huge, misshapen, black and towering. It stirred not, but seemed gathered up in the gloom, like some gigantic monster ready to spring upon the traveller.

The hair of the affrighted pedagogue rose upon his head with terror. What was to be done? To turn and fly was now too late; and besides, what chance was there of escaping ghost or goblin, if such it was, which could ride upon the wings of the wind? Summoning up, therefore, a show of courage, he demanded in stammering accents—'Who are you?' He received no reply. He repeated his demand in a still more agitated voice. Still there was no answer. Once more he cudgelled the sides of the inflexible Gunpowder, and, shutting his eyes, broke forth with involuntary fervour into a psalm tune. Just then the shadowy object of alarm put itself in motion, and with a scramble and a bound, stood at once in the middle of the road. Though the night was dark and dismal, yet the form of the unknown might now in some degree be ascertained. He appeared to be a horseman of large dimensions, and mounted on a black horse of powerful frame. He made no offer of molestation or sociability, but kept aloof on one side of the road, jogging along on the blind side of old Gunpowder, who had now got over his fright and waywardness.

Ichabod, who had no relish for this strange midnight companion, and bethought himself of the adventure of Brom Bones with the Galloping Hessian, now quickened his steed, in hopes of leaving him behind. The stranger, however, quickened his horse to an equal pace. Ichabod pulled up, and fell into a walk, thinking to lag behind—the other did the same. His heart began to sink within him; he endeavoured to resume his psalm tune, but his parched tongue clove to the roof of his mouth, and he could not utter a stave. There was something in the moody and dogged silence of this pertinacious companion that was mysterious and appalling. It was soon fearfully accounted for. On mounting a rising ground, which brought the figure of his fellow-traveller in relief against the sky, gigantic in height, and muffled in a cloak, Ichabod was horror-struck on perceiving that he was headless!—but his horror was still more increased on observing that the head, which should have rested on his shoulders, was carried before him on the pommel of the saddle: his terror rose to desperation; he rained a shower of kicks and blows upon Gunpowder, hoping, by a sudden movement, to give his companion the slip—but the spectre started full jump with him. Away then they dashed, through thick and thin; stones flying and sparks flashing at every bound. Ichabod's flimsy garments fluttered in the air, as he stretched his long lank body away over his horse's head, in the eagerness of his flight.

They had now reached the road which turns off to Sleepy Hollow; but Gunpowder, who seemed possessed with a demon, instead of keeping up it, made an opposite turn, and plunged headlong down the hill to the left. This road leads through a sandy hollow, shaded by trees for about a quarter of a mile, where it crosses the bridge famous in goblin story, and just beyond swells the green knoll on which stands the whitewashed church.

As yet the panic of the steed had given his unskilful rider an apparent advantage in the chase; but just as he had got half way through the hollow, the girths of the saddle gave way, and he felt it slipping from under him. He seized it by the pommel, and endeavoured to hold it firm, but in vain; and had just time to save himself by clasping old Gunpowder round the neck, when the saddle fell to the earth, and he heard it trampled under-foot by his pursuer. For a moment the terror of Hans Van Ripper's wrath passed across his mind—for it was his Sunday saddle; but this was no time for petty fears; the goblin was hard on his haunches; and (unskilful rider that he was!) he had much ado to maintain his seat; sometimes slipping on one side, sometimes on the other, and sometimes jolted on the high ridge of his horse's back-bone, with a violence that he verily feared would cleave him asunder.

An opening in the trees now cheered him with the hopes that the church bridge was at hand. The wavering reflection of a silver star in the bosom of the brook told him that he was not mistaken. He saw the walls of the church dimly glaring under the trees beyond. He recollected the place where Brom Bones' ghostly competitor had disappeared. 'If I can but reach that bridge,' thought Ichabod, 'I am safe.' Just then he heard the black steed panting and blowing close behind him; he even fancied that he felt his hot breath. Another convulsive kick in the ribs, and old Gunpowder sprang upon the bridge; he thundered over the resounding planks; he gained the opposite side; and now Ichabod cast a look behind to see if his pursuer should vanish, according to rule, in a flash of fire and brimstone. Just then he saw the goblin rising in his stirrups, and in the very act of hurling his head at him. Ichabod endeavoured to dodge the horrible missile, but too late. It encountered his cranium with a tremendous crash—he was tumbled headlong into the dust, and Gunpowder, the black steed, and the goblin rider passed by like a whirlwind.

He heard the black steed panting and blowing close behind him . . .

The next morning the old horse was found without his saddle, and with the bridle under his feet, soberly cropping the grass at his master's gate. Ichabod did not make his appearance at breakfast—dinner-hour came, but no Ichabod. The boys assembled at the school-house, and strolled idly about the banks of the brook; but no schoolmaster. Hans Van Ripper now began to feel some uneasiness about the fate of poor Ichabod and his saddle. An inquiry was set on foot, and after diligent investigation they came upon his traces. In one part of the road leading to the church was found the saddle trampled in the dirt; the tracks of horses' hoofs deeply dented in the road, and evidently at furious speed, were traced to the bridge, beyond which, on the bank of a broad part of the brook, where the water ran deep and black, was found the hat of the unfortunate Ichabod, and close beside it a shattered pumpkin.

The brook was searched, but the body of the schoolmaster was not to be discovered. Hans Van Ripper, as executor of his estate, examined the bundle which contained all his worldly effects. They consisted of two shirts and a half; two stocks for the neck; a pair or two of worsted stockings; an old pair of corduroy small-clothes; a rusty razor; a book of psalm tunes, full of dog's ears; and a broken pitch-pipe. As to the books and furniture of the school-house, they belonged to the community, excepting Cotton Mather's *History of Witchcraft*, a New England Almanac, and a book of dreams and fortune-telling; in which last was a sheet of foolscap much scribbled and blotted in several fruitless attempts to make a copy of verses in honour of the heiress of Van Tassel. These magic books and the poetic scrawl were forthwith consigned to the flames by Hans Van Ripper; who from that time forward determined to send his children no more to school, observing, that he never knew any good come of this same reading and writing. Whatever money the schoolmaster possessed, and he had received his quarter's pay but a day or two before, he must have had about his person at the time of his disappearance.

The mysterious event caused much speculation at the church on the following Sunday. Knots of gazers and gossips were collected in the churchyard, at the bridge, and at the spot where the hat and pumpkin had been found. The stories of Brouwer, of Bones, and a whole budget of others, were called to mind; and when they had diligently considered them all, and compared them with the symptoms of the present case, they shook their heads, and came to the conclusion that Ichabod had been carried off by the Galloping Hessian. As he was a bachelor, and in nobody's debt, nobody troubled his head any more about him: the school was removed to a different quarter of the Hollow, and another pedagogue reigned in his stead.

It is true, an old farmer, who had been down to New York on a visit several years after, and from whom this account of the ghostly adventure was received, brought home the intelligence that Ichabod Crane was still alive; that he had left the neighbourhood, partly through fear of the goblin and Hans Van Ripper, and partly in mortification at having been suddenly dismissed by the heiress; that he had changed his quarters to a distant part of the country; had kept school and studied law at the same time; had been admitted to the bar, turned politician, electioneered, written for the newspapers, and finally had been made a justice of the Ten-pound Court. Brom Bones, too, who shortly after his rival's disappearance conducted the blooming Katrina in triumph to the altar, was observed to look exceedingly knowing whenever the story of Ichabod was related, and always burst into a hearty laugh at the mention of the pumpkin; which led some to suspect that he knew more about the matter than he chose to tell.

The old country wives, however, who are the best judges of these matters, maintain to this day that Ichabod was spirited away by supernatural means; and it is a favourite story often told about the neighbourhood round the winter evening fire. The bridge became more than ever an object of superstitious awe, and that may be the reason why the road has been altered of late years, so as to approach the church by the border of the mill-pond. The school-house being deserted, soon fell to decay, and was reported to be haunted by the ghost of the unfortunate pedagogue; and the plough-boy, loitering homeward of a still summer evening, has often fancied his voice at a distance, chanting a melancholy psalm tune among the tranquil solitudes of Sleepy Hollow.

POSTSCRIPT

FOUND IN THE HANDWRITING OF MR KNICKERBOCKER

THE preceding tale is given, almost in the precise words in which I heard it related at a Corporation meeting of the ancient city of Manhattoes, at which were present many of its sagest and most illustrious burghers. The narrator was a pleasant, shabby, gentlemanly old fellow, in pepper-and-salt clothes, with a sadly humorous face; and one whom I strongly suspected of being poor,—he made such efforts to be entertaining. When his story was concluded, there was much laughter and approbation, particularly from two or three deputy aldermen, who had been asleep the greater part of the time. There was, however, one tall, dry-looking old gentleman, with beetling eyebrows, who maintained a grave and rather a severe face throughout: now and then folding his arms, inclining his head, and looking down upon the floor, as if turning a doubt over in his mind. He was one of your wary men, who never laugh, but upon good grounds—when they have reason and the law on their side. When the mirth of the rest of the company had subsided, and silence was restored, he leaned one arm on the elbow of his chair, and sticking the other a-kimbo, demanded, with a slight but exceedingly sage motion of the head, and contraction of the brow, what was the moral of the story, and what it went to prove?

The story-teller, who was just putting a glass of wine to his lips, as a refreshment after his toils, paused for a moment, looked at his inquirer with an air of infinite deference, and, lowering the glass slowly to the table, observed that the story was intended most logically to prove:

'That there is no situation in life but has its advantages and pleasures—provided we will but take a joke as we find it:

'That, therefore, he that runs races with goblin troopers is likely to have rough riding of it.

'Ergo, for a country schoolmaster to be refused the hand of a Dutch heiress is a certain step to high preferment in the state.'

The cautious old gentleman knit his brows tenfold closer after this explanation, being sorely puzzled by the ratiocination of the syllogism: while, methought, the one in pepper-and-salt eyed him with something of a triumphant leer. At length he observed that all this was very well; but still he thought the story a little on the extravagant—there were one or two points on which he had his doubts.

'Faith, sir,' replied the story-teller, 'as to that matter, I don't believe one half of it myself.' D. K.

Andrew Lang

THE HOUSE OF STRANGE STORIES

THE House of Strange Stories, as I prefer to call it (though it is not known by that name in the country), seems the very place for a ghost. Yet, though so many peoples have dwelt upon its site and in its chambers, though the ancient Elizabethan oak, and all the queer tables and chairs that a dozen generations have bequeathed, might well be tenanted by ancestral spirits, and disturbed by rappings, it is a curious fact that there is *not* a ghost in the House of Strange Stories. On my earliest visit to this mansion, I was disturbed, I own, by a not unpleasing expectancy. There *must*, one argued, be a shadowy lady in green in the bedroom, or, just as one was falling asleep, the spectre of a Jesuit would creep out of the priest's hole, where he was starved to death in the 'spacious times of great Elizabeth,' and would search for a morsel of bread.

'Does the priest of your "priest-hole" walk?' I asked the squire one winter evening in the House of Strange Stories.

Darkness had come to the rescue of the pheasants about four in the afternoon, and all of us, men and women, were sitting at afternoon tea in the firelit study, drowsily watching the flicker of the flame on the black panelling. The characters will introduce themselves, as they take part in the conversation.

'No,' said the squire, 'even the priest does not walk. Somehow very few of the Jesuits have left ghosts in country houses. They are just the customers you would expect to "walk," but they don't. . . .'

'The only ghost *I* ever came across, or, rather, came within measurable distance of, never appeared at all so far as one knew,' remarked the Girton girl.

'Miss Lebas has a story,' said the squire. 'Won't she tell us her story?'

The ladies murmured, 'Do, please.'

'It really cannot be called a ghost-story,' remarked Miss Lebas, 'it was only an uncomfortable kind of coincidence, and I never think of it without a shudder. But I know there is not any reason at all why it should make any of *you* shudder; so don't be disappointed.

'It was the Long Vacation before last, and I went on a reading-party to Bantry Bay. Term-time was drawing near, and Bantry Bay was getting pretty cold, when I received an invitation from Lady Garryowen to stay with them at Dundellan on my way south. They were two very dear, old, hospitable Irish ladies, the last of their race, Lady Garryowen and her sister, Miss Patty. They were *so* hospitable that, though I did not know it, Dundellan was quite full when I reached it, overflowing with young people. The house has nothing very remarkable about it: a grey, plain building, with remains of the château about it, and a high park wall. In the garden wall there is a small round tower, just like those in the precinct wall at St Andrews. The ground floor is not used. On the first floor there is a furnished chamber with a deep round niche, almost a separate room, like that in Queen Mary's apartments in Holy Rood. The first floor has long been fitted up as a bedroom and dressing-room, but it had not been occupied, and a curious old spinning-wheel in the corner (which has nothing to do with my story, if you can call it a story), must have been unused since 1798, at least. I reached Dublin late; our train should have arrived at half-past six—it was ten before we toiled into the station. The Dundellan carriage was waiting for me, and, after an hour's drive, I reached the house. The dear old ladies had sat up for me, and I went to bed as soon as possible, in a very comfortable room. I fell asleep at once, and did not waken till broad daylight, between seven and eight, when, as my eyes wandered about, I saw, by the pictures on the wall, and the names on the books beside my bed, that Miss Patty must have given up her own room to me. I was quite sorry and, as I dressed, determined to get her to let me change into any den rather than accept this sacrifice. I went downstairs, and found breakfast ready, but neither Lady Garryowen nor Miss Patty. Looking out of the window into the garden, I heard, for the only time in my life, the wild Irish *keen* over the dead, and saw the old nurse wailing and wringing her hands and hurrying to the house. As soon as she entered she told me, with a burst of grief, and in language I shall not try to imitate, that Miss Patty was dead.

'When I arrived the house was so full that there was literally no room for me. But "Dundellan was never beaten yet," the old ladies had said. There was still the room in the tower. But this room had such an evil reputation for being "haunted" that the servants could hardly be got to go near it, at least after dark, and the dear old ladies never dreamed of sending any of their guests to pass a bad night in a place with a bad name. Miss Patty, who had the courage of a Bayard, did not think twice. She went herself to sleep in the haunted tower, and left her room to me. And when the old nurse went to call her in the morning, she could not waken Miss Patty. She was dead. Heart-disease, they called it. Of course,' added the Girton girl, 'as I said, it was only a coincidence. But the Irish servants could not be persuaded that Miss Patty had not seen whatever the thing was that they believed to be in the garden tower. I don't know what it was. You see the context was dreadfully vague, a mere fragment.'

There was a little silence after the Girton girl's story.

'I never heard before in my life,' said the maiden aunt, at last, 'of any host or hostess who took the haunted room themselves, when the house happened to be full. They always send the stranger within their gates to it, and then pretend to be vastly surprised when he does not have a good night. I had several bad nights myself once. In Ireland too.'

'Tell us all about it, Judy,' said her brother, the squire.

'No,' murmured the maiden aunt. 'You would only laugh at me. There was no ghost. I didn't hear anything. I didn't see anything. I didn't even *smell* anything, as they do in that horrid book, *The Haunted Hotel*.'

'Then why had you such bad nights?'

'Oh, I *felt*,' said the maiden aunt, with a little shudder.

'What did you *feel*, Aunt Judy?'

'I *know* you will laugh,' said the maiden aunt, abruptly entering on her nervous narrative. 'I felt all the time *as if somebody was looking through the window*. Now, you know, there *couldn't* be anybody. It was in an Irish country house where I had just arrived, and my room was on the second floor. The window was old-fashioned and narrow, with a deep recess. As soon as I went to bed, my dears, I *felt* that some one was looking through the window, and meant to come in. I got up, and bolted the window, though I knew it was impossible for anybody to climb up there, and I drew the curtains, but I could not fall asleep. If ever I began to dose, I would waken with a start, and turn and look in the direction of the window. I did not sleep all night, and next night, though I was dreadfully tired, it was just the same thing. So I had to take my hostess into my confidence, though it was extremely disagreeable, my dears, to seem so foolish. I only told her that I thought the air, or something, must disagree with me, for I could not sleep. Then, as some one was leaving the house that day, she implored me to try another room, where I slept beautifully, and afterwards had a very pleasant visit. But, the day I went away, my hostess asked me if I had been kept awake by anything in particular, for instance, by a feeling that some one was trying to come in at the window. Well, I admitted that I *had* a nervous feeling of that sort, and she said that she was very sorry, and that every one who lay in the room had exactly the same sensation. She supposed they must all have heard the history of the room, in childhood, and forgotten that they had heard it, and then been consciously reminded of it by reflex action. It seems, my dears, that that is the new scientific way of explaining all these things, presentiments and dreams and wraiths, and all that sort of thing. We have seen them before, and remember them without being aware of it. So I said I'd never heard the history of the room; but she said I *must* have, and so must all the people who felt as if some one was coming in by the window. And I said that it was rather a curious thing they should *all* forget they knew it, and *all* be reminded of it without being aware of it, and that, if she did not mind, I'd like to be reminded of it again. So she said that these objections had all been replied to (just as clergymen always say in sermons), and then she told me the history of the room. It only came to this, that, three generations before, the family butler (whom every one had always thought a most steady, respectable man), dressed himself up like a ghost, or like his notion of a ghost, and got a ladder, and came in by the window to steal the diamonds of the lady of the house, and he frightened her to death, poor woman! That was all. But, ever since, people who sleep in the room don't sleep, so to speak, and keep thinking that some one is coming in by the casement. That's all; and I told you it was not an interesting story, but perhaps you will find more interest in the scientific explanation of all these things.'

The story of the maiden aunt, so far as it recounted her own experience, did not contain anything to which the judicial faculties of the mind refused assent. Probably the Bachelor of Arts felt that something a good deal more unusual was wanted, for he instantly started, without being asked, on the following narrative:

'I also was staying,' said the Bachelor of Arts, 'at the home of my friends, the aristocracy in Scotland. The name of the house, and the precise rank in the peerage of my illustrious host, it is not necessary for me to give. All, however, who know those more than feudal and baronial halls, are aware that the front of the castle looks forth on a somewhat narrow drive, bordered by black and funereal pines. On the night of my arrival at the castle, although I went late to bed, I did not feel at all sleepy. Something, perhaps, in the mountain air, or in the vicissitudes of *baccarat*, may have banished slumber. I had been in luck, and a pile of sovereigns and notes lay, in agreeable confusion, on my dressing-table. My feverish blood declined to be tranquillized, and at last I drew up the blind, threw open the latticed window, and looked out on the drive and the pine-wood. The faint and silvery blue of dawn was just wakening in the sky, and a setting moon hung, with a peculiarly ominous and wasted appearance, above the crests of the forest. But conceive my astonishment when I beheld, on the drive, and right under my window, a large and well-appointed hearse, with two white horses, with plumes complete, and attended by mutes, whose black staffs were tipped with silver that glittered pallid in the dawn.

'I exhausted my ingenuity in conjectures as to the presence of this remarkable vehicle with the white horses, so unusual, though, when one thinks of it, so appropriate to the chariot of Death. Could some belated visitor have arrived in a hearse, like the lady in Miss Ferrier's novel? Could one of the domestics have expired, and was it the intention of my host to have the body thus honourably removed without casting a gloom over his guests?

'Wild as these hypotheses appeared, I could think of nothing better, and was just about to leave the window, and retire to bed, when the driver of the strange carriage, who had hitherto sat motionless, turned, and looked me full in the face. Never shall I forget the appearance of this man, whose sallow countenance, close-shaven dark skin, and small, black moustache, combined with I know not what of martial in his air, struck into me a certain indefinable alarm. No sooner had he caught my eye, than he gathered up his reins, just raised his whip, and started the mortuary vehicle at a walk down the road. I followed it with my eyes till a bend in the avenue hid it from my sight. So wrapt up was my spirit in the exercise of the single sense of vision that it was not till the hearse became lost to view that I noticed the entire absence of sound which accompanied its departure. Neither had the bridles and trappings of the white horses jingled as the animals shook their heads, nor had the wheels of the hearse crashed upon the gravel of the avenue. I was compelled by all these circumstances to believe that what I had looked upon was not of this world, and, with a beating heart, I sought refuge in sleep.

'Next morning, feeling far from refreshed, I arrived among the latest at a breakfast which was a desultory and movable feast. Almost all the men had gone forth to hill, forest, or river, in pursuit of the furred, finned, or feathered denizens of the wilds——'

'You speak,' interrupted the schoolboy, 'like a printed book! I like to hear you speak like that. Drive on, old man! Drive on your hearse!'

The Bachelor of Arts 'drove on,' without noticing this interruption. 'I tried to "lead up" to the hearse,' he said, 'in conversation with the young ladies of the castle. I endeavoured to assume the languid and preoccupied air of the guest who, in ghost-stories, has had a bad night with the family spectre. I drew the conversation to the topic of apparitions, and even to warnings of death. I knew that every family worthy of the name has its omen: the Oxenhams a white bird, another house a brass band, whose airy music is poured forth by invisible performers, and so on. Of course I expected some one to cry, "Oh, *we've* got a hearse with white horses," for that is the kind of heirloom an ancient house regards with complacent pride. But nobody offered any remarks on the local omen, and even when I drew near the

'The driver of the strange carri

topic of *hearses*, one of the girls, my cousin, merely quoted, "Speak not like a death's-head, good Doll" (my name is Adolphus), and asked me to play at lawn-tennis.

'In the evening, in the smoking-room, it was no better, nobody had ever heard of an omen in this particular castle. Nay, when I told my story, for it came to that at last, they only laughed at me, and said I must have dreamed it. Of course I expected to be wakened in the night by some awful apparition, but nothing disturbed me. I never slept better, and hearses were the last things I thought of during the remainder of my visit. Months passed, and I had almost forgotten the vision, or dream, for I began to feel apprehensive that, after all, it *was* a dream. So costly and elaborate an apparition as a hearse, with white horses and plumes complete, could never have been got up, regardless

ed and looked me full in the face'

of expense, for one occasion only, and to frighten one undergraduate, yet it was certain that the hearse was not "the old family coach." My entertainers had undeniably never heard of it in their lives before. Even tradition at the castle said nothing of a spectral hearse, though the house was credited with a white lady deprived of her hands, and a luminous boy.'

Here the Bachelor of Arts paused, and a shower of chaff began.

'Is that really all?' asked the Girton girl. 'Why, this is the third ghost-story to-night without any ghost in it!'

'I don't remember saying that it *was* a ghost-story,' replied the Bachelor of Arts; 'but I thought a little anecdote of a mere "warning" might not be unwelcome.'

'But where does the warning come in?' asked the schoolboy.

'That's just what I was arriving at,' replied the narrator, 'when I was interrupted with as little ceremony as if I had been Mr Gladstone in the middle of a most important speech. I was going to say that, in the Easter Vacation after my visit to the castle, I went over to Paris with a friend, a fellow of my college. We drove to the *Hôtel d'Alsace* (I believe there is no hotel of that name; if there is, I beg the spirited proprietor's pardon, and assure him that nothing personal is intended). We marched upstairs with our bags and baggage, and jolly high stairs they were. When we had removed the soil of travel from our persons, my friend called out to me, "I say, Jones, why shouldn't we go down by the lift?" "All right," said I, and my friend walked to the door of the mechanical apparatus, opened it, and got in. I followed him, when the porter whose business it is to "personally conduct" the inmates of the hotel, entered also, and was closing the door.

'His eyes met mine, and I knew him in a moment. I had seen him once before. His sallow face, black, closely shaven chin, furtive glance, and military bearing, were the face and the glance and bearing of the driver of that awful hearse!

'In a moment—more swiftly than I can tell you—I pushed past the man, threw open the door, and just managed, by a violent effort, to drag my friend on to the landing. Then the lift rose with a sudden impulse, fell again, and rushed, with frightful velocity, to the basement of the hotel, whence we heard an appalling crash, followed by groans. We rushed downstairs, and the horrible spectacle of destruction that met our eyes I shall never forget. The unhappy porter was expiring in agony; but the warning had saved my life and my friend's.'

'*I was that friend*,' said I—the collector of these anecdotes; 'and so far I can testify to the truth of Jones's story.'

At this moment, however, the gong for dressing sounded, and we went to our several apartments, after this emotional specimen of 'Evenings at Home.'

R. L. Stevenson

THE BOTTLE IMP

THERE was a man of the Island of Hawaii, whom I shall call Keawe; for the truth is, he still lives, and his name must be kept secret; but the place of his birth was not far from Honaunau, where the bones of Keawe the Great lie hidden in a cave. This man was poor, brave, and active; he could read and write like a schoolmaster; he was a first-rate mariner besides, sailed for some time in the island steamers, and steered a whale-boat on the Hamakua coast. At length it came in Keawe's mind to have a sight of the great world and foreign cities, and he shipped on a vessel bound to San Francisco.

This is a fine town, with a fine harbour, and rich people uncountable; and, in particular, there is one hill which is covered with palaces. Upon this hill Keawe was one day taking a walk with his pocket full of money, viewing the great houses upon either hand with pleasure. 'What fine houses these are!' he was thinking, 'and how happy must those people be who dwell in them, and take no care for the morrow!' The thought was in his mind when he came abreast of a house that was smaller than some others, but all finished and beautiful like a toy; the steps of that house shone like silver, and the borders of the garden bloomed like garlands, and the windows were bright like diamonds; and Keawe stopped and wondered at the excellence of all he saw. So stopping, he was aware of a man that looked forth upon him through a window so clear that Keawe could see him as you see a fish in a pool upon the reef. The man was elderly, with a bald head and a black beard, and his face was heavy with sorrow, and he bitterly sighed. And the truth of it is, that as Keawe looked in upon the man, and the man looked out upon Keawe, each envied the other.

All of a sudden, the man smiled and nodded, and beckoned Keawe to enter, and met him at the door of the house.

'This is a fine house of mine,' said the man, and bitterly sighed. 'Would you not care to view the chambers?'

So he led Keawe all over it, from the cellar to the roof, and there was nothing there that was not perfect of its kind, and Keawe was astonished.

'Truly,' said Keawe, 'this is a beautiful house; if I lived in the like of it, I should be laughing all day long. How comes it, then, that you should be sighing?'

'There is no reason,' said the man, 'why you should not have a house in all points similar to this, and finer, if you wish. You have some money, I suppose?'

'I have fifty dollars,' said Keawe; 'but a house like this will cost more than fifty dollars.'

The man made a computation. 'I am sorry you have no more,' said he, 'for it may raise you trouble in the future; but it shall be yours at fifty dollars.'

'The house?' asked Keawe.

'No, not the house,' replied the man; 'but the bottle. For, I must tell you, although I appear to you so rich and fortunate, all my fortune, and this house itself and its garden, came out of a bottle not much bigger than a pint. This is it.'

And he opened a lockfast place, and took out a round-bellied bottle with a long neck; the glass of it was white like milk, with changing rainbow colours in the grain. Within-sides something obscurely moved, like a shadow and a fire.

'This is the bottle,' said the man; and, when Keawe laughed, 'You do not believe me?' he added. 'Try, then, for yourself. See if you can break it.'

So Keawe took the bottle up and dashed it on the floor till he was weary; but it jumped on the floor like a child's ball, and was not injured.

'This is a strange thing,' said Keawe. 'For by the touch of it, as well as by the look, the bottle should be of glass.'

'Of glass it is,' replied the man, sighing more heavily than ever; 'but the glass of it was tempered in the flames of hell. An imp lives in it, and that is the shadow we behold there moving: or so I suppose. If any man buy this bottle the imp is at his command; all that he desires—love, fame, money, houses like this house, ay, or a city like this city—all are his at the word uttered. Napoleon had this bottle, and by it he grew to be the king of the world; but he sold it at the last, and fell. Captain Cook had this bottle, and by it he found his way to so many islands; but he, too, sold it, and was slain upon Hawaii. For once it is sold, the power goes and the protection; and unless a man remain content with what he has, ill will befall him.'

'And yet you talk of selling it yourself?' Keawe said.

'I have all I wish, and I am growing elderly,' replied the man. 'There is one thing the imp cannot do—he cannot prolong life; and, it would not be fair to conceal from you, there is a drawback to the bottle; for if a man die before he sells it, he must burn in hell for ever.'

'To be sure, that is a drawback and no mistake,' cried Keawe. 'I would not meddle with the thing. I can do without a house, thank God; but there is one thing I could not be doing with one particle, and that is to be damned.'

'Dear me, you must not run away with things,' returned the man. 'All you have to do is to use the power of the imp in moderation, and then sell it to someone else, as I do to you, and finish your life in comfort.'

'Well, I observe two things,' said Keawe. 'All the time you keep sighing like a maid in love, that is one; and, for the other, you sell this bottle very cheap.'

'I have told you already why I sigh,' said the man. 'It is because I fear my health is breaking up; and, as you said yourself, to die and go to the devil is a pity for anyone. As for why I sell so cheap, I must explain to you there is a peculiarity about the bottle. Long ago, when the devil brought it first upon earth, it was extremely expensive, and was sold first of all to Prester John for many millions of dollars; but it cannot be sold at all, unless sold at a loss. If you sell it for as much as you paid for it, back it comes to you again like a homing pigeon. It follows that the price has kept falling in these centuries, and the bottle is now remarkably cheap. I bought it myself from one of my great neighbours on this hill, and the price I paid was only ninety dollars. I could sell it for as high as eighty-nine dollars and ninety-nine cents, but not a penny dearer, or back the thing must come to me. Now, about this there are two bothers. First, when you offer a bottle so singular for eighty odd dollars people suppose you to be jesting. And second—but there is no hurry about that—and I need not go into it. Only remember it must be coined money that you sell it for.'

'How am I to know that this is all true?' asked Keawe.

'Some of it you can try at once,' replied the man. 'Give me your fifty dollars, take the bottle, and wish your fifty dollars back into your pocket. If that does not happen, I pledge you my honour I will cry off the bargain and restore your money.'

'You are not deceiving me?' said Keawe.

The man bound himself with a great oath.

'Well, I will risk that much,' said Keawe, 'for that can do no harm.' And he paid over his money to the man, and the man handed him the bottle.

'Imp of the bottle,' said Keawe, 'I want my fifty dollars back.' And sure enough he had scarce said the word before his pocket was as heavy as ever.

'To be sure this is a wonderful bottle,' said Keawe.

'And now good morning to you, my fine fellow, and the devil go with you for me!' said the man.

'Hold on,' said Keawe, 'I don't want any more of this fun. Here, take your bottle back.'

'You have bought it for less than I paid for it,' replied the man, rubbing his hands. 'It is yours now; and, for my part, I am only concerned to see the back of you.' And with that he rang for his Chinese servant, and had Keawe shown out of the house.

Now, when Keawe was in the street with the bottle under his arm, he began to think. 'If all is true about this bottle, I may have made a losing bargain,' thinks he. 'But perhaps the man was only fooling me.' The first thing he did was to count his money; the sum was exact—forty-nine dollars American money, and one

Chili piece. 'That looks like the truth,' said Keawe. 'Now I will try another part.'

The streets in that part of the city were as clean as a ship's decks, and though it was noon, there were no passengers. Keawe set the bottle in the gutter and walked away. Twice he looked back, and there was the milky, round-bellied bottle where he left it. A third time he looked back, and turned a corner; but he had scarce done so, when something knocked upon his elbow, and, behold! it was the long neck sticking up; and as for the round belly, it was jammed into the pocket of his pilot-coat.

'And that looks like the truth,' said Keawe.

The next thing he did was to buy a corkscrew in a shop, and go apart into a secret place in the fields. And there he tried to draw the cork, but as often as he put the screw in, out it came again, and the cork as whole as ever.

'This is some new sort of cork,' said Keawe, and all at once he began to shake and sweat, for he was afraid of that bottle.

On his way back to the port-side, he saw a shop where a man sold shells and clubs from the wild islands, old heathen deities, old coined money, pictures from China and Japan, and all manner of things that sailors bring in their sea-chests. And here he had an idea. So he went in and offered the bottle for a hundred dollars. The man of the shop laughed at him at the first, and offered him five; but, indeed, it was a curious bottle—such glass was never blown in any human glassworks, so prettily the colours shone under the milky white, and so strangely the shadow hovered in the midst; so, after he had disputed awhile after the manner of his kind, the shopman gave Keawe sixty silver dollars for the thing, and set it on a shelf in the midst of his window. 'Now,' said Keawe, 'I have sold that for sixty which I bought for fifty—or, to say truth, a little less, because one of my dollars was from Chili. Now I shall know the truth upon another point.'

So he went back on board his ship, and, when he opened his chest, there was the bottle, and had come more quickly than himself. Now Keawe had a mate on board whose name was Lopaka.

'What ails you,' said Lopaka, 'that you stare in your chest?'

They were alone in the ship's forecastle, and Keawe bound him to secrecy, and told all.

'This is a very strange affair,' said Lopaka; 'and I fear you will be in trouble about this bottle. But there is one point very clear —that you are sure of the trouble, and you had better have the profit in the bargain. Make up your mind what you want with it; give the order, and if it is done as you desire, I will buy the bottle myself; for I have an idea of my own to get a schooner, and go trading through the islands.'

'That is not my idea,' said Keawe; 'but to have a beautiful house and garden on the Kona Coast, where I was born, the sun shining in at the door, flowers in the garden, glass in the windows, pictures on the walls, and toys and fine carpets on the tables, for all the world like the house I was in this day—only a storey higher, and with balconies all about like the King's palace; and to live there without care and make merry with my friends and relatives.'

'Well,' said Lopaka, 'let us carry it back with us to Hawaii; and if all comes true, as you suppose, I will buy the bottle, as I said, and ask a schooner.'

Upon that they were agreed, and it was not long before the ship returned to Honolulu, carrying Keawe and Lopaka and the bottle. They were scarce come ashore when they met a friend upon the beach who began at once to condole with Keawe.

'I do not know what I am to be condoled about,' said Keawe.

'Is it possible you have not heard,' said the friend, 'your uncle—that good old man—is dead, and your cousin—that beautiful boy—was drowned at sea?'

Keawe was filled with sorrow, and, beginning to weep and to lament, he forgot about the bottle. But Lopaka was thinking to himself, and presently when Keawe's grief was a little abated, 'I have been thinking,' said Lopaka. 'Had not your uncle lands in Hawaii, in the district of Kaü?'

'No,' said Keawe, 'not in Kaü; they are on the mountainside —a little way south of Hookena.'

'These lands will now be yours?' asked Lopaka.

'And so they will,' says Keawe, and began again to lament for his relatives.

'No,' said Lopaka, 'do not lament at present. I have a thought in my mind. How if this should be the doing of the bottle? For here is the place ready for your house.'

'If this be so,' cried Keawe, 'it is a very ill way to serve me by killing my relatives. But it may be, indeed; for it was in just such a station that I saw the house with my mind's eye.'

'The house, however, is not yet built,' said Lopaka.

'No, nor like to be!' said Keawe; 'for though my uncle has some coffee and ava and bananas, it will not be more than will keep me in comfort; and the rest of that land is the black lava.'

'Let us go to the lawyer,' said Lopaka; 'I have still this idea in my mind.'

Now, when they came to the lawyer's, it appeared Keawe's uncle had grown monstrous rich in the last days, and there was a fund of money.

'And here is the money for the house!' cried Lopaka.

'If you are thinking of a new house,' said the lawyer, 'here is the card of a new architect, of whom they tell me great things.'

'Better and better!' cried Lopaka. 'Here is all made plain for us. Let us continue to obey orders.'

So they went to the architect, and he had drawings of houses on his table.

'You want something out of the way,' said the architect. 'How do you like this?' and he handed a drawing to Keawe.

Now, when Keawe set eyes on the drawing, he cried out aloud, for it was the picture of his thought exactly drawn.

'I am in for this house,' thought he. 'Little as I like the way it comes to me, I am in for it now, and I may as well take the good along with the evil.'

So he told the architect all that he wished, and how he would have that house furnished, and about the pictures on the wall and the knick-knacks on the tables; and he asked the man plainly for how much he would undertake the whole affair.

The architect put many questions, and took his pen and made a computation; and when he had done he named the very sum that Keawe had inherited.

Lopaka and Keawe looked at one another and nodded.

'It is quite clear,' thought Keawe, 'that I am to have this house, whether or no. It comes from the devil, and I fear I will get little good by that; and of one thing I am sure, I will make no more wishes as long as I have this bottle. But with the house I am saddled and I may as well take the good along with the evil.'

So he made his terms with the architect, and they signed a paper; and Keawe and Lopaka took ship again and sailed to Australia; for it was concluded between them they should not interfere at all, but leave the architect and the bottle imp to build and to adorn that house at their own pleasure.

The voyage was a good voyage, only all the time Keawe was holding in his breath, for he had sworn he would utter no more wishes, and take no more favours from the devil. The time was up when they got back. The architect told them that the house was ready, and Keawe and Lopaka took a passage in the *Hall*, and went down Kona way to view the house, and see if all had been done fitly according to the thought that was in Keawe's mind.

Now, the house stood on the mountain-side, visible to ships. Above, the forest ran up into the clouds of rain; below, the black lava fell in cliffs, where the kings of old lay buried. A garden bloomed about that house with every hue of flowers; and there was an orchard of papaia on the one hand and an orchard of breadfruit on the other, and right in front, toward the sea, a ship's mast had been rigged up and bore a flag. As for the house, it was three storeys high, with great chambers and broad balconies on each. The windows were of glass, so excellent that it was as clear as water and as bright as day. All manner of furniture adorned the chambers. Pictures hung upon the wall in golden frames: pictures of ships, and men fighting, and of the most beautiful women, and of singular places; nowhere in the world are there pictures of so bright a colour as those Keawe found hanging in his house. As for the knick-knacks, they were extraordinary fine; chiming clocks and musical boxes, little men with nodding heads, books filled with pictures, weapons of price from all quarters of the world, and the most elegant puzzles to entertain the leisure of a solitary man. And as no one would care to live in such chambers, only to walk through and view them, the balconies were made so broad that a whole town might have lived upon them in delight; and Keawe knew not which to prefer, whether the back porch, where you got the land breeze, and looked upon the orchards and the flowers, or the front balcony, where you could drink the wind of the sea, and look down the steep wall of the mountain and see the *Hall* going by once a week or so between Hookena and the hills of Pele, or the schooners plying up the coast for wood and ava and bananas.

When they had viewed all, Keawe and Lopaka sat on the porch.

'Well,' asked Lopaka, 'is it all as you designed?'

'Words cannot utter it,' said Keawe. 'It is better than I dreamed, and I am sick with satisfaction.'

'There is but one thing to consider,' said Lopaka; 'all this may be quite natural, and the bottle imp have nothing whatever to say to it. If I were to buy the bottle, and got no schooner after all, I should have put my hand in the fire for nothing. I gave you my word, I know; but yet I think you would not grudge me one more proof.'

'I have sworn I would take no more favours,' said Keawe. 'I have gone already deep enough.'

'This is no favour I am thinking of,' replied Lopaka. 'It is only to see the imp himself. There is nothing to be gained by that, and so nothing to be ashamed of; and yet, if I once saw him, I should be sure of the whole matter. So indulge me so far, and let me see the imp; and, after that, here is the money in my hand, and I will buy it.'

'There is only one thing I am afraid of,' said Keawe. 'The imp may be very ugly to view; and if you once set eyes upon him you might be very undesirous of the bottle.'

'I am a man of my word,' said Lopaka. 'And here is the money betwixt us.'

'Very well,' replied Keawe. 'I have a curiosity myself. So come, let us have one look at you, Mr Imp.'

Now as soon as that was said, the imp looked out of the bottle, and in again, swift as a lizard; and there sat Keawe and Lopaka turned to stone. The night had quite come, before either found

The imp looked out of the bottle . . . and there sat Keawe and Lopaka turned to stone

a thought to say or voice to say it with; and then Lopaka pushed the money over and took the bottle.

'I am a man of my word,' said he, 'and had need to be so, or I would not touch this bottle with my foot. Well, I shall get my schooner and a dollar or two for my pocket; and then I will be rid of this devil as fast as I can. For, to tell you the plain truth, the look of him has cast me down.'

'Lopaka,' said Keawe, 'do not you think any worse of me than you can help; I know it is night, and the roads bad, and the pass by the tombs an ill place to go by so late, but I declare since I have seen that little face, I cannot eat or sleep or pray till it is gone from me. I will give you a lantern, and a basket to put the bottle in, and any picture or fine thing in all my house that takes your fancy;—and be gone at once, and go sleep at Hookena with Nahinu.'

'Keawe,' said Lopaka, 'many a man would take this ill; above all, when I am doing you a turn so friendly, as to keep my word and buy the bottle; and for that matter, the night and the dark, and the way by the tombs, must be all tenfold more dangerous to a man with such a sin upon his conscience, and such a bottle under his arm. But for my part, I am so extremely terrified myself, I have not the heart to blame you. Here I go then; and I pray God you may be happy in your house, and I fortunate with my schooner, and both get to Heaven in the end in spite of the devil and his bottle.'

So Lopaka went down the mountain; and Keawe stood in his front balcony, and listened to the clink of the horse's shoes, and watched the lantern go shining down the path, and along the cliff of caves where the old dead are buried; and all the time he trembled and clasped his hands, and prayed for his friend, and gave glory to God that he himself was escaped out of that trouble.

But the next day came very brightly, and that new house of his was so delightful to behold that he forgot his terrors. One day followed another, and Keawe dwelt there in perpetual joy. He had his place on the back porch; it was there he ate and lived, and read the stories in the Honolulu newspapers; but when anyone came by they would go in and view the chambers and the pictures. And the fame of the house went far and wide; it was called *Ka-Hale Nui*—the Great House—in all Kona; and sometimes the Bright House, for Keawe kept a Chinaman, who was all day dusting and furbishing; and the glass, and the gilt, and the fine stuffs, and the pictures, shone as bright as the morning. As for Keawe himself, he could not walk in the chambers without singing, his heart was so enlarged; and when ships sailed by upon the sea, he would fly his colours on the mast.

So time went by, until one day Keawe went upon a visit as far as Kailua to certain of his friends. There he was well feasted; and left as soon as he could the next morning, and rode hard, for he was impatient to behold his beautiful house; and, besides, the night then coming on was the night in which the dead of old days go abroad in the sides of Kona; and having already meddled with the devil, he was the more chary of meeting with the dead. A little beyond Honaunau, looking far ahead, he was aware of a woman bathing in the edge of the sea; and she seemed a well-grown girl, but he thought no more of it. Then he saw her white shift flutter as she put it on, and then her red holoku; and by the time he came abreast of her she was done with her toilet, and had come up from the sea, and stood by the track-side in her red holoku, and she was all freshened with the bath, and her eyes shone and were kind. Now Keawe no sooner beheld her than he drew rein.

'I thought I knew every one in this country,' said he. 'How comes it that I do not know you?'

'I am Kokua, daughter of Kiano,' said the girl, 'and I have just returned from Oahu. Who are you?'

'I will tell you who I am in a little,' said Keawe, dismounting from his horse, 'but not now. For I have a thought in my mind, and if you knew who I was, you might have heard of me, and would not give me a true answer. But tell me, first of all, one thing: Are you married?'

At this Kokua laughed out aloud. 'It is you who ask questions,' she said. 'Are you married yourself?'

'Indeed, Kokua, I am not,' replied Keawe, 'and never thought to be until this hour. But here is the plain truth. I have met you here at the roadside, and I saw your eyes which are like the stars, and my heart went to you as swift as a bird. And so now, if you want none of me, say so, and I will go to my own place; but if you think me no worse than any other young man, say so, too, and I will turn aside to your father's for the night, and tomorrow I will talk with the good man.'

Kokua said never a word, but she looked at the sea and laughed.

'Kokua,' said Keawe, 'if you say nothing, I will take that for the good answer; so let us be stepping to your father's door.'

She went on ahead of him, still without speech; only sometimes she glanced back and glanced away again, and she kept the strings of her hat in her mouth.

Now, when they had come to the door, Kiano came out on his veranda, and cried out and welcomed Keawe by name. At that the girl looked over, for the fame of the great house had come to her ears; and, to be sure, it was a great temptation. All that evening they were very merry together; and the girl was as bold as brass under the eyes of her parents, and made a mock of Keawe, for she had a quick wit. The next day he had a word with Kiano, and found the girl alone.

'Kokua,' said he, 'you made a mock of me all the evening; and it is still time to bid me go. I would not tell you who I was, because I have so fine a house, and I feared you would think too much of that house and too little of the man who loves you. Now you know all, and if you wish to have seen the last of me, say so at once.'

'No,' said Kokua; but this time she did not laugh, nor did Keawe ask for more.

This was the wooing of Keawe; things had gone quickly; but so an arrow goes, and the ball of a rifle swifter still, and yet both may strike the target. Things had gone fast, but they had gone far also, and the thought of Keawe rang in the maiden's head; she heard his voice in the breach of the surf upon the lava, and for this young man that she had seen but twice she would have left father and mother and her native islands. As for Keawe himself, his horse flew up the path of the mountain under the cliff of tombs, and the sound of the hoofs, and the sound of Keawe singing to himself for pleasure, echoed in the caverns of the dead. He came to the Bright House, and still he was singing. He sat and ate in the broad balcony, and the Chinaman wondered at his master, to hear how he sang between the mouthfuls. The sun went down into the sea, and the night came; and Keawe walked the balconies by lamplight, high on the mountains, and the voice of his singing startled men on ships.

'Here am I now upon my high place,' he said to himself. 'Life may be no better; this is the mountain top: and all shelves about me toward the worse. For the first time I will light up the chambers, and bathe in my fine bath with the hot water and the cold, and sleep alone in the bed of my bridal chamber.'

So the Chinaman had word, and he must rise from sleep and light the furnaces; and as he wrought below, beside the boilers, he heard his master singing and rejoicing above him in the lighted chambers. When the water began to be hot the Chinaman cried to his master; and Keawe went into the bathroom; and the Chinaman heard him sing as he filled the marble basin; and heard him sing, and the singing broken, as he undressed; until of a sudden, the song ceased. The Chinaman listened, and listened; he called up the house to Keawe to ask if all were well, and Keawe answered him, 'Yes,' and bade him go to bed; but there was no more singing in the Bright House; and all night long, the Chinaman heard his master's feet go round and round the balconies without repose.

Now the truth of it was this: as Keawe undressed for his bath, he spied upon his flesh a patch like a patch of lichen on a rock, and it was then that he stopped singing. For he knew the likeness of that patch, and knew that he was fallen in the Chinese Evil (leprosy).

Now, it is a sad thing for any man to fall into this sickness. And it would be a sad thing for any one to leave a house so beautiful and so commodious, and depart from all his friends to the north coast of Molokai between the mighty cliff and the sea-breakers. But what was that to the case of the man Keawe, he who had met his love but yesterday, and won her but that morning, and now saw all his hopes break, in a moment, like a piece of glass?

Awhile he sat upon the edge of the bath; then sprang, with a cry, and ran outside; and to and fro, to and fro, along the balcony, like one despairing.

'Very willingly could I leave Hawaii, the home of my fathers,' Keawe was thinking. 'Very lightly could I leave my house, the high-placed, the many-windowed, here upon the mountains. Very bravely could I go to Molokai, to Kalaupapa by the cliffs, to live with the smitten and to sleep there, far from my fathers. But what wrong have I done, what sin lies upon my soul, that I should have encountered Kokua coming cool from the seawater in the evening? Kokua, the soul ensnarer! Kokua, the light of my life! Her may I never wed, her may I look upon no longer, her may I no more handle with my loving hand; and it is for this, it is for you, O Kokua! that I pour my lamentations!'

Now you are to observe what sort of a man Keawe was, for he might have dwelt there in the Bright House for years, and no one been the wiser of his sickness; but he reckoned nothing of that, if he must lose Kokua. And again, he might have wed Kokua even as he was; and so many would have done, because they have the souls of pigs; but Keawe loved the maid manfully, and he would do her no hurt and bring her in no danger.

A little beyond the midst of the night, there came in his mind the recollection of that bottle. He went round to the back porch, and called to memory the day when the devil had looked forth; and at the thought ice ran in his veins.

'A dreadful thing is the bottle,' thought Keawe, 'and dreadful is the imp, and it is a dreadful thing to risk the flames of hell. But what other hope have I to cure my sickness or to wed Kokua? What!' he thought, 'would I beard the devil once, only to get me a house, and not face him again to win Kokua?'

Thereupon he called to mind it was the next day the *Hall* went by on her return to Honolulu. 'There must I go first,' he thought, 'and see Lopaka. For the best hope that I have now is to find that same bottle I was so pleased to be rid of.'

Never a wink could he sleep; the food stuck in his throat; but he sent a letter to Kiano, and about the time when the steamer would be coming, rode down beside the cliff of the tombs. It rained; his horse went heavily; he looked up at the black mouths of the caves, and he envied the dead that slept there and were done with trouble; and called to mind how he had galloped by the day before, and was astonished. So he came down to Hookena, and there was all the country gathered for the steamer as usual. In the shed before the store they sat and jested and passed the news; but there was no matter of speech in Keawe's bosom, and he sat in their midst and looked without on the rain falling on the houses, and the surf beating among the rocks, and the sighs arose in his throat.

'Keawe of the Bright House is out of spirits,' said one to another. Indeed, and so he was, and little wonder.

Then the *Hall* came, and the whale-boat carried him on board. The after-part of the ship was full of Haoles (whites) who had been to visit the volcano, as their custom is; and the midst was crowded with Kanakas, and the fore-part with wild bulls from Hilo and horses from Kaü; but Keawe sat apart from all in his sorrow, and watched for the house of Kiano. There it sat, low upon the shore in the black rocks, and shaded by the cocoa-palms, and there by the door was a red holoku, no greater than a fly, and going to and fro with a fly's busyness. 'Ah, queen of my heart,' he cried, 'I'll venture my dear soul to win you!'

Soon after, darkness fell, and the cabins were lit up, and the Haoles sat and played at the cards and drank whisky as their custom is; but Keawe walked the deck all night; and all the next day, as they steamed under the lee of Maui or of Molokai, he was still pacing to and fro like a wild animal in a menagerie.

Towards evening they passed Diamond Head, and came to the pier of Honolulu. Keawe stepped out among the crowd and began to ask for Lopaka. It seemed he had become the owner of a schooner—none better in the islands—and was gone upon an adventure as far as Pola-Pola or Kahiki; so there was no help to be looked for from Lopaka. Keawe called to mind a friend of his, a lawyer in the town (I must not tell his name), and inquired of him. They said he had grown suddenly rich, and had a fine new house upon Waikiki shore; and this put a thought in Keawe's head, and he called a hack and drove to the lawyer's house.

The house was all brand new, and the trees in the garden no greater than walking-sticks, and the lawyer, when he came, had the air of a man well pleased.

'What can I do to serve you?' said the lawyer.

'You are a friend of Lopaka's,' replied Keawe, 'and Lopaka purchased from me a certain piece of goods that I thought you might enable me to trace.'

The lawyer's face became very dark. 'I do not profess to misunderstand you, Mr Keawe,' said he, 'though this is an ugly business to be stirring in. You may be sure I know nothing, but yet I have a guess, and if you would apply in a certain quarter I think you might have news.'

And he named the name of a man, which, again, I had better not repeat. So it was for days, and Keawe went from one to another, finding everywhere new clothes and carriages, and fine new houses and men everywhere in great contentment, although to be sure, when he hinted at his business their faces would cloud over.

'No doubt I am upon the track,' thought Keawe. 'These new clothes and carriages are all the gifts of the little imp, and these glad faces are the faces of men who have taken their profit and got rid of the accursed thing in safety. When I see pale cheeks and hear sighing, I shall know that I am near the bottle.'

So it befell at last that he was recommended to a Haole in Beritania Street. When he came to the door, about the hour of the evening meal, there were the usual marks of the new house, and the young garden, and the electric light shining in the windows; but when the owner came, a shock of hope and fear ran through Keawe; for here was a young man, white as a corpse, and black about the eyes, the hair shedding from his head, and such a look in his countenance as a man may have when he is waiting for the gallows.

'Here it is, to be sure,' thought Keawe, and so with this man he noways veiled his errand. 'I am come to buy the bottle,' said he.

At the word, the young Haole of Beritania Street reeled against the wall.

'The bottle!' he gasped. 'To buy the bottle!' Then he seemed to choke, and seizing Keawe by the arm carried him into a room and poured out wine in two glasses.

'Here is my respects,' said Keawe, who had been much about with Haoles in his time. 'Yes,' he added, 'I am come to buy the bottle. What is the price by now?'

At that word the young man let his glass slip through his fingers, and looked upon Keawe like a ghost.

'The price,' says he; 'the price! You do not know the price?'

'It is for that I am asking you,' returned Keawe. 'But why

are you so much concerned? Is there anything wrong about the price?'

'It has dropped a great deal in value since your time, Mr Keawe,' said the young man, stammering.

'Well, well, I shall have the less to pay for it,' says Keawe. 'How much did it cost you?'

The young man was as white as a sheet. 'Two cents,' said he.

'What?' cried Keawe, 'two cents? Why, then, you can only sell it for one. And he who buys it——' The words died upon Keawe's tongue; he who bought it could never sell it again, the bottle and the bottle imp must abide with him until he died, and when he died must carry him to the red end of hell.

The young man of Beritania Street fell upon his knees. 'For God's sake buy it!' he cried. 'You can have all my fortune in the bargain. I was mad when I bought it at that price. I had embezzled money at my store; I was lost else; I must have gone to jail.'

'Poor creature,' said Keawe, 'you would risk your soul upon so desperate an adventure, and to avoid the proper punishment of your own disgrace; and you think I could hesitate with love in front of me. Give me the bottle, and the change which I make sure you have all ready. Here is a five-cent piece.'

It was as Keawe supposed; the young man had the change ready in a drawer; the bottle changed hands, and Keawe's fingers were no sooner clasped upon the stalk than he had breathed his wish to be a clean man. And, sure enough, when he got home to his room, and stripped himself before a glass, his flesh was whole like an infant's. And here was the strange thing: he had no sooner seen this miracle than his mind was changed within him, and he cared naught for the Chinese Evil, and little enough for Kokua; and had but the one thought, that here he was bound to the bottle imp for time and for eternity, and had no better hope but to be a cinder for ever in the flames of hell. Away ahead of him he saw them blaze with his mind's eye, and his soul shrank, and darkness fell upon the light.

When Keawe came to himself a little, he was aware it was the night when the band played at the hotel. Thither he went, because he feared to be alone; and there, among happy faces, walked to and fro, and heard the tunes go up and down, and saw Berger beat the measure, and all the while he heard the flames crackle, and saw the red fire burning in the bottomless pit. Of a sudden the band played *Hiki-ao-ao*, that was a song that he had sung with Kokua, and at the strain courage returned to him.

'It is done now,' he thought, 'and once more let me take the good along with the evil.'

So it befell that he returned to Hawaii by the first steamer, and as soon as it could be managed he was wedded to Kokua, and carried her up the mountain-side to the Bright House.

Now it was so with these two, that when they were together, Keawe's heart was stilled; but so soon as he was alone, he fell into a brooding horror, and heard the flames crackle, and saw the red fire burn in the bottomless pit. The girl, indeed, had come to him wholly; her heart leapt in her side at sight of him, her hand clung to his; and she was so fashioned from the hair upon her head to the nails upon her toes that none could see her without joy. She was pleasant in her nature. She had the good word always. Full of song she was, and went to and fro in the Bright House, the brightest thing in its three storeys, carolling like the birds. And Keawe beheld and heard her with delight, and then must shrink upon one side, and weep and groan to think upon the price that he had paid for her; and then he must dry his eyes, and wash his face, and go and sit with her on the broad balconies, joining in her songs, and, with a sick spirit, answering her smiles.

There came a day when her feet began to be heavy and her songs more rare; and now it was not Keawe only that would weep apart, but each would sunder from the other and sit in opposite balconies with the whole width of the Bright House betwixt. Keawe was so sunk in his despair, he scarce observed the change and was only glad he had more hours to sit alone and brood upon his destiny, and was not so frequently condemned to pull a smiling face on a sick heart. But one day, coming softly through the house, he heard the sound of a child sobbing, and there was Kokua rolling her face upon the balcony floor, and weeping like the lost.

'You do well to weep in this house, Kokua,' he said. 'And yet

I would give the head off my body that you (at least) might have been happy.'

'Happy!' she cried. 'Keawe, when you lived alone in your Bright House, you were the word of the island for a happy man; laughter and song were in your mouth, and your face was as bright as the sunrise. Then you wedded poor Kokua; and the good God knows what is amiss in her—but from that day you have not smiled. Oh!' she cried, 'what ails me? I thought I was pretty, and I knew I loved him. What ails me that I throw this cloud upon my husband?'

'Poor Kokua,' said Keawe. He sat down by her side, and sought to take her hand; but that she plucked away. 'Poor Kokua,' he said, again. 'My poor child—my pretty. And I had thought all this while to spare you! Well, you shall know all. Then, at least, you will pity poor Keawe; then you will understand how much he loved you in the past—that he dared hell for your possession—and how much he loves you still (the poor condemned one), that he can yet call up a smile when he beholds you.'

With that, he told her all, even from the beginning.

'You have done this for me?' she cried. 'Ah, well, then what do I care!'—and she clasped and wept upon him.

'Ah, child!' said Keawe, 'and yet, when I consider of the fire of hell, I care a good deal!'

'Never tell me,' said she; 'no man can be lost because he loved Kokua, and no other fault. I tell you, Keawe, I shall save you with these hands, or perish in your company. What! you loved me, and gave your soul, and you think I will not die to save you in return?'

'Ah, my dear! you might die a hundred times, and what difference would that make?' he cried, 'except to leave me lonely till the time comes of my damnation?'

'You know nothing,' said she. 'I was educated in a school in Honolulu; I am no common girl. And I tell you, I shall save my lover. What is this you say about a cent? But all the world is not American. In England they have a piece they call a farthing, which is about half a cent. Ah! sorrow!' she cried, 'that makes it scarcely better, for the buyer must be lost, and we shall find none so brave as my Keawe! But, then, there is France; they have a small coin there which they call a centime, and these go five to the cent or thereabout. We could not do better. Come, Keawe, let us go to the French islands; let us go to Tahiti, as fast as ships can bear us. There we have four centimes, three centimes, two centimes, one centime; four possible sales to come and go on; and two of us to push the bargain. Come, my Keawe! kiss me, and banish care. Kokua will defend you.'

'Gift of God!' he cried. 'I cannot think that God will punish me for desiring aught so good! Be it as you will, then; take me where you please: I put my life and my salvation in your hands.'

Early the next day Kokua was about her preparations. She took Keawe's chest that he went with sailoring; and first she put the bottle in a corner; and then packed it with the richest of their clothes and the bravest of the knick-knacks in the house. 'For,' said she, 'we must seem to be rich folks, or who will believe in the bottle?' All the time of her preparation she was as gay as a bird; only when she looked upon Keawe, the tears would spring in her eye, and she must run and kiss him. As for Keawe, a weight was off his soul; now that he had his secret shared, and some hope in front of him, he seemed like a new man, his feet went lightly on the earth, and his breath was good to him again. Yet was terror still at his elbow; and ever and again, as the wind blows out a taper, hope died in him, and he saw the flames toss and the red fire burn in hell.

It was given out in the country they were gone pleasuring to the States, which was thought a strange thing, and yet not so strange as the truth, if any could have guessed it. So they went to Honolulu in the *Hall*, and thence in the *Umatilla* to San Francisco with a crowd of Haoles, and at San Francisco took their passage by the mail brigantine, the *Tropic Bird*, for Papeete, the chief place of the French in the south islands. Thither they came, after a pleasant voyage, on a fair day of the Trade Wind, and saw the reef with the surf breaking, and Motuiti with its palms, and the schooner riding withinside, and the white houses of the town low down along the shore among green trees, and overhead the mountains and the clouds of Tahiti, the wise island.

It was judged the most wise to hire a house, which they did

accordingly, opposite the British Consul's, to make a great parade of money, and themselves conspicuous with carriages and horses. This it was very easy to do, so long as they had the bottle in their possession; for Kokua was more bold than Keawe, and, whenever she had a mind, called on the imp for twenty or a hundred dollars. At this rate they soon grew to be remarked in the town; and the strangers from Hawaii, their riding and their driving, the fine holokus and the rich lace of Kokua, became the matter of much talk.

They got on well after the first with the Tahitian language, which is indeed like to the Hawaiian, with a change of certain letters; and as soon as they had any freedom of speech, began to push the bottle. You are to consider it was not an easy subject to introduce it; it was not easy to persuade people you were in earnest, when you offered to sell them for four centimes the spring of health and riches inexhaustible. It was necessary besides to explain the dangers of the bottle; and either people disbelieved the whole thing and laughed, or they thought the more of the darker part, became overcast with gravity, and drew away from Keawe and Kokua, as from persons who had dealings with the devil. So far from gaining ground, these two began to find they were avoided in the town; the children ran away from them screaming, a thing intolerable to Kokua; Catholics crossed themselves as they went by, and all persons began with one accord to disengage themselves from their advances.

Depression fell upon their spirits. They would sit at night in their new house, after a day's weariness, and not exchange one word, or the silence would be broken by Kokua bursting suddenly into sobs. Sometimes they would pray together; sometimes they would have the bottle out upon the floor, and sit all the evening watching how the shadow hovered in the midst. At such times they would be afraid to go to rest. It was long ere slumber came to them, and if either dozed off, it would be to wake and find the other silently weeping in the dark, or, perhaps, to wake alone, the other having fled from the house and the neighbourhood of that bottle, to pace under the bananas in the little garden, or to wander on the beach by moonlight.

One night it was so when Kokua awoke. Keawe was gone. She felt in the bed and his place was cold. Then fear fell upon her, and she sat up in bed. A little moonshine filtered through the shutters. The room was bright, and she could spy the bottle on the floor. Outside it blew high, the great trees of the avenue cried aloud, and the fallen leaves rattled in the veranda. In the midst of this Kokua was aware of another sound; whether of a beast or of a man she could scarce tell, but it was as sad as death, and cut her to the soul. Softly she arose, set the door ajar, and looked forth into the moonlit yard. There, under the bananas, lay Keawe, his mouth in the dust, and as he lay he moaned.

It was Kokua's first thought to run forward and console him; her second potently withheld her. Keawe had borne himself before his wife like a brave man; it became her little in the hour of weakness to intrude upon his shame. With the thought she drew back into the house.

'Heaven!' she thought, 'how careless have I been—how weak! It is he, not I, that stands in this eternal peril; it was he, not I, that took the curse upon his soul. It is for my sake, and for the love of a creature of so little worth and such poor help, that he now beholds so close to him the flames of hell—ay, and smells the smoke of it, lying without there in the wind and moonlight. Am I so dull of spirit that never till now I have surmised my duty, or have I seen it before and turned aside? But now, at least, I take up my soul in both the hands of my affection; now I say farewell to the white steps of heaven and the waiting faces of my friends. A love for a love, and let mine be equalled with Keawe's! A soul for a soul, and be it mine to perish!'

She was a deft woman with her hands, and was soon apparelled. She took in her hands the change—the precious centimes they kept ever at their side; for this coin is little used, and they had made provision at a Government office. When she was forth in the avenue, clouds came on the wind and the moon was blackened. The town slept, and she knew not whither to turn till she heard one coughing in the shadow of the trees.

'Old man,' said Kokua, 'what do you here abroad in the cold night?'

The old man could scarce express himself for coughing, but she made out that he was old and poor, and a stranger in the island.

'Will you do me a service?' said Kokua. 'As one stranger to another, and as an old man to a young woman, will you help a daughter of Hawaii?'

'Ah,' said the old man. 'So you are the witch from the Eight Islands, and even my old soul you seek to entangle. But I have heard of you, and defy your wickedness.'

'Sit down here,' said Kokua, 'and let me tell you a tale.' And she told him the story of Keawe from the beginning to the end.

'And now,' said she, 'I am his wife, whom he bought with his soul's welfare. And what should I do? If I went to him myself and offered to buy it, he would refuse. But if you go, he will sell it eagerly; I will await you here: you will buy it for four centimes, and I will buy it again for three. And the Lord strengthen a poor girl!'

'If you meant falsely,' said the old man, 'I think God would strike you dead.'

'He would!' cried Kokua. 'Be sure he would. I could not be so treacherous—God would not suffer it.'

'Give me the four centimes and await me here,' said the old man.

Now, when Kokua stood alone in the street, her spirit died. The wind roared in the trees, and it seemed to her the rushing of the flames of hell; the shadows tossed in the light of the street lamp, and they seemed to her the snatching hands of evil ones. If she had had the strength, she must have run away, and if she had had the breath she must have screamed aloud; but, in truth, she could do neither, and stood and trembled in the avenue, like an affrighted child.

Then she saw the old man returning, and he had the bottle in his hand.

'I have done your bidding,' said he. 'I left your husband weeping like a child; to-night he will sleep easy.' And he held the bottle forth.

'Before you give it me,' Kokua panted, 'take the good with the evil—ask to be delivered from your cough.'

'I am an old man,' replied the other, 'and too near the gate of the grave to take a favour from the devil. But what is this? Why do you not take the bottle? Do you hesitate?'

'Not hesitate!' cried Kokua. 'I am only weak. Give me a moment. It is my hand resists, my flesh shrinks back from the accursed thing. One moment only!'

The old man looked upon Kokua kindly. 'Poor child!' said he, 'you fear; your soul misgives you. Well, let me keep it. I am old, and can never more be happy in this world, and as for the next——'

'Give it me!' gasped Kokua. 'There is your money. Do you think I am so base as that? Give me the bottle.'

'God bless you, child,' said the old man.

Kokua concealed the bottle under her holoku, said farewell to the old man, and walked off along the avenue, she cared not whither. For all roads were now the same to her, and led equally to hell. Sometimes she walked, and sometimes ran; sometimes she screamed out loud in the night, and sometimes lay by the wayside in the dust and wept. All that she had heard of hell came back to her; she saw the flames blaze, and she smelt the smoke, and her flesh withered on the coals.

Near day she came to her mind again, and returned to the house. It was even as the old man said—Keawe slumbered like a child. Kokua stood and gazed upon his face.

'Now, my husband,' said she, 'it is your turn to sleep. When you wake it will be your turn to sing and laugh. But for poor Kokua, alas! that meant no evil—for poor Kokua no more sleep, no more singing, no more delight, whether in earth or Heaven.'

With that she lay down in the bed by his side, and her misery was so extreme that she fell in a deep slumber instantly.

Late in the morning her husband woke her and gave her the good news. It seemed he was silly with delight, for he paid no heed to her distress, ill though she dissembled it. The words stuck in her mouth, it mattered not; Keawe did the speaking. She ate not a bite, but who was to observe it? for Keawe cleared the dish. Kokua saw and heard him, like some strange thing in a dream; there were times when she forgot or doubted, and put her hands to her brow; to know herself doomed and hear her husband babble, seemed so monstrous.

All this while Keawe was eating and talking, and planning the time of their return, and thanking her for saving him, and fondling her, and calling her the true helper after all. He laughed at the old man that was fool enough to buy that bottle.

'A worthy old man he seemed,' Keawe said. 'But no one can judge by appearances. For why did the old reprobate require the bottle?'

'My husband,' said Kokua humbly, 'his purpose may have been good.'

Keawe laughed like an angry man.

'Fiddle-de-dee!' cried Keawe. 'An old rogue, I tell you; and an old ass to boot. For the bottle was hard enough to sell at four centimes; and at three it will be quite impossible. The margin is not broad enough, the thing begins to smell of scorching—brrr!' said he, and shuddered. 'It is true I bought it myself at a cent, when I knew not there were smaller coins. I was a fool for my pains; there will never be found another: and whoever has that bottle now will carry it to the pit.'

'O my husband!' said Kokua. 'Is it not a terrible thing to save oneself by the eternal ruin of another? It seems to me, I could not laugh. I would be humbled. I would be filled with melancholy. I would pray for the poor holder.'

Then Keawe, because he felt the truth of what she said, grew the more angry. 'Heighty-teighty!' cried he. 'You may be filled with melancholy if you please. It is not the mind of a good wife. If you thought at all of me, you would sit shamed.'

Thereupon he went out, and Kokua was alone.

What chance had she to sell that bottle at two centimes? None, she perceived. And if she had any, here was her husband hurrying her away to a country where there was nothing lower than a cent. And here—on the morrow of her sacrifice—was her husband leaving her and blaming her.

She would not even try to profit by what time she had, but sat in the house, and now had the bottle out and viewed it with unutterable fear, and now, with loathing, hid it out of sight.

By and by, Keawe came back, and would have her take a drive.

'My husband, I am ill,' she said. 'I am out of heart. Excuse me, I can take no pleasure.'

Then was Keawe more wroth than ever. With her, because he thought she was brooding over the case of the old man; and with himself, because he thought she was right, and was ashamed to be so happy.

'This is your truth,' cried he, 'and this your affection! Your husband is just saved from eternal ruin, which he encountered for the love of you—and you can take no pleasure! Kokua, you have a disloyal heart.'

He went forth again furious, and wandered in the town all day. He met friends, and drank with them; they hired a carriage and drove into the country, and there drank again. All the time Keawe was ill at ease, because he was taking his pastime while his wife was sad, and because he knew in his heart that she was more right than he; and the knowledge made him drink the deeper.

Now there was an old brutal Haole drinking with him, one that had been a boatswain of a whaler, a runaway, a digger in gold mines, a convict in prisons. He had a low mind and a foul mouth; he loved to drink and to see others drunken; and he pressed the glass upon Keawe. Soon there was no more money in the company.

'Here you!' says the boatswain, 'you are rich, you have been always saying. You have a bottle or some foolishness.'

'Yes,' says Keawe, 'I am rich; I will go back and get some money from my wife, who keeps it.'

'That's a bad idea, mate,' says the boatswain. 'Never you trust a petticoat with dollars. They're all as false as water; you keep an eye on her.'

Now, this word stuck in Keawe's mind; for he was muddled with what he had been drinking.

'I should not wonder but she was false, indeed,' thought he. 'Why else should she be so cast down at my release? But I will show her I am not the man to be fooled. I will catch her in the act.'

Accordingly, when they were back in town, Keawe bade the boatswain wait for him at the corner, by the old calaboose, and went forward up the avenue alone to the door of his house. The night had come again; there was a light within, but never a sound, and Keawe crept about the corner, opened the back door softly, and looked in.

There was Kokua on the floor, the lamp at her side; before her was a milk-white bottle, with a round belly and a long neck; and as she viewed it, Kokua wrung her hands.

A long time Keawe stood and looked in the doorway. At first he was struck stupid; and then fear fell upon him that the bargain had been made amiss, and the bottle had come back to him as it came at San Francisco; and at that his knees were loosened, and the fumes of the wine departed from his head like mists off a river in the morning. And then he had another thought; and it was a strange one, that made his cheeks to burn.

'I must make sure of this,' thought he.

So he closed the door, and went softly round the corner again, and then came noisily in, as though he were but now returned. And lo! by the time he opened the front door no bottle was to be seen; and Kokua sat in a chair and started up like one awakened out of sleep.

'I have been drinking all day and making merry,' said Keawe. 'I have been with good companions, and now I only come back for money, and return to drink and carouse with them again.'

Both his face and voice were as stern as judgment, but Kokua was too troubled to observe.

'You do well to use your own, my husband,' said she, and her words trembled.

'Oh, I do well in all things,' said Keawe, and he went straight to the chest and took out money. But he looked besides in the corner where they kept the bottle, and there was no bottle there.

At that the chest heaved upon the floor like a sea-billow, and the house span about him like a wreath of smoke, for he saw he was lost now, and there was no escape. 'It is what I feared,' he thought; 'it is she who has bought it.'

And then he came to himself a little and rose up; but the sweat streamed on his face as thick as the rain and as cold as the well-water.

'Kokua,' said he, 'I said to you today what ill became me. Now I return to carouse with my jolly companions,' and at that he laughed a little quietly. 'I will take more pleasure in the cup if you forgive me.'

She clasped his knees in a moment; she kissed his knees with flowing tears.

'Oh,' she cried, 'I asked but a kind word!'

'Let us never one think hardly of the other,' said Keawe, and was gone out of the house.

Now, the money that Keawe had taken was only some of that store of centime pieces they had laid in at their arrival. It was very sure he had no mind to be drinking. His wife had given her soul for him, now he must give his for her; no other thought was in the world with him.

At the corner, by the old calaboose, there was the boatswain waiting.

'My wife has the bottle,' said Keawe, 'and, unless you help me to recover it, there can be no more money and no more liquor to-night.'

'You do not mean to say you are serious about that bottle?' cried the boatswain.

'There is the lamp,' said Keawe. 'Do I look as if I was jesting?'

'That is so,' said the boatswain. 'You look as serious as a ghost.'

'Well, then,' said Keawe, 'here are two centimes; you must go to my wife in the house, and offer her these for the bottle, which (if I am not much mistaken) she will give you instantly. Bring it to me here, and I will buy it back from you for one; for that is the law with this bottle, that it still must be sold for a less sum. But whatever you do, never breathe a word to her that you have come from me.'

'Mate, I wonder are you making a fool of me?' asked the boatswain.

'It will do you no harm if I am,' returned Keawe.

'That is so, mate,' said the boatswain.

'And if you doubt me,' added Keawe, 'you can try. As soon as you are clear of the house, wish to have your pocket full of money, or a bottle of the best rum, or what you please, and you will see the virtue of the thing.'

'Very well, Kanaka,' says the boatswain. 'I will try; but if you are having your fun out of me, I will take my fun out of you with a belaying pin.'

So the whaler-man went off up the avenue; and Keawe stood and waited. It was near the same spot where Kokua had waited the night before; but Keawe was more resolved, and never faltered in his purpose; only his soul was bitter with despair.

It seemed a long time he had to wait before he heard a voice singing in the darkness of the avenue. He knew the voice to be the boatswain's; but it was strange how drunken it appeared upon a sudden.

Next, the man himself came stumbling into the light of the lamp. He had the devil's bottle buttoned in his coat; another bottle was in his hand; and even as he came in view he raised it to his mouth and drank.

'You have it,' said Keawe. 'I see that.'

'Hands off!' cried the boatswain, jumping back. 'Take a step near me, and I'll smash your mouth. You thought you could make a cat's-paw of me, did you?'

'What do you mean?' cried Keawe.

'Mean?' cried the boatswain. 'This is a pretty good bottle, this is; that's what I mean. How I got it for two centimes I can't make out; but I'm sure you shan't have it for one.'

'You mean you won't sell?' gasped Keawe.

'No, *sir*!' cried the boatswain. 'But I'll give you a drink of the rum, if you like.'

'I tell you,' said Keawe, 'the man who has that bottle goes to hell.'

'I reckon I'm going anyway,' returned the sailor; 'and this bottle's the best thing to go with I've struck yet. No, sir!' he cried again, 'this is my bottle now, and you can go and fish for another.'

'Can this be true?' Keawe cried. 'For your own sake, I beseech you, sell it me!'

'I don't value any of your talk,' replied the boatswain. 'You thought I was a flat; now you see I'm not; and there's an end. If you won't have a swallow of the rum, I'll have one myself. Here's your health, and good night to you!'

So off he went down the avenue towards town, and there goes the bottle out of the story.

But Keawe ran to Kokua light as the wind; and great was their joy that night; and great, since then, has been the peace of all their days in the Bright House.

E. Nesbit

MAN-SIZE IN MARBLE

Although every word of this story is as true as despair, I do not expect people to believe it. Nowadays a 'rational explanation' is required before belief is possible. Let me, then, at once offer the 'rational explanation' which finds most favour among those who have heard the tale of my life's tragedy. It is held that we were 'under a delusion,' Laura and I, on that 31st of October; and that this supposition places the whole matter on a satisfactory and believable basis. The reader can judge, when he, too, has heard my story, how far this is an 'explanation,' and in what sense it is 'rational.' There were three who took part in this: Laura and I and another man. The other man still lives, and can speak to the truth of the least credible part of my story.

I never in my life knew what it was to have as much money as I required to supply the most ordinary needs—good colours, books, and cab-fares—and when we were married we knew quite well that we should only be able to live at all by 'strict punctuality and attention to business.' I used to paint in those days, and Laura used to write, and we felt sure we could keep the pot at least simmering. Living in town was out of the question, so we went to look for a cottage in the country, which should be at once sanitary and picturesque. So rarely do these two qualities meet in one cottage that our search was for some time quite fruitless. But when we got away from friends and house-agents, on our honeymoon, our wits grew clear again, and we knew a pretty cottage when at last we saw one.

It was at Brenzett—a little village set on a hill over against the southern marshes. We had gone there, from the seaside village where we were staying, to see the church, and two fields from the church we found this cottage. It stood quite by itself, about two miles from the village. It was a long, low building, with rooms sticking out in unexpected places. There was a bit of stone-work—ivy-covered and moss-grown, just two old rooms, all that was left of a big house that had once stood there—and round this stone-work the house had grown up. Stripped of its roses and jasmine it would have been hideous. As it stood it was charming, and after a brief examination we took it. It was absurdly cheap. There was a jolly old-fashioned garden, with grass paths, and no end of hollyhocks and sunflowers, and big lilies. From the window you could see the marsh-pastures, and beyond them the blue, thin line of the sea.

We got a tall old peasant woman to do for us. Her face and figure were good, though her cooking was of the homeliest; but she understood all about gardening, and told us all the old names of the coppices and cornfields, and the stories of the smugglers and highwaymen, and, better still, of the 'things that walked,' and of the 'sights' which met one in lonely glens of a starlight night. We soon came to leave all the domestic business to Mrs Dorman, and to use her legends in little magazine stories which brought in the jingling guinea.

We had three months of married happiness, and did not have a single quarrel. One October evening I had been down to smoke a pipe with the doctor—our only neighbour—a pleasant young Irishman. Laura had stayed at home to finish a comic sketch. I left her laughing over her own jokes, and came in to find her a crumpled heap of pale muslin, weeping on the window seat.

'Good heavens, my darling, what's the matter?' I cried, taking her in my arms. 'What is the matter? Do speak.'

'It's Mrs Dorman,' she sobbed.

'What has she done?' I inquired, immensely relieved.

'She says she must go before the end of the month, and she says her niece is ill; she's gone down to see her now, but I don't believe that's the reason, because her niece is always ill. I believe someone has been setting her against us. Her manner was so queer——'

'Never mind, Pussy,' I said; 'whatever you do, don't cry, or

I shall have to cry too to keep you in countenance, and then you'll never respect your man again.'

'But you see,' she went on, 'it is really serious, because these village people are so sheepy, and if one won't do a thing you may be quite sure none of the others will. And I shall have to cook the dinners and wash up the hateful greasy plates; and you'll have to carry cans of water about and clean the boots and knives—and we shall never have any time for work or earn any money or anything.'

I represented to her that even if we had to perform these duties the day would still present some margin for other toils and recreations. But she refused to see the matter in any but the greyest light.

'I'll speak to Mrs Dorman when she comes back, and see if I can't come to terms with her,' I said. 'Perhaps she wants a rise. It will be all right. Let's walk up to the church.'

The church was a large and lonely one, and we loved to go there, especially upon bright nights. The path skirted a wood, cut through it once, and ran along the crest of the hill through two meadows, and round the churchyard wall, over which the old yews loomed in black masses of shadow.

This path, which was partly paved, was called 'the bier-walk,' for it had long been the way by which the corpses had been carried to burial. The churchyard was richly treed, and was shaded by great elms which stood just outside and stretched their majestic arms in benediction over the happy dead. A large, low porch let one into the building by a Norman doorway and a heavy oak door studded with iron. Inside, the arches rose into darkness, and between them the reticulated windows, which stood out white in the moonlight. In the chancel, the windows were of rich glass, which showed in faint light their noble colouring, and made the black oak of the choir pews hardly more solid than the shadows. But on each side of the altar lay a grey marble figure of a knight in full plate armour lying upon a low slab, with hands held up in everlasting prayer, and these figures, oddly enough, were always to be seen if there was any glimmer of light in the church. Their names were lost, but the peasants told of them that they had been fierce and wicked men, marauders by land and sea, who had been the scourge of their time, and had been guilty of deeds so foul that the house they had lived in—the big house, by the way, that had stood on the site of our cottage—had been stricken by lightning and the vengeance of Heaven. But for all that, the gold of their heirs had bought them a place in the church. Looking at the bad, hard faces reproduced in the marble, this story was easily believed.

The church looked at its best and weirdest on that night, for the shadows of the yew trees fell through the windows upon the floor of the nave and touched the pillars with tattered shade. We sat down together without speaking, and watched the solemn beauty of the old church with some of that awe which inspired its early builders. We walked to the chancel and looked at the sleeping warriors. Then we rested some time on the stone seat in the porch, looking out over the stretch of quiet moonlit meadows, feeling in every fibre of our being the peace of the night and of our happy love; and came away at last with a sense that even scrubbing and black-leading were but small troubles at their worst.

Mrs Dorman had come back from the village, and I at once invited her to a *tête-à-tête*.

'Now, Mrs Dorman,' I said, when I had got her into my painting room, 'what's all this about your not staying with us?'

'I should be glad to get away, sir, before the end of the month,' she answered, with her usual placid dignity.

'Have you any fault to find, Mrs Dorman?'

'None at all, sir: you and your lady have always been most kind, I'm sure——'

'Well, what is it? Are your wages not high enough?'

'No, sir, I gets quite enough.'

'Then why not stay?'

'I'd rather not'—with some hesitation—'my niece is ill.'

'But your niece has been ill ever since we came. Can't you stay for another month?'

'No, sir, I'm bound to go by Thursday.'

And this was Monday!

'Well, I must say, I think you might have let us know before. There's no time now to get anyone else, and your mistress is not fit to do heavy housework. Can't you stay till next week?'

'I might be able to come back next week.'

'But why must you go this week?' I persisted. 'Come out with it.'

Mrs Dorman drew the little shawl, which she always wore, tightly across her bosom, as though she were cold. Then she said, with a sort of effort:

'They say, sir, as this was a big house in Catholic times, and there was a many deeds done here.'

The nature of the 'deeds' might be vaguely inferred from the inflection of Mrs Dorman's voice—which was enough to make one's blood run cold. I was glad that Laura was not in the room. She was always nervous, as highly-strung natures are, and I felt that these tales about our house, told by this old peasant woman, with her impressive manner and contagious credulity, might have made our home less dear to my wife.

'Tell me all about it, Mrs Dorman,' I said; 'you needn't mind about telling me. I'm not like the young people who make fun of such things.'

Which was partly true.

'Well, sir'—she sank her voice—'you may have seen in the church, beside the altar, two shapes.'

'You mean the effigies of the knights in armour,' I said cheerfully.

'I mean them two bodies, drawed out man-size in marble,' she returned, and I had to admit that her description was a thousand times more graphic than mine, to say nothing of a certain weird force and uncanniness about the phrase 'drawed out man-size in marble.'

'They do say, as on All Saints' Eve them two bodies sits up on their slabs, and gets off of them, and then walks down the aisle, *in their marble*'—(another good phrase, Mrs Dorman)—'and as the church clock strikes eleven they walks out of the church door, and over the graves, and along the bier-walk, and if it's a wet night there's the marks of their feet in the morning.'

'And where do they go?' I asked, rather fascinated.

'They comes back here to their home, sir, and if anyone meets them——'

'Well, what then?' I asked.

But no—not another word could I get from her, save that her niece was ill and she must go.

'Whatever you do, sir, lock the door early on All Saints' Eve, and make the cross-sign over the doorstep and on the windows.'

'But has anyone ever seen these things?' I persisted. 'Who was here last year?'

'No one, sir; the lady as owned the house only stayed here in summer, and she always went to London a full month afore *the* night. And I'm sorry to inconvenience you and your lady, but my niece is ill and I must go Thursday.'

I could have shaken her for her absurd reiteration of that obvious fiction, after she had told me her real reasons.

I did not tell Laura the legend of the shapes that 'walked in their marble,' partly because a legend concerning our house might perhaps trouble my wife, and partly, I think, from some more occult reason. This was not quite the same to me as any other story, and I did not want to talk about it till the day was over. I had very soon ceased to think of the legend, however. I was painting a portrait of Laura, against the lattice window, and I could not think of much else. I had got a splendid background of yellow and grey sunset, and was working away with enthusiasm at her face. On Thursday Mrs Dorman went. She relented, at parting, so far as to say:

'Don't you put yourself about too much, ma'am, and if there's any little thing I can do next week I'm sure I shan't mind.'

Thursday passed off pretty well. Friday came. It is about what happened on that Friday that this is written.

I got up early, I remember, and lighted the kitchen fire, and had just achieved a smoky success when my little wife came running down as sunny and sweet as the clear October morning itself. We prepared breakfast together, and found it very good fun. The housework was soon done, and when brushes and brooms and pails were quiet again the house was still indeed.

It is wonderful what a difference one makes in a house. We really missed Mrs Dorman, quite apart from considerations concerning pots and pans. We spent the day in dusting our books and putting them straight, and dined on cold steak and coffee. Laura was, if possible, brighter and gayer and sweeter than usual, and I began to think that a little domestic toil was really good for her. We had never been so merry since we were married, and the walk we had that afternoon was, I think, the happiest time of all my life. When we had watched the deep scarlet clouds slowly pale into leaden grey against a pale green sky and saw the white mists curl up along the hedgerows in the distant marsh we came back to the house hand in hand.

'You are sad, my darling,' I said, half-jestingly, as we sat down together in our little parlour. I expected a disclaimer, for my own silence had been the silence of complete happiness. To my surprise she said:

'Yes, I think I am sad, or, rather, I am uneasy. I don't think I'm very well. I have shivered three or four times since we came in; and it is not cold, is it?'

'No,' I said, and hoped it was not a chill caught from the treacherous mists that roll up from the marshes in the dying night. No—she said, she did not think so. Then, after a silence, she spoke suddenly:

'Do you ever have presentiments of evil?'

'No,' I said, smiling, 'and I shouldn't believe in them if I had.'

'I do,' she went on, 'the night my father died I knew it, though he was right away in the North of Scotland.' I did not answer in words.

She sat looking at the fire for some time in silence, gently stroking my hand. At last she sprang up, came behind me, and, drawing my head back, kissed me.

'There, it's over now,' she said. 'What a baby I am! Come, light the candles, and we'll have some of these new Rubinstein duets.'

And we spent a happy hour or two at the piano.

At about half past ten I began to long for the good-night pipe, but Laura looked so white that I felt it would be brutal of me to fill our sitting-room with the fumes of strong cavendish.

'I'll take my pipe outside,' I said.

'Let me come, too.'

'No, sweetheart, not tonight; you're much too tired. I shan't be long. Get to bed, or I shall have an invalid to nurse tomorrow as well as the boots to clean.'

I kissed her and was turning to go when she flung her arms round my neck and held me as if she would never let me go again. I stroked her hair.

'Come, Pussy, you're over-tired. The housework has been too much for you.'

She loosened her clasp a little and drew a deep breath.

'No. We've been very happy today, Jack, haven't we? Don't stay out too long.'

'I won't, my dearie.'

I strolled out of the front door, leaving it unlatched. What a night it was! The jagged masses of heavy dark cloud were rolling at intervals from horizon to horizon, and thin white wreaths covered the stars. Through all the rush of the cloud river the moon swam, breasting the waves and disappearing again in the darkness.

I walked up and down, drinking in the beauty of the quiet earth and the changing sky. The night was absolutely silent. Nothing seemed to be abroad. There was no scurrying of rabbits, or twitter of the half-asleep birds. And though the clouds went sailing across the sky, the wind that drove them never came low enough to rustle the dead leaves in the woodland paths. Across the meadows I could see the church tower standing out black and grey against the sky. I walked there thinking over our three months of happiness.

I heard a bell-beat from the church. Eleven already! I turned to go in, but the night held me. I could not go back into our warm rooms yet. I would go up to the church.

I looked in at the low window as I went by. Laura was half lying on her chair in front of the fire. I could not see her face, only her little head showed dark against the pale blue wall. She was quite still. Asleep, no doubt.

I walked slowly along the edge of the wood. A sound broke the stillness of the night, it was a rustling in the wood. I stopped and listened. The sound stopped too. I went on, and now distinctly heard another step than mine answer mine like an echo. It was a poacher or a wood-stealer, most likely, for these were not unknown in our Arcadian neighbourhood. But whoever it was, he was a fool not to step more lightly. I turned into the wood and now the footstep seemed to come from the path I had just left. It must be an echo, I thought. The wood looked perfect in the moonlight. The large dying ferns and the brushwood showed where through thinning foliage the pale light came down. The tree trunks stood up like Gothic columns all around me. They reminded me of the church, and I turned into the bier-walk, and passed through the corpse-gate between the graves to the low porch.

I paused for a moment on the stone seat where Laura and I had watched the fading landscape. Then I noticed that the door of the church was open, and I blamed myself for having left it unlatched the other night. We were the only people who ever cared to come to the church except on Sundays, and I was vexed to think that through our carelessness the damp autumn airs had had a chance of getting in and injuring the old fabric. I went in. It will seem strange, perhaps, that I should have gone half way up the aisle before I remembered—with a sudden chill, followed by as sudden a rush of self-contempt—that this was the very day and hour when, according to tradition, the 'shapes drawed out man-size in marble' began to walk.

Having thus remembered the legend, and remembered it with a shiver, of which I was ashamed, I could not do otherwise than walk up towards the altar, just to look at the figures—as I said to myself; really what I wanted was to assure myself, first, that I did not believe the legend, and secondly, that it was not true. I was rather glad that I had come. I thought now I could tell Mrs Dorman how vain her fancies were, and how peacefully the marble figures slept on through the ghastly hour. With my hands in my pockets I passed up the aisle. In the grey dim light the eastern end of the church looked larger than usual, and the arches above the two tombs looked larger too. The moon came out and showed me the reason. I stopped short, my heart gave a leap that nearly choked me, and then sank sickeningly.

The 'bodies drawed out man-size' *were gone*! and their marble slabs lay wide and bare in the vague moonlight that slanted through the east window.

Were they really gone, or was I mad? Clenching my nerves, I stooped and passed my hand over the smooth slabs and felt their flat unbroken surface. Had someone taken the things away? Was it some vile practical joke? I would make sure, anyway. In an instant I had made a torch of newspaper, which happened to be in my pocket, and, lighting it, held it high above my head. Its yellow glare illumined the dark arches and those slabs. The figures *were* gone. And I was alone in the church; or was I alone?

And then a horror seized me, a horror indefinable and indescribable—an overwhelming certainty of supreme and accomplished calamity. I flung down the torch and tore along the aisle and out through the porch, biting my lips as I ran to keep myself from shrieking aloud. Oh, was I mad—or what was this that possessed me? I leaped the churchyard wall and took the straight cut across the fields, led by the light from our windows. Just as I got over the first stile a dark figure seemed to spring out of the ground. Mad still with that certainty of misfortune, I made for the thing that stood in my path, shouting, 'Get out of the way, can't you!'

But my push met with a more vigorous resistance than I had expected. My arms were caught just above the elbow and held as in a vice, and the raw-boned Irish doctor actually shook me.

'Let me go, you fool,' I gasped. 'The marble figures have gone from the church; I tell you they've gone.'

He broke into a ringing laugh. 'I'll have to give you a draught tomorrow, I see. Ye've bin smoking too much and listening to old wives' tales.'

'I tell you, I've seen the bare slabs.'

'Well, come back with me. I'm going up to old Palmer's—his daughter's ill; we'll look in at the church and let me see the bare slabs.'

'You go, if you like,' I said, a little less frantic for his laughter; 'I'm going home to my wife.'

'Rubbish, man,' said he; 'd'ye think I'll permit of that? Are ye to go saying all yer life that ye've seen solid marble endowed with vitality, and me to go all me life saying ye were a coward? No, sir—ye shan't do ut.'

The night air—a human voice—and I think also the physical contact with this six feet of solid common sense, brought me back to my ordinary self, and the word 'coward' was a mental shower-bath.

'Come on, then,' I said sullenly; 'perhaps you're right.'

He still held my arm tightly. We got over the stile and back to the church. All was still as death. The place smelt very damp and earthly. We walked up the aisle. I am not ashamed to confess that I shut my eyes: I knew the figures would not be there. I heard Kelly strike a match.

'Here they are, ye see, right enough; ye've been dreaming or drinking, asking yer pardon for the imputation.'

I opened my eyes. By Kelly's expiring vesta I saw two shapes lying 'in their marble' on their slabs. I drew a deep breath.

'I'm awfully indebted to you,' I said. 'It must have been some trick of light, or I have been working rather hard, perhaps that's it. I was quite convinced they were gone.'

'I'm aware of that,' he answered rather grimly; 'ye'll have to be careful of that brain of yours, my friend, I assure ye.'

He was leaning over and looking at the right-hand figure, whose stony face was the most villainous and deadly in expression.

'By Jove,' he said, 'something has been afoot here—this hand is broken.'

And so it was. I was certain that it had been perfect the last time Laura and I had been there.

'Perhaps someone has *tried* to remove them,' said the young doctor.

'Come along,' I said, 'or my wife will be getting anxious. You'll come in and have a drop of whisky and drink confusion to ghosts and better sense to me.'

Her hands were tightly clenched. In one of them she held something fast

'I ought to go up to Palmer's, but it's so late now I'd best leave it till the morning,' he replied.

I think he fancied I needed him more than did Palmer's girl, so, discussing how such an illusion could have been possible, and deducing from this experience large generalities concerning ghostly apparitions, we walked up to our cottage. We saw, as we walked up the garden path, that bright light streamed out of the front door, and presently saw that the parlour door was open, too. Had she gone out?

'Come in,' I said, and Dr Kelly followed me into the parlour.

It was all ablaze with candles, not only the wax ones, but at least a dozen guttering, glaring tallow dips, stuck in vases and ornaments in unlikely places. Light, I knew, was Laura's remedy for nervousness. Poor child! Why had I left her? Brute that I was.

We glanced round the room, and at first we did not see her. The window was open, and the draught set all the candles flaring one way. Her chair was empty and her handkerchief and book lay on the floor. I turned to the window. There, in the recess of the window, I saw her. Oh, my child, my love, had she gone to that window to watch for me? And what had come into the room behind her? To what had she turned with that look of frantic fear and horror? Oh, my little one, had she thought that it was I whose step she heard, and turned to meet—what?

She had fallen back across a table in the window, and her body lay half on it and half on the window-seat, and her head hung down over the table, the brown hair loosened and fallen to the carpet. Her lips were drawn back, and her eyes wide, wide open. They saw nothing now. What had they seen last?

The doctor moved towards her, but I pushed him aside and sprang to her; caught her in my arms and cried:

'It's all right, Laura! I've got you safe, wifie.'

She fell into my arms in a heap. I clasped her and kissed her, and called her by pet names, but I think I knew all the time that she was dead. Her hands were tightly clenched. In one of them she held something fast. When I was quite sure that she was dead, and that nothing mattered at all any more, I let him open her hand to see what she held.

It was a grey marble finger.

Sir Arthur Conan Doyle

THE STRIPED CHEST

'WHAT do you make of her, Allardyce?' I asked.

My second mate was standing beside me upon the poop, with his short, thick legs astretch, for the gale had left a considerable swell behind it, and our two quarter-boats nearly touched the water with every roll. He steadied his glass against the mizzen-shrouds, and he looked long and hard at this disconsolate stranger every time she came reeling up on to the crest of a roller and hung balanced for a few seconds before swooping down upon the other side. She lay so low in the water that I could only catch an occasional glimpse of a pea-green line of bulwark.

She was a brig, but her mainmast had been snapped short off some ten feet above the deck, and no effort seemed to have been made to cut away the wreckage, which floated, sails and yards, like the broken wing of a wounded gull, upon the water beside her. The foremast was still standing, but the fore-topsail was flying loose, and the headsails were streaming out in long white pennons in front of her. Never have I seen a vessel which appeared to have gone through rougher handling.

But we could not be surprised at that, for there had been times during the last three days when it was a question whether our own barque would ever see land again. For thirty-six hours we had kept her nose to it, and if the *Mary Sinclair* had not been as good a sea-boat as ever left the Clyde, we could not have gone through. And yet here we were at the end of it with the loss only of our gig and of part of the starboard bulwark. It did not astonish us, however, when the smother had cleared away, to find that others had been less lucky, and that this mutilated brig, staggering about upon a blue sea, and under a cloudless sky, had been left, like a blinded man after a lightning flash, to tell of the terror which is past.

Allardyce, who was a slow and methodical Scotsman, stared long and hard at the little craft, while our seamen lined the bulwark or clustered upon the fore shrouds to have a view of the stranger. In latitude 20° and longitude 10°, which were about our bearings, one becomes a little curious as to whom one meets, for one has left the main lines of Atlantic commerce to the north. For ten days we had been sailing over a solitary sea.

'She's derelict, I'm thinking,' said the second mate.

I had come to the same conclusion, for I could see no sign of life upon her deck, and there was no answer to the friendly wavings from our seamen. The crew had probably deserted her under the impression that she was about to founder.

'She can't last long,' continued Allardyce, in his measured way. 'She may put her nose down and her tail up any minute. The water's lipping up to the edge of her rail.'

'What's her flag?' I asked.

'I'm trying to make out. It's got all twisted and tangled with the halyards. Yes, I've got it now, clear enough. It's the Brazilian flag, but it's wrong side up.'

She had hoisted a signal of distress, then, before her people had abandoned her. Perhaps they had only just gone. I took the mate's glass and looked round over the tumultuous face of the deep blue Atlantic, still veined and starred with white lines and spoutings of foam. But nowhere could I see anything human beyond ourselves.

'There may be living men aboard,' said I.

'There may be salvage,' muttered the second mate.

'Then we will run down upon her lee side, and lie to.'

We were not more than a hundred yards from her when we swung our foreyard aback, and there we were, the barque and the brig, ducking and bowing like two clowns in a dance.

'Drop one of the quarter-boats,' said I. 'Take four men, Mr Allardyce, and see what you can learn of her.'

But just at that moment my first officer, Mr Armstrong, came on deck, for seven bells had struck, and it was but a few minutes off his watch. It would interest me to go myself to this abandoned vessel and to see what there might be aboard of her. So, with a word to Armstrong, I swung myself over the side, slipped down the falls, and took my place in the sheets of the boat.

It was but a little distance, but it took some time to traverse, and so heavy was the roll, that often, when we were in the trough of the sea, we could not see either the barque which we had left or the brig which we were approaching. The sinking sun did not penetrate down there, and it was cold and dark in the hollows of the waves, but each passing billow heaved us up into the warmth and the sunshine once more. At each of these moments, as we hung upon a white-capped ridge between the two dark valleys, I caught a glimpse of the long, pea-green line, and the nodding foremast of the brig, and I steered so as to come round by her stern, so that we might determine which was the best way of boarding her. As we passed her we saw the name *Nossa Sehnora da Vittoria* painted across her dripping counter.

'The weather side, sir,' said the second mate. 'Stand by with the boathook, carpenter!' An instant later we had jumped over the bulwarks, which were hardly higher than our boat, and found ourselves upon the deck of the abandoned vessel.

Our first thought was to provide for our own safety in case—as seemed very probable—the vessel should settle down beneath our feet. With this object two of our men held on to the painter of the boat, and fended her off from the vessel's side, so that she might be ready in case we had to make a hurried retreat. The carpenter was sent to find out how much water there was, and whether it was still gaining, while the other seaman, Allardyce and myself, made a rapid inspection of the vessel and her cargo.

The deck was littered with wreckage and with hen-coops, in which the dead birds were washing about. The boats were gone, with the exception of one, the bottom of which had been stove, and it was certain that the crew had abandoned the vessel. The cabin was in a deck house, one side of which had been beaten in by a heavy sea. Allardyce and I entered it, and found the captain's table as he had left it, his books and papers—all Spanish or Portuguese—scattered over it, with piles of cigarette ash everywhere. I looked about for the log, but could not find it.

'As likely as not he never kept one,' said Allardyce. 'Things are pretty slack aboard a South American trader, and they don't do more than they can help. If there was one it must have been taken away with him in the boat.'

'I should like to take all these books and papers,' said I. 'Ask the carpenter how much time we have.'

His report was reassuring. The vessel was full of water, but some of the cargo was buoyant, and there was no immediate danger of her sinking. Probably she would never sink, but would drift about as one of those terrible, unmarked reefs which have sent so many stout vessels to the bottom.

'In that case there is no danger in your going below, Mr Allardyce,' said I. 'See what you can make of her, and find out how much of her cargo may be saved. I'll look through these papers while you are gone.'

The bills of lading, and some notes and letters which lay upon the desk, sufficed to inform me that the Brazilian brig *Nossa Sehnora da Vittoria* had cleared from Bahia a month before. The name of the captain was Texeira, but there was no record as to the number of the crew. She was bound for London, and a glance at the bills of lading was sufficient to show me that we were not likely to profit much in the way of salvage. Her cargo consisted of nuts, ginger, and wood, the latter in the shape of great logs of valuable tropical growths. It was these, no doubt, which had prevented the ill-fated vessel from going to the bottom, but they were of such a size as to make it impossible for us to extract them. Besides these, there were a few fancy goods, such as a number of ornamental birds for millinery purposes, and a hundred cases of preserved fruits. And then, as I turned over the papers, I came upon a short note in English, which arrested my attention.

'It is requested,' said the note, 'that the various old Spanish and Indian curiosities, which came out of the Santarem collection, and which are consigned to Prontfoot and Neuman, of Oxford Street, London, should be put in some place where there may be no danger of these very valuable and unique articles being injured or tampered with. This applies most particularly to the treasure-chest of Don Ramirez di Leyra, which must on no account be placed where anyone can get at it.'

The treasure-chest of Don Ramirez! Unique and valuable articles! Here was a chance of salvage after all! I had risen to my feet with the paper in my hand, when my Scotch mate appeared in the doorway.

'I'm thinking all isn't quite as it should be aboard of this ship, sir,' said he. He was a hard-faced man, and yet I could see that he had been startled.

'What's the matter?'

'Murder's the matter, sir. There's a man here with his brains beaten out.'

'Killed in the storm?' said I.

'Maybe so, sir. But I'll be surprised if you think so after you have seen him.'

'Where is he, then?'

'This way, sir; here in the main-deck house.'

There appeared to have been no accommodation below in the brig, for there was the afterhouse for the captain, another by the main hatchway with the cook's galley attached to it, and a third in the forecastle for the men. It was to this middle one that the mate led me. As you entered, the galley, with its litter of tumbled pots and dishes, was upon the right, and upon the left was a small room with two bunks for the officers. Then beyond there was a place about twelve feet square, which was littered with flags and spare canvas. All round the walls were a number of packets done up in coarse cloth and carefully lashed to the woodwork. At the other end was a great box, striped red and white, though the red was so faded and the white so dirty that it was only where the light fell directly upon it that one could see the colouring. The box was, by subsequent measurement, four feet three inches in length, three feet two inches in height, and three feet across—considerably larger than a seaman's chest.

But it was not to the box that my eyes or my thoughts were turned as I entered the store-room. On the floor, lying across the litter of bunting, there was stretched a small, dark man with a short, curling beard. He lay as far as it was possible from the box, with his feet towards it and his head away. A crimson patch was printed upon the white canvas on which his head was resting, and little red ribbons wreathed themselves round his swarthy neck and trailed away on to the floor, but there was no sign of a wound that I could see, and his face was as placid as that of a sleeping child.

It was only when I stooped that I could perceive his injury, and then I turned away with an exclamation of horror. He had been pole-axed; apparently by some person standing behind him. A frightful blow had smashed in the top of his head and penetrated deeply into his brain. His face might well be placid, for death must have been absolutely instantaneous, and the position of the wound showed that he could never have seen the person who had inflicted it.

'Is that foul play or accident, Captain Barclay?' asked my second mate, demurely.

'You are quite right, Mr Allardyce. The man has been murdered, struck down from above by a sharp and heavy weapon. But who was he, and why did they murder him?'

'He was a common seaman, sir,' said the mate. 'You can see that if you look at his fingers.' He turned out his pockets as he spoke and brought to light a pack of cards, some tarred string, and a bundle of Brazilian tobacco.

'Hullo, look at this!' said he.

It was a large, open knife with a stiff spring blade which he had picked up from the floor. The steel was shining and bright, so that we could not associate it with the crime, and yet the dead man had apparently held it in his hand when he was struck down, for it still lay within his grasp.

'It looks to me, sir, as if he knew he was in danger, and kept his knife handy,' said the mate. 'However, we can't help the poor beggar now. I can't make out these things that are lashed to the wall. They seem to be idols and weapons and curios of all sorts done up in old sacking.'

'That's right,' said I. 'They are the only things of value that we are likely to get from the cargo. Hail the barque and tell them to send the other quarter-boat to help us to get the stuff aboard.'

While he was away I examined this curious plunder which had come into our possession. The curiosities were so wrapped up that I could only form a general idea as to their nature, but the striped box stood in a good light where I could thoroughly examine it. On the lid, which was clamped and cornered with metal-work, there was engraved a complex coat of arms, and beneath it was a line of Spanish which I was able to decipher as meaning, 'The treasure-chest of Don Ramirez di Leyra, Knight of the Order of Saint James, Governor and Captain-General of Terra Firma and of the Province of Veraquas.' In one corner was the date 1606, and on the other a large white label, upon which was written in English, 'You are earnestly requested, upon no account, to open this box.' The same warning was repeated underneath in Spanish. As to the lock, it was a very complex and heavy one of engraved steel, with a Latin motto, which was above a seaman's comprehension.

By the time I had finished this examination of the peculiar box, the other quarter-boat with Mr Armstrong, the first officer, had come alongside, and we began to carry out and place in her the various curiosities which appeared to be the only objects worth moving from the derelict ship. When she was full I sent her back to the barque, and then Allardyce and I, with a carpenter and one seaman, shifted the striped box, which was the only thing left, to our boat, and lowered it over, balancing it upon the two middle thwarts, for it was so heavy that it would have given the boat a dangerous tilt had we placed it at either end. As to the dead man, we left him where we had found him.

The mate had a theory that, at the moment of the desertion of the ship, this fellow had started plundering, and that the captain, in an attempt to preserve discipline, had struck him down with a hatchet or some other heavy weapon. It seemed more probable than any other explanation, and yet it did not entirely satisfy me either. But the ocean is full of mysteries, and we were content to leave the fate of the dead seaman of the Brazilian brig to be added to that long list which every sailor can recall.

The heavy box was slung up by ropes on to the deck of the *Mary Sinclair*, and was carried by four seamen into the cabin, where, between the table and the after-lockers, there was just space for it to stand. There it remained during supper, and after that meal the mates remained with me, and discussed over a glass of grog the event of the day. Mr Armstrong was a long, thin, vulture-like man, an excellent seaman, but famous for his nearness and cupidity. Our treasure-trove had excited him greatly, and already he had begun with glistening eyes to reckon up how much it might be worth to each of us when the shares of the salvage came to be divided.

'If the paper said that they were unique, Mr Barclay, then they may be worth anything that you like to name. You wouldn't believe the sums that the rich collectors give. A thousand pounds is nothing to them. We'll have something to show for our voyage, or I am mistaken.'

'I don't think that,' said I. 'As far as I can see they are not very different from any other South American curios.'

'Well, sir, I've traded there for fourteen voyages, and I have never seen anything like that chest before. That's worth a pile of money, just as it stands. But it's so heavy, that surely there must be something valuable inside it. Don't you think that we ought to open it and see?'

'If you break it open you will spoil it, as likely as not,' said the second mate.

Armstrong squatted down in front of it, with his head on one side, and his long, thin nose within a few inches of the lock.

'The wood is oak,' said he, 'and it has shrunk a little with age. If I had a chisel or a strong-bladed knife I could force the lock back without doing any damage at all.'

The mention of a strong-bladed knife made me think of the dead seaman upon the brig.

'I wonder if he could have been on the job when someone came to interfere with him,' said I.

'I don't know about that, sir, but I am perfectly certain that I could open the box. There's a screwdriver here in the locker. Just hold the lamp, Allardyce, and I'll have it done in a brace of shakes.'

'Wait a bit,' said I, for already, with eyes which gleamed with curiosity and with avarice, he was stooping over the lid. 'I don't see that there is any hurry over this matter. You've read that card which warns us not to open it. It may mean anything or it may mean nothing, but somehow I feel inclined to obey it. After all, whatever is in it will keep, and if it is valuable it will be worth as much if it is opened in the owner's offices as in the cabin of the *Mary Sinclair*.'

The first officer seemed bitterly disappointed at my decision.

'Surely, sir, you are not superstitious about it,' said he, with a slight sneer upon his thin lips. 'If it gets out of our own hands, and we don't see for ourselves what is inside it, we may be done out of our rights; besides——'

'That's enough, Mr Armstrong,' said I, abruptly. 'You may have every confidence that you will get your rights, but I will not have that box opened to-night.'

'Why, the label itself shows that the box has been examined by Europeans,' Allardyce added. 'Because a box is a treasure-box is no reason that it has treasures inside it now. A good many folk have had a peep into it since the days of the old Governor of Terra Firma.'

Armstrong threw the screwdriver down upon the table and shrugged his shoulders.

'Just as you like,' said he; but for the rest of the evening, although we spoke upon many subjects, I noticed that his eyes were continually coming round, with the same expression of curiosity and greed, to the old striped box.

And now I come to that portion of my story which fills me even now with a shuddering horror when I think of it. The main cabin had the rooms of the officers round it, but mine was the farthest away from it at the end of the little passage which led to the companion. No regular watch was kept by me, except in cases of emergency, and the three mates divided the watches among them. Armstrong had the middle watch, which ends at four in the morning, and he was relieved by Allardyce. For my part I have always been one of the soundest of sleepers, and it is rare for anything less than a hand upon my'shoulder to arouse me.

And yet I was aroused that night, or rather in the early grey of the morning. It was just half-past four by my chronometer when something caused me to sit up in my berth wide awake and with every nerve tingling. It was a sound of some sort, a crash with a human cry at the end of it, which still jarred upon my ears. I sat listening, but all was now silent. And yet it could not have been imagination, that hideous cry, for the echo of it still rang in my head, and it seemed to have come from some place quite close to me. I sprang from my bunk, and, pulling on some clothes, I made my way into the cabin.

At first I saw nothing unusual there. In the cold, grey light I made out the red-clothed table, the six rotating chairs, the walnut lockers, the swinging barometer, and there, at the end, the big striped chest. I was turning away with the intention of going upon deck and asking the second mate if he had heard anything when my eyes fell suddenly upon something which projected from under the table. It was the leg of a man—a leg with a long sea-boot upon it. I stooped, and there was a figure sprawling upon his face, his arms thrown forward and his body twisted. One glance told me that it was Armstrong, the first officer, and a second that he was a dead man. For a few moments I stood gasping. Then I rushed on to the deck, called Allardyce to my assistance, and came back with him into the cabin.

Together we pulled the unfortunate fellow from under the table, and as we looked at his dripping head we exchanged glances, and I do not know which was the paler of the two.

'The same as the Spanish sailor,' said I.

'The very same. God preserve us! It's that infernal chest! Look at Armstrong's hand!'

He held up the mate's right hand, and there was the screw-driver which he had wished to use the night before.

'He's been at the chest, sir. He knew that I was on deck and you asleep. He knelt down in front of it, and he pushed the lock back with that tool. Then something happened to him, and he cried out so that you heard him.'

'Allardyce,' I whispered, 'what *could* have happened to him?'

The second mate put his hand upon my sleeve and drew me into his cabin.

'We can talk here, sir, and we don't know who may be listening to us in there. What do you suppose is in that box, Captain Barclay?'

'I give you my word, Allardyce, that I have no idea.'

'Well, I can only find one theory which will fit all the facts. Look at the size of the box. Look at all the carving and metal-work which may conceal any number of holes. Look at the weight of it; it took four men to carry it. On the top of that, remember that two men have tried to open it, and both have come to their end through it. Now, sir, what can it mean except one thing?'

'You mean there is a man in it?'

'Of course there is a man in it. You know how it is in these South American States, sir. A man may be President one week and hunted like a dog the next. They are for ever flying for their lives. My idea is that there is some fellow in hiding there, who is armed and desperate, and who will fight to the death before he is taken.'

'But his food and drink?'

'It's a roomy chest, sir, and he may have some provisions stowed away. As to his drink, he had a friend among the crew upon the brig who saw that he had what he needed.'

'You think, then, that the label asking people not to open the box was simply written in his interest?'

'Yes, sir, that is my idea. Have you any other way of explaining the facts?'

I had to confess that I had not.

'The question is what are we to do?' I asked.

'The man's a dangerous ruffian who sticks at nothing. I'm thinking it wouldn't be a bad thing to put a rope round the chest and tow it alongside for half an hour; then we could open it at our ease. Or if we just tied the box up and kept him from getting any water maybe that would do as well. Or the carpenter could put a coat of varnish over it and stop all the blowholes.'

'Come, Allardyce,' said I, angrily. 'You don't seriously mean to say that a whole ship's company are going to be terrorized by a single man in a box. If he's there, I'll engage to fetch him out!' I went to my room and came back with my revolver in my hand. 'Now, Allardyce,' said I. 'Do you open the lock, and I'll stand on guard.'

'For God's sake, think what you are doing, sir!' cried the mate. 'Two men have lost their lives over it, and the blood of one not yet dry upon the carpet.'

'The more reason why we should revenge him.'

'Well, sir, at least let me call the carpenter. Three are better than two, and he is a good stout man.'

He went off in search of him, and I was left alone with the striped chest in the cabin. I don't think that I'm a nervous man, but I kept the table between me and this solid old relic of the Spanish Main. In the growing light of morning the red and white striping was beginning to appear, and the curious scrolls and wreaths of metal and carving which showed the loving pains which cunning craftsmen had expended upon it. Presently the carpenter and the mate came back together, the former with a hammer in his hand.

'It's a bad business, this, sir,' said he, shaking his head, as he looked at the body of the mate. 'And you think there's someone hiding in the box?'

'There's no doubt about it,' said Allardyce, picking up the screwdriver and setting his jaw like a man who needs to brace his courage. 'I'll drive the lock back if you will both stand by. If he rises let him have it on the head with your hammer, carpenter! Shoot at once, sir, if he raises his hand. Now!'

He had knelt down in front of the striped chest, and passed the blade of the tool under the lid. With a sharp snick the lock flew back. 'Stand by!' yelled the mate, and with a heave he threw open the massive top of the box. As it swung up, we all three sprang back, I with my pistol levelled, and the carpenter with the hammer above his head. Then, as nothing happened, we each took a step forward and peeped in. The box was empty.

Not quite empty either, for in one corner was lying an old yellow candlestick, elaborately engraved, which appeared to be as old as the box itself. Its rich yellow tone and artistic shape suggested that it was an object of value. For the rest there was

As nothing happened we each took a step forward and peeped in

nothing more weighty or valuable than dust in the old striped treasure-chest.

'Well, I'm blessed!' cried Allardyce, staring blankly into it. 'Where does the weight come in, then?'

'Look at the thickness of the sides and look at the lid. Why, it's five inches through. And see that great metal spring across it.'

'That's for holding the lid up,' said the mate. 'You see, it won't lean back. What's that German printing on the inside?'

'It means that it was made by Johann Rothstein of Augsburg, in 1606.'

'And a solid bit of work, too. But it doesn't throw much light on what has passed, does it, Captain Barclay? That candlestick looks like gold. We shall have something for our trouble after all.'

He leant forward to grasp it, and from that moment I have

never doubted as to the reality of inspiration, for on the instant I caught him by the collar and pulled him straight again. It may have been some story of the Middle Ages which had come back to my mind, or it may have been that my eye had caught some red which was not that of rust upon the upper part of the lock, but to him and to me it will always seem an inspiration, so prompt and sudden was my action.

'There's devilry here,' said I. 'Give me the crooked stick from the corner.'

It was an ordinary walking-cane with a hooked top. I passed it over the candlestick and gave it a pull. With a flash a row of polished steel fangs shot out from below the upper lip, and the great striped chest snapped at us like a wild animal. Clang came the huge lid into its place, and the glasses on the swinging rack sang and tinkled with the shock. The mate sat down on the edge of the table and shivered like a frightened horse.

'You've saved my life, Captain Barclay!' said he.

So this was the secret of the striped treasure-chest of old Don Ramirez di Leyra, and this was how he preserved his ill-gotten gains from the Terra Firma and the Province of Veraquas. Be the thief ever so cunning he could not tell that golden candlestick from the other articles of value, and the instant that he laid hand upon it the terrible spring was unloosed and the murderous steel spikes were driven into his brain, while the shock of the blow sent the victim backwards and enabled the chest to automatically close itself. How many, I wondered, had fallen victims to the ingenuity of the Mechanic of Augsburg. And as I thought of the possible history of that grim striped chest my resolution was very quickly taken.

'Carpenter, bring three men and carry this on deck.'

'Going to throw it overboard, sir?'

'Yes, Mr Allardyce. I'm not superstitious as a rule, but there are some things which are more than a sailor can be called upon to stand.'

'No wonder that brig made heavy weather, Captain Barclay, with such a thing on board. The glass is dropping fast, sir, and we are only just in time.'

So we did not even wait for the three sailors, but we carried it out, the mate, the carpenter, and I, and we pushed it with our own hands over the bulwarks. There was a white spout of water, and it was gone. There it lies, the striped chest, a thousand fathoms deep, and if, as they say, the sea will some day be dry land, I grieve for the man who finds that old box and tries to penetrate into its secret.

Sir Arthur Quiller-Couch

A PAIR OF HANDS

'YES,' said Miss Le Petyt, gazing into the deep fireplace and letting her hands and her knitting lie for the moment idle in her lap. 'Oh, yes, I have seen a ghost. In fact I have lived in a house with one for quite a long time.'

'How you *could*——!' began one of my host's daughters; and '*You*, Aunt Emily?' cried the other at the same moment.

Miss Le Petyt, gentle soul, withdrew her eyes from the fireplace and protested with a gay little smile. 'Well, my dears, I am not quite the coward you take me for. And, as it happens, mine was the most harmless ghost in the world. In fact'—and here she looked at the fire again—'I was quite sorry to lose her.'

'It was a woman, then? Now *I* think,' said Miss Blanche, 'that female ghosts are the horridest of all. They wear little shoes with high red heels, and go about *tap*, *tap*, wringing their hands.'

'This one wrung her hands, certainly. But I don't know about the high red heels, for I never saw her feet. Perhaps she was like the Queen of Spain, and hadn't any. And as for the hands, it all depends *how* you wring them. There's an elderly shopwalker at Knightsbridge, for instance——'

'Don't be prosy, dear, when you know that we're just dying to hear the story.'

Miss Le Petyt turned to me with a small deprecating laugh. 'It's such a little one.'

'The story, or the ghost?'

'Both.'

And this was Miss Le Petyt's story:

'It happened when I lived down in Cornwall, at Tresillack on the south coast. Tresillack was the name of the house, which stood quite alone at the head of a coombe, within sound of the sea but without sight of it; for though the coombe led down to a wide open beach, it wound and twisted half a dozen times on its way, and its overlapping sides closed the view from the house, which was advertised as "secluded". I was very poor in those days. Your father and all of us were poor then, as I trust, my dears, you will never be; but I was young enough to be romantic and wise enough to like independence, and this word "secluded" took my fancy.

'The misfortune was that it had taken the fancy, or just suited the requirements, of several previous tenants. You know, I dare say, the kind of person who rents a secluded house in the country? Well, yes, there are several kinds; but they seem to agree in being odious. No one knows where they come from, though they soon remove all doubt about where they're "going to", as the children say. "Shady" is the word, is it not? Well, the previous tenants of Tresillack (from first to last a bewildering series) had been shady with a vengeance.

'I knew nothing of this when I first made application to the landlord, a solid yeoman inhabiting a farm at the foot of the coombe, on a cliff overlooking the beach. To him I presented myself fearlessly as a spinster of decent family and small but assured income, intending a rural life of combined seemliness and economy. He met my advances politely enough, but with an air of suspicion which offended me. I began by disliking him for it: afterwards I set it down as an unpleasant feature in the local character. I was doubly mistaken. Farmer Hosking was slow-witted, but as honest a man as ever stood up against hard times; and a more open and hospitable race than the people on that coast I never wish to meet. It was the caution of a child who had burnt his fingers, not once but many times. Had I known what I afterwards learned of Farmer Hosking's tribulations as landlord of a "secluded country residence", I should have approached him with the bashfulness proper to my suit and faltered as I undertook to prove the bright exception in a long line of painful experiences. He had bought the Tresillack estate twenty years before—on mortgage, I fancy—because the land adjoined his own and would pay him for tillage. But the house was a nuisance, an incubus: and had been so from the beginning.

'"Well, miss," he said, "you're welcome to look over it; a pretty enough place, inside and out. There's no trouble about keys, because I've put in a housekeeper, a widow-woman, and she'll show you round. With your leave I'll step up the coombe so far with you, and put you in your way." As I thanked him he paused and rubbed his chin. "There's one thing I must tell you, though. Whoever takes the house must take Mrs Carkeek along with it."

'"Mrs Carkeek?" I echoed dolefully. "Is that the housekeeper?"

'"Yes: she was wife to my late hind. I'm sorry, miss," he added, my face telling him no doubt what sort of woman I expected Mrs Carkeek to be; "but I had to make it a rule after—after some things that happened. And I dare say you won't find her so bad. Mary Carkeek's a sensible comfortable woman, and knows the place. She was in service there to Squire Kendall when he sold up and went: her first place it was."

'"I may as well see the house, anyhow," said I dejectedly. So we started to walk up the coombe. The path, which ran beside a little chattering stream, was narrow for the most part, and Farmer Hosking, with an apology, strode on ahead to beat aside the brambles. But whenever its width allowed us to walk side by side I caught him from time to time stealing a shy inquisitive glance under his rough eyebrows. Courteously though he bore himself, it was clear that he could not sum me up to his satisfaction or bring me square with his notion of a tenant for his "secluded country residence".

'I don't know what foolish fancy prompted it, but about halfway up the coombe I stopped short and asked:

'"There are no ghosts, I suppose?"

'It struck me, a moment after I had uttered it, as a supremely silly question; but he took it quite seriously. "No; I never heard tell of any *ghosts*." He laid a queer sort of stress on the word. "There's always been trouble with servants, and maids' tongues will be runnin'. But Mary Carkeek lives up there alone, and she seems comfortable enough."

'We walked on. By and by he pointed with his stick. "It don't look like a place for ghosts, now, do it?"

'Certainly it did not. Above an untrimmed orchard rose a terrace of turf scattered with thorn-bushes, and above this a terrace of stone, upon which stood the prettiest cottage I had ever seen. It was long and low and thatched; a deep verandah ran from end to end. Clematis, Banksia roses and honeysuckle climbed the posts of this verandah, and big blooms of the Maréchal Niel were clustered along its roof, beneath the lattices of the bedroom windows. The house was small enough to be called a cottage, and rare enough in features and in situation to confer distinction on any tenant. It suggested what in those days we should have called "elegant" living. And I could have clapped my hands for joy.

'My spirits mounted still higher when Mrs Carkeek opened the door to us. I had looked for a Mrs Gummidge, and I found a healthy middle-aged woman with a thoughtful but contented face, and a smile which, without a trace of obsequiousness, quite bore out the farmer's description of her. She was a comfortable woman; and while we walked through the rooms together (for Mr Hosking waited outside) I "took to" Mrs Carkeek. Her speech was direct and practical; the rooms, in spite of their faded furniture, were bright and exquisitely clean; and somehow the very atmosphere of the house gave me a sense of well-being, of feeling at home and cared for; yes, *of being loved*. Don't laugh, my dears; for when I've done you may not think this fancy altogether foolish.

'I stepped out into the verandah, and Farmer Hosking pocketed the pruning-knife which he had been using on a bush of jasmine.

'"This is better than anything I had dreamed of," said I.

'"Well, miss, that's not a wise way of beginning a bargain, if you'll excuse me."

'He took no advantage, however, of my admission; and we struck the bargain as we returned down the coombe to his farm, where the hired chaise waited to convey me back to the market-town. I had meant to engage a maid of my own, but now it occurred to me that I might do very well with Mrs Carkeek. This, too, was settled in the course of the next day or two, and within the week I had moved into my new home.

'I can hardly describe to you the happiness of my first month at Tresillack; because (as I now believe) if I take the reasons which I had for being happy, one by one, there remains over something which I cannot account for. I was moderately young, entirely healthy; I felt myself independent and adventurous; the season was high summer, the weather glorious, the garden in all the pomp of June, yet sufficiently unkempt to keep me busy, give me a sharp appetite for meals, and send me to bed in that drowsy stupor which comes of the odours of earth. I spent the most of my time out-of-doors, winding up the day's work as a rule with a walk down the cool valley, along the beach and back.

'I soon found that all housework could be safely left to Mrs Carkeek. She did not talk much; indeed her only fault (a rare one in housekeepers) was that she talked too little, and even when I addressed her seemed at times unable to give me her attention. It was as though her mind strayed off to some small job she had forgotten, and her eyes wore a listening look, as though she waited for the neglected task to speak and remind her. But as a matter of fact she forgot nothing. Indeed, my dears, I was never so well attended to in my life.

'Well, that is what I'm coming to. That, so to say, is just *it*. The woman not only had the rooms swept and dusted, and my meals prepared to the moment. In a hundred odd little ways this orderliness, these preparations, seemed to read my desires. Did I wish the roses renewed in a bowl upon the dining-table, sure enough at the next meal they would be replaced by fresh ones. Mrs Carkeek (I told myself) must have surprised and interpreted a glance of mine. And yet I could not remember having glanced at the bowl in her presence. And how on earth had she guessed the very roses, the very shapes and colours I had lightly wished for? This is only an instance, you understand. Every day, and from morning to night, I happened on others, each slight enough, but all together bearing witness to a ministering intelligence as subtle as it was untiring.

'I am a light sleeper, as you know, with an uncomfortable

knack of waking with the sun and roaming early. No matter how early I rose at Tresillack, Mrs Carkeek seemed to have prevented me. Finally I had to conclude that she arose and dusted and tidied as soon as she judged me safely a-bed. For once, finding the drawing-room (where I had been sitting late) "redded up" at four in the morning, and no trace of a plate of raspberries which I had carried thither after dinner and left overnight, I determined to test her, and walked through to the kitchen, calling her by name. I found the kitchen as clean as a pin, and the fire laid, but no trace of Mrs Carkeek. I walked upstairs and knocked at her door. At the second knock a sleepy voice cried out, and presently the good woman stood before me in her nightgown, looking (I thought) very badly scared.

'"No," I said, "it's not a burglar. But I've found out what I wanted, that you do your morning's work over-night. But you mustn't wait for me when I choose to sit up. And now go back to your bed like a good soul, whilst I take a run down to the beach."

'She stood blinking in the dawn. Her face was still white.

'"Oh, miss," she gasped, "I made sure you must have seen something!"

'"And so I have," I answered, "but it was neither burglars nor ghosts."

'"Thank God!" I heard her say as she turned her back to me in her grey bedroom—which faced the north. And I took this for a carelessly pious expression and ran downstairs, thinking no more of it.

'A few days later I began to understand.

'The plan of Tresillack house (I must explain) was simplicity itself. To the left of the hall as you entered was the dining-room; to the right the drawing-room, with a boudoir beyond. The foot of the stairs faced the front door, and beside it, passing a glazed inner door, you found two others right and left, the left opening on the kitchen, the right on a passage which ran by a store-cupboard under the bend of the stairs to a neat pantry with the usual shelves and linen-press, and under the window (which faced north) a porcelain basin and brass tap. On the first morning of my tenancy I had visited this pantry and turned the tap; but no water ran. I supposed this to be accidental. Mrs Carkeek had to wash up glassware and crockery, and no doubt Mrs Carkeek would complain of any failure in the water-supply.

'But the day after my surprise visit (as I called it) I had picked a basketful of roses, and carried them into the pantry as a handy place to arrange them in. I chose a china bowl and went to fill it at the tap. Again the water would not run.

'I called Mrs Carkeek. "What is wrong with this tap?" I asked. "The rest of the house is well enough supplied."

'"I don't know, miss. I never use it."

'"But there must be a reason; and you must find it a great nuisance washing up the plate and glasses in the kitchen. Come around to the back with me, and we'll have a look at the cisterns."

'"The cisterns'll be all right, miss. I assure you I don't find it a trouble."

'But I was not to be put off. The back of the house stood but ten feet from a wall which was really but a stone face built against the cliff cut away by the architect. Above the cliff rose the kitchen-garden, and from its lower path we looked over the wall's parapet upon the cisterns. There were two—a very large one, supplying the kitchen and the bathroom above the kitchen; and a small one, obviously fed by the other, and as obviously leading, by a pipe which I could trace, to the pantry. Now the big cistern stood almost full, and yet the small one, though on a lower level, was empty.

'"It's as plain as daylight," said I. "The pipe between the two is choked." And I clambered onto the parapet.

'"I wouldn't, miss. The pantry tap is only cold water, and no use to me. From the kitchen boiler I gets it hot, you see."

'"But I want the pantry water for my flowers." I bent over and groped. "I thought as much!" said I, as I wrenched out a thick plug of cork and immediately the water began to flow. I turned triumphantly on Mrs Carkeek, who had grown suddenly red in the face. Her eyes were fixed on the cork in my hand. To keep it more firmly wedged in its place somebody had wrapped it round with a rag of calico print; and, discoloured though the rag was, I seemed to recall the pattern (a lilac sprig). Then, as our eyes met, it occurred to me that only two mornings before Mrs Carkeek had worn a print gown of that same sprigged pattern.

'I had the presence of mind to hide this very small discovery, sliding over it with some quite trivial remark; and presently Mrs Carkeek regained her composure. But I own I felt disappointed in her. It seemed such a paltry thing to be disingenuous over. She had deliberately acted a fib before me; and why? Merely because she preferred the kitchen to the pantry tap. It was childish. "But servants are all the same," I told myself. "I must take Mrs Carkeek as she is; and, after all, she is a treasure."

'On the second night after this, and between eleven and twelve o'clock, I was lying in bed and reading myself sleepy over a novel of Lord Lytton's, when a small sound disturbed me. I listened. The sound was clearly that of water trickling; and I set it down to rain. A shower (I told myself) had filled the water-pipes which drained the roof. Somehow I could not fix the sound. There was a water-pipe against the wall just outside my window. I rose and drew up the blind.

'To my astonishment no rain was falling; no rain had fallen. I felt the slate window-sill; some dew had gathered there—no more. There was no wind, no cloud: only a still moon high over the eastern slope of the coombe, the distant plash of waves, and the fragrance of many roses. I went back to bed and listened again. Yes, the trickling sound continued, quite distinct in the silence of the house, not to be confused for a moment with the dull murmur of the beach. After a while it began to grate on my nerves. I caught up my candle, flung my dressing-gown about me, and stole softly downstairs.

'Then it was simple. I traced the sound to the pantry. "Mrs Carkeek has left the tap running," said I: and, sure enough, I found it so—a thin trickle steadily running to waste in the porcelain basin. I turned off the tap, went contentedly back to my bed, and slept.

'——for some hours. I opened my eyes in darkness, and at

once knew what had awakened me. The tap was running again. Now it had shut easily in my hand, but not so easily that I could believe it had slipped open again of its own accord. "This is Mrs Carkeek's doing," said I; and am afraid I added "Bother Mrs Carkeek!"

'Well, there was no help for it: so I struck a light, looked at my watch, saw that the hour was just three o'clock, and descended the stairs again. At the pantry door I paused. I was not afraid—not one little bit. In fact the notion that anything might be wrong had never crossed my mind. But I remember thinking, with my hand on the door, that if Mrs Carkeek were in the pantry I might happen to give her a severe fright.

'I pushed the door open briskly. Mrs Carkeek was not there. But something *was* there, by the porcelain basin—something which might have sent me scurrying upstairs two steps at a time, but which as a matter of fact held me to the spot. My heart seemed to stand still—so still! And in the stillness I remember setting down the brass candlestick on a tall nest of drawers beside me.

'Over the porcelain basin and beneath the water trickling from the tap I saw two hands.

'That was all—two small hands, a child's hands. I cannot tell you how they ended.

'No: they were not cut off. I saw them quite distinctly: just a pair of small hands and the wrists, and after that—nothing. They were moving briskly—washing themselves clean. I saw the water trickle and splash over them—not *through* them—but just as it would on real hands. They were the hands of a little girl, too. Oh, yes, I was sure of that at once. Boys and girls wash their hands differently. I can't just tell you what the difference is, but it's unmistakable.

'I saw all this before my candle slipped and fell with a crash. I had set it down without looking—for my eyes were fixed on the basin—and had balanced it on the edge of the nest of drawers. After the crash, in the darkness there, with the water running, I suffered some bad moments. Oddly enough, the thought uppermost with me was that I *must* shut off that tap before escaping. I

Something was there, by the porcelain basin . . .

had to. And after a while I picked up all my courage, so to say, between my teeth, and with a little sob thrust out my hand and did it. Then I fled.

'The dawn was close upon me: and as soon as the sky reddened I took my bath, dressed and went downstairs. And there at the pantry door I found Mrs Carkeek, also dressed, with my candlestick in her hand.

'"Ah!" said I, "you picked it up."

'Our eyes met. Clearly Mrs Carkeek wished me to begin, and I determined at once to have it out with her.

'"And you knew all about it. That's what accounts for your plugging up the cistern."

'"You saw . . . ?" she began.

'"Yes, yes. And you must tell me all about it—never mind how bad. Is——is it—murder?"

'"Law bless you, miss, whatever put such horrors in your head?"

'"She was washing her hands."

'"Ah, so she does, poor dear! But—murder! And dear little Miss Margaret, that wouldn't go to hurt a fly!"

'"Miss Margaret?"

'"Eh, she died at seven year. Squire Kendall's only daughter; and that's over twenty year ago. I was her nurse, miss, and I know—diphtheria it was; she took it down in the village."

'"But how do you know it is Margaret?"

'"Those hands—why, how could I mistake, that used to be her nurse?"

'"But why does she wash them?"

'"Well, miss, being always a dainty child—and the housework, you see——"

'I took a long breath. "Do you mean to tell me that all this tidying and dusting——" I broke off. "Is it *she* who has been taking this care of me?"

'Mrs Carkeek met my look steadily.

'"Who else, miss?"

'"Poor little soul!"

'"Well now"—Mrs Carkeek rubbed my candlestick with the

edge of her apron—"I'm so glad you take it like this. For there isn't really nothing to be afraid of—is there?" She eyed me wistfully. "It's my belief she loves you, miss. But only to think what a time she must have had with the others!"

'"The others?" I echoed.

'"The other tenants, miss: the ones afore you."

'"Were they bad?"

'"They was awful. Didn't Farmer Hosking tell you? They carried on fearful—one after another, and each one worse than the last."

'"What was the matter with them? Drink?"

'"Drink, miss, with some of 'em. There was the Major—he used to go mad with it, and run about the coombe in his night-shirt. Oh, scandalous! And his wife drank too—that is, if she ever *was* his wife. Just think of that tender child washing up after their nasty doings!"

'I shivered.

'"But that wasn't the worst, miss—not by a long way. There was a pair here—from the colonies, or so they gave out—with two children, a boy and gel, the eldest scarce six. Poor mites!"

'"Why, what happened?"

'"They beat those children, miss—your blood would boil!—*and* starved, *and* tortured 'em, it's my belief. You could hear their screams, I've been told, away back in the high road, and that's the best part of half a mile. Sometimes they was locked up without food for days together. But it's my belief that little Miss Margaret managed to feed them somehow. Oh, I can see her, creeping to the door and comforting!"

'"But perhaps she never showed herself when these awful people were here, but took to flight until they left."

'"You didn't never know her, miss. The brave she was! She'd have stood up to lions. She've been here all the while: and only to think what her innocent eyes and ears must have took in! There was another couple——" Mrs Carkeek sunk her voice.

'"Oh, hush!" said I, "if I'm to have any peace of mind in this house!"

'"But you won't go, miss? She loves you, I know she do. And

think what you might be leaving her to—what sort of tenant might come next. For she can't go. She've been here ever since her father sold the place. He died soon after. You mustn't go!"

'Now I had resolved to go, but all of a sudden I felt how mean this resolution was.

'"After all," said I, "there's nothing to be afraid of."

'"That's it, miss; nothing at all. I don't even believe it's so very uncommon. Why, I've heard my mother tell of farmhouses where the rooms were swept every night as regular as clockwork, and the floors sanded, and the pots and pans scoured, and all while the maids slept. They put it down to the piskies; but we know better, miss, and now we've got the secret between us we can lie easy in our beds, and if we hear anything, say 'God bless the child!' and go to sleep."

'"Mrs Carkeek," said I, "there's only one condition I have to make."

'"What's that?"

'"Why, that you let me kiss you."

'"Oh, you dear!" said Mrs Carkeek as we embraced: and this was as close to familiarity as she allowed herself to go in the whole course of my aquaintance with her.

'I spent three years at Tresillack, and all that while Mrs Carkeek lived with me and shared the secret. Few women, I dare to say, were ever so completely wrapped around with love as we were during those three years. It ran through my waking life like a song: it smoothed my pillow, touched and made my table comely, in summer lifted the heads of the flowers as I passed, and in winter watched the fire with me and kept it bright.

'Why did I ever leave Tresillack? Because one day, at the end of five years, Farmer Hosking brought me word that he had sold the house—or was about to sell it; I forget which. There was no avoiding it, at any rate; the purchaser being a Colonel Kendall, a brother of the old Squire.

'"A married man?" I asked.

'"Yes, miss; with a family of eight. As pretty children as ever you see, and the mother a good lady. It's the old home to Colonel Kendall."

'"I see. And that is why you feel bound to sell."

'"It's a good price, too, that he offers. You mustn't think but I'm sorry enough——"

'"To turn me out? I thank you, Mr Hosking; but you are doing the right thing."

'Since Mrs Carkeek was to stay, the arrangement lacked nothing of absolute perfection—except, perhaps, that it found no room for me.

'"*She*—Margaret—will be happy," I said; "with her cousins, you know."

'"Oh yes, miss, she will be happy, sure enough," Mrs Carkeek agreed.

'So when the time came I packed up my boxes, and tried to be cheerful. But on the last morning, when they stood corded in the hall, I sent Mrs Carkeek upstairs upon some poor excuse, and stepped alone into the pantry.

'"Margaret!" I whispered.

'There was no answer at all. I had scarcely dared to hope for one. Yet I tried again, and, shutting my eyes this time, stretched out both hands and whispered:

'"Margaret!"

'And I will swear to my dying day that two little hands stole and rested—for a moment only—in mine.'

F. Anstey

THE LIGHTS OF SPENCER PRIMMETT'S EYES

A WORTHIER and more estimable young man than Spencer Primmett it would have been difficult to find in the whole of London. He was in one of the Government Departments, in which he occupied an exceptionally good position for one of his years, while he was also in enjoyment of a very comfortable private income.

His principal ambition was to eschew any conduct which might possibly have the effect of rendering him conspicuous, in which laudable object he had so far succeeded admirably.

There was nothing whatever remarkable about his countenance, which was mild and rather round; or his demeanour, which was correct without assumption; or his opinions, which were those of all well-regulated persons.

Wherefore mothers and *chaperons* generally regarded him with favour as a highly eligible *parti*—a fact of which he was modestly but fully aware.

He had indeed but one defect, and that of so gradual a growth that he was pardonable for being the last to perceive it. He was excessively near-sighted. For some time it had struck him more and more forcibly that the British climate was becoming mistier than at any previous period in his recollection, and he was surprised that none of his friends and acquaintances were observant enough to notice so obvious an atmospherical deterioration.

But there came an afternoon when Spencer Primmett was compelled to admit that his own observation was less acute than he had imagined. For while paying a call—a social duty which he was ever punctilious in discharging—on the Bellinghams in Cornwall Gardens, he was not a little mortified by the discovery that he had been wasting much time and many blandishments in a

. . . he had been wasting much time . . . to induce a foot-stool to sit up and beg for a biscuit

futile endeavour to induce a foot-stool to sit up and beg for a biscuit.

This led him to infer that there might be some slight imperfection in his eyesight, which, to avoid all chance of some really ludicrous blunder, he would do well to rectify by purchasing an eyeglass.

He had another and even stronger motive for taking such a step. Hilda and Rhoda Bellingham were both extremely attractive girls, and of late his thoughts had begun to dwell, not unpleasingly, upon the possibility of his falling in love with one of them. But which? For the life of him he could not determine, being by no means sure, now that he came to consider, whether he had ever seen either at all distinctly.

Ordinary prudence suggested that it would be advisable to be better acquainted with the features of each before committing himself by any definite advances to either. It would be a pity to find out, when it was too late to retract, that he had pledged himself to the plainer of the two.

So he tried several opticians in turn, but none of them had an eyeglass, or even a *pince-nez*, in stock that could do anything more than increase the dimness of his natural sight, and at last he took the course which he should have taken at first, and consulted a leading oculist.

After a prolonged examination, the oculist informed him that he was 'abnormally astigmatic,' which seems a harsh thing for any man to say of a fellow-creature.

However, he wrote him out a prescription for a pair of special glasses of differing powers, and this Spencer took to be made up by the firm to whom he was recommended.

A few days afterwards, on returning from Whitehall to his rooms, he found awaiting him a neat little parcel containing a pair of spectacles, and accompanied by the account, which came to more than he had anticipated. He would have preferred, too, a pair of *pince-nez* to spectacles, which he knew have a tendency to add years without the corresponding experience, and it was not without anxiety that he fitted them on and inspected himself in a hand-glass which lay on his dressing-table.

It was a considerable relief to him to find that they were not by any means unbecoming. Indeed, his eyes, now that they were framed and glazed, as it were, looked larger and more brilliant; the glasses gave him an air of higher intelligence and deeper thoughtfulness than he had previously discerned in his expression, while they were so light and so easily adjusted that he was scarcely aware of having them on.

But it was less from vanity than an uncontrollable impatience to see what the Miss Bellinghams were really like that he called a hansom and gave the address of Cornwall Gardens.

As he drove westward, facing the sunset sky, he was delightfully conscious of the extraordinary degree to which his powers of vision had improved. No longer was the sun a mere scarlet blur for him, but a clear golden disc surrounded by mauve and crimson clouds, while more immediate objects had become defined with a sharpness that revealed much that hitherto would have altogether escaped him.

For instance, he remarked for the first time the singular incompetency of London cabmen, evidenced by the fact that the drivers of almost all the hansoms he met seemed to have the greatest difficulty in controlling their horses. It impressed him as an additional proof of the decadence in our national character.

Fortunately his own cabman was an exception to the general rule, and brought him to his destination without mishap.

Spencer learnt on inquiry that Mrs Bellingham was at home, and he followed the butler upstairs to the drawing-room with a thrill of excitement. For he might find the daughters of the house there as well, and then he would know at last whether it was Hilda or Rhoda who would prove to be his actual enchantress.

They were at home, as it happened, and greeted him with a cordiality sufficiently charming to remove all doubt, had he felt any, which he did not, of the gratification he was affording them. He accepted a cup of tea and a seat by the fire, and, as often and intently as he could without infringing the ordinary rules of good breeding, he studied the features of the two graceful girls who sat opposite to him in the lamplight. Thanks to his recent acquisition, he could now see them perfectly, and was delighted to find that they surpassed all his previous conceptions.

Even then he had as much difficulty as ever in making up his mind which of the two was the more irresistibly engaging, they were both so adorably pretty in their different styles; but at least he saw now that there *was* a difference.

So he sat there talking—rather pleasantly, he thought—to all three ladies, with the sense that he was making an increasingly favourable impression. Indeed, before long he began to fear that he was inspiring a deeper sentiment in both the Miss Bellinghams than he had any right or intention to do at that stage of their acquaintance.

Without being unduly conceited, he could not help observing that, whenever he turned to address Miss Bellingham, she regarded him with a kind of spellbound subjection closely resembling fascination; whereas Miss Rhoda, on the other hand, seemed powerless to meet his eye at all.

These were trifles, no doubt—but not without significance. He was wondering whether he had not better go, when the dog, which had been previously snoring soundly in its basket, created a diversion by waking up and coming out for its usual saucer of weak and milky tea.

This time Spencer made no mistake; he knew it was not a foot-stool, or even a door-mat, but a Maltese terrier a trifle out of condition. So he beamed upon it with affable recognition, and called it by its name, which was 'Lulu'. But instead of responding to his advances, the animal uttered a sharp howl and fled into the back drawing-room with every sign of abject terror.

Spencer said he could not understand it, as he generally got on so well with dogs, and the Bellinghams agreed that it was most unaccountable, and began to talk of something else.

But somehow the incident caused a certain constraint. Hilda and Rhoda chattered on, it was true, but in rather a random and desultory manner, while their mother's silence was marked by a want of repose which was unusual in one so essentially a woman of the world.

So he cut short his visit, after staying little more than an hour, heartily wishing that the dog had not chosen to make such a fool of itself, just when things were going so well.

On thinking over it afterwards, he recalled sundry symptoms which almost led him to the distressing conclusion that the Bellingham family was inclined to be slightly hysterical.

Spencer had forgotten that he had to dine out that evening at a house in Lancaster Gate, and did not get back to his rooms until just before eight, which obliged him to dress in frantic haste. Even then he arrived quite a quarter of an hour after everybody else, so that he could hardly expect anything but the chilling reception which he certainly got.

He was consoled, however, by the discovery that the Bellinghams were among the guests, and that it would be his privilege to take Miss Bellingham in to dinner. He would have been equally pleased had she been her sister, for both were looking more bewitching than ever in those brilliantly-lighted rooms.

Still, as he advanced eagerly to claim her, he felt at once that something had come between them; he distinctly noticed her flinch, as though with repressed aversion, as he offered her his arm with a playful allusion to his good fortune.

And when they were seated at the dinner-table, on which innumerable electric lamps, artistically disposed around the walls, shed a soft but still dazzling radiance, he could not feast his eyes on her face so constantly as he desired and expected, for the reason that she seldom looked at him in speaking, and then only by an obvious effort. Was it merely his disordered fancy, or did she invariably turn away her head on such occasions with something suspiciously like a shudder?

At the first opportunity she turned away from him altogether to enter into an animated conversation with her right-hand neighbour, leaving him with nothing of her to contemplate except her left shoulder till dessert.

He tried his other neighbour, but she was anything but forthcoming, and after one or two perfunctory replies, evidently preferred to be entertained by her allotted partner.

So, in his utter isolation, Spencer was free to let his thoughts dwell on Miss Rhoda, who was seated exactly opposite. He wished now that it had been she who had fallen to his lot; she would not have treated him, he was sure, with this inexcusable caprice, she was much too kindhearted, and, besides, she was quite as pretty as Hilda, if not actually prettier.

He directed a glance of half-humorous, half-melancholy appeal for sympathy across the table at her, which he intended should establish a secret bond of intelligence between them, but he found an unexpected difficulty in catching her eye. Even when he succeeded in doing so, he only knew it because he saw her start and bite her lower lip hard, as if to control some rising emotion which too obviously was not maidenly confusion, since she neither blushed nor accorded him the discreetest smile of recognition.

What in the world was the matter with them both? It was impossible that he could have done anything since that afternoon to account for the change in their conduct. Surely they could not be influenced by the fact that that little overfed beast of a terrier of theirs had exhibited a perfectly unreasonable antipathy to him! He had thought modern young women possessed more commonsense.

And presently it was apparent to him, as he allowed his eyes to wander idly round the table, that he must be generally unpopular—or how was it that every face on which his gaze casually lighted seemed to freeze instantly into petrifaction? He had arrived a little late, he knew, but, hang it all! he could not think he had spoilt the dinner so much as all *that*! And even if he had, it was most unchristian of them to carry unforgiveness further than the fish! It was horrible to sit there, feeling like an apologetic skeleton. He had never felt less at home at a dinner-party in all his life.

Even on rising, Rhoda had no look nor word for him, and, as soon as the ladies had departed, Mr Bellingham began to tell a story that gave every promise of lasting for a considerable time.

Spencer had never met him before, and, had he been the parent of anybody but Hilda and Rhoda, might have been tempted to regard him as an insufferable old bore. As it was, in his anxiety to propitiate at least one member of the family, he leaned forward, drinking in every detail of the narrative with an air of absorbed and eager interest which was perhaps a little overdone.

At all events, he did not propitiate the old gentleman—he merely put him out. For Mr Bellingham grew more and more uneasy under Spencer's ardent attention, until at length he brought his monologue to a lame and evidently premature conclusion.

Primmett made really heroic efforts during the awkward silences that ensued to put the company at their ease by throwing out intelligent remarks from time to time on some topic of the day. But, although he was confident that he said nothing that was not perfectly safe in any gathering, somehow his blameless platitudes seemed to burst on his hearers like bombshells. Every one appeared to have a positive dread of being drawn into conversation with him. He noticed those he addressed directly blinking nervously as they returned some monosyllabic reply, while others evaded his advances by studiously looking in any other direction but his own.

He affected the nerves of the very servants, for, as he turned towards a footman who was offering him coffee, the man suddenly let the tray fall with a crash.

Spencer was glad when the host proposed that they should go upstairs, though, even when he reached the drawing-room, he was no happier. Before he could obtain the explanation for which he was hoping from Rhoda or Hilda, he was introduced to two or three older ladies, all of whom responded to his agreeable nothings with absent minds and roving eyes, and before he could escape from these compulsory amenities, he had the misery of seeing the Bellinghams take their leave.

He left himself as soon afterwards as he was able, and it struck him that his hostess was almost indecently glad to get rid of him.

Spencer walked back to his rooms in a pitiable frame of mind. He was conscious of having shed a kind of blight on the whole dinner-party—but how or why he was at a loss to imagine.

Was there, unknown to him, some discreditable rumour in circulation with regard to his private character? But that was impossible, for his conscience assured him that he had done nothing that could have given occasion for the slightest scandal.

Then why—*why* did the Bellinghams and everybody else shrink from him as though he were some accursed thing? Was he to go through life henceforth as an object of universal repugnance—he, who by nature was so eminently sociable and desirous of winning esteem? Would he never find any one to look him in the face again with the old friendliness and approval? If so, it seemed hard that he should not even know why this fate had befallen him!

Still gloomily pondering over his probable future, he regained his sitting-room, where, resting his elbow upon the mantelpiece, he stood staring hopelessly down at the cheerily burning fire.

Suddenly, on looking up, he beheld his own reflection in the bevelled mirror of the overmantel, and recoiled in positive terror.

For the eyes that met his own were no human eyes—they were two glowing caverns in which flickered lurid flames, as though his brain were being slowly consumed by an infernal fire!

The effect was simply appalling. He realised at once that no man with such eyes as those could ever hope to inspire the object of his affection with any feelings but instinctive distrust, and even horror. Gaze at her as tenderly and pleadingly as he might, it was impossible to prevent his ardour from impressing her as unpleasantly volcanic.

And yet, how could he have been thus transformed into a fiend of peculiarly repulsive aspect without being even aware of the process?

Then all at once he remembered his spectacles. They fitted him so comfortably that after he had once grown accustomed to the improvement in his sight, he had ungratefully forgotten their very existence. However, he found that he was still wearing them.

Was it just barely possible that *they*— He removed them hurriedly, and, on closely approaching the mirror, discovered with inexpressible relief that his eyes were no longer illumined by their former baleful glare.

He put them on once more, and, placing a lamp between

himself and the mirror, observed the result at some distance. The right lens was slightly concave, and threw rays as blinding as those of a search-light, while the left, which was convex, blazed like some illuminated globe of distilled water in a chemist's window!

After repeated experiments, he ascertained that—to himself at least—this disquieting phenomenon was apparent in the mirror only when a strong artificial light struck his spectacles at particular angles of refraction, which accounted for his failure to notice it by daylight, or even while dressing for dinner.

But he had no difficulty in understanding *now* why the cab-horses had shied that afternoon as his spectacles reflected all the glories of the sunset; why the Bellinghams' dog had fled in dismay from the unearthly radiance of his eyes, and the Bellinghams themselves had been so susceptible to their mesmeric influence; or why, in short, throughout that fearful evening he had been innocently producing the effect of a human basilisk or a Medusa head!

He felt he could not go about doing that any more—it made him altogether too remarkable.

And so, in another instant he had torn those costly but perfidious spectacles from his ears, and ground the glasses to splinters under his heel. . . .

Since that day he has not had the courage to try any others—but he is rewarded for his sacrifice by the knowledge that he can now permit his eyes to rest on both the Miss Bellinghams without reducing them to a cataleptic condition. The only drawback is that he is as unable as ever to distinguish one from the other.

Which is possibly the reason why there has been no intimation, as yet, of his engagement to either.

H. G. Wells

THE DOOR IN THE WALL

I

One confidential evening, not three months ago, Lionel Wallace told me this story of the Door in the Wall. And at the time I thought that so far as he was concerned it was a true story.

He told it me with such a direct simplicity of conviction that I could not do otherwise than believe in him. But in the morning, in my own flat, I woke to a different atmosphere; and as I lay in bed and recalled the things he had told me, stripped of the glamour of his earnest slow voice, denuded of the focused, shaded table light, the shadowy atmosphere that wrapped about him and me, and the pleasant bright things, the dessert and glasses and napery of the dinner we had shared, making them for the time a bright little world quite cut off from everyday realities, I saw it all as frankly incredible. 'He was mystifying!' I said, and then: 'How well he did it! . . . It isn't quite the thing I should have expected him, of all people, to do well.'

Afterwards as I sat up in bed and sipped my morning tea, I found myself trying to account for the flavour of reality that perplexed me in his impossible reminiscences, by supposing they did in some way suggest, present, convey—I hardly know which word to use—experiences it was otherwise impossible to tell.

Well, I don't resort to that explanation now. I have got over my intervening doubts. I believe now, as I believed at the moment of telling, that Wallace did to the very best of his ability strip the truth of his secret for me. But whether he himself saw, or only thought he saw, whether he himself was the possessor of an inestimable privilege or the victim of a fantastic dream, I cannot pretend to guess. Even the facts of his death, which ended my doubts for ever, throw no light on that.

That much the reader must judge for himself.

I forget now what chance comment or criticism of mine moved so reticent a man to confide in me. He was, I think, defending himself against an imputation of slackness and unreliability I had made in relation to a great public movement, in which he had disappointed me. But he plunged suddenly. 'I have,' he said, 'a preoccupation . . .

'I know,' he went on, after a pause, 'I have been negligent. The fact is—it isn't a case of ghosts or apparitions—but—it's an odd thing to tell of, Redmond—I am haunted. I am haunted by something—that rather takes the light out of things, that fills me with longings . . .'

He paused, checked by that English shyness that so often overcomes us when we would speak of moving or grave or beautiful things. 'You were at Saint Athelstan's all through,' he said, and for a moment that seemed to me quite irrelevant. 'Well . . .' and he paused. Then very haltingly at first, but afterwards more easily, he began to tell of the thing that was hidden in his life, the haunting memory of a beauty and a happiness that filled his heart with insatiable longings, that made all the interests and spectacle of worldly life seem dull and tedious and vain to him.

Now that I have the clue to it, the thing seems written visibly in his face. I have a photograph in which that look of detachment has been caught and intensified. It reminds me of what a woman once said of him—a woman who had loved him greatly. 'Suddenly,' she said, 'the interest goes out of him. He forgets you. He doesn't care a rap for you—under his very nose . . .'

Yet the interest was not always out of him, and when he was holding his attention to a thing Wallace could contrive to be an extremely successful man. His career, indeed, is set with successes. He left me behind him long ago; he soared up over my head, and cut a figure in the world that I couldn't cut—anyhow. He was still a year short of forty, and they say now that he would have been in office and very probably in the new Cabinet if he had lived. At school he always beat me without effort—as it were by nature. We were at school together at Saint Athelstan's College in West Kensington for almost all our school-time. He came into the school as my co-equal, but he left far above me, in a blaze of scholarships and brilliant performance. Yet I think I made a fair average running. And it was at school I heard first of the 'Door in the Wall'—that I was to hear of a second time only a month before his death.

To him at least the Door in the Wall was a real door, leading through a real wall to immortal realities. Of that I am now quite assured.

And it came into his life quite early, when he was a little fellow between five and six. I remember how, as he sat making his confession to me with a slow gravity, he reasoned and reckoned the date of it. 'There was,' he said, 'a crimson Virginia creeper in it—all one bright uniform crimson, in a clear amber sunshine against a white wall. That came into the impression somehow, though I don't clearly remember how, and there were horse-chestnut leaves upon the clean pavement outside the green door. They were blotched yellow and green, you know, not brown nor dirty, so that they must have been new fallen. I take it that means October. I look out for horse-chestnut leaves every year and I ought to know.

'If I'm right in that, I was about five years and four months old.'

He was, he said, rather a precocious little boy—he learned to talk at an abnormally early age, and he was so sane and 'old-fashioned,' as people say, that he was permitted an amount of initiative that most children scarcely attain by seven or eight. His mother died when he was two, and he was under the less vigilant and authoritative care of a nursery governess. His father was a stern, preoccupied lawyer, who gave him little attention and expected great things of him. For all his brightness he found life grey and dull, I think. And one day he wandered.

He could not recall the particular neglect that enabled him to get away, nor the course he took among the West Kensington roads. All that had faded among the incurable blurs of memory. But the white wall and the green door stood out quite distinctly

As his memory of that childish experience ran, he did at the very first sight of that door experience a peculiar emotion, an attraction, a desire to get to the door and open it and walk in. And at the same time he had the clearest conviction that either it was unwise or it was wrong of him—he could not tell which—to yield to this attraction. He insisted upon it as a curious thing that he knew from the very beginning—unless memory has played him the queerest trick—that the door was unfastened, and that he could go in as he chose.

I seem to see the figure of that little boy, drawn and repelled. And it was very clear in his mind, too, though why it should be so was never explained, that his father would be very angry if he went in through that door.

Wallace described all these moments of hesitation to me with the utmost particularity. He went right past the door, and then, with his hands in his pockets and making an infantile attempt to whistle, strolled right along beyond the end of the wall. There he recalls a number of mean dirty shops, and particularly that of a plumber and decorator with a dusty disorder of earthenware pipes, sheet lead, ball taps, pattern books of wallpaper, and tins of enamel. He stood pretending to examine these things, and *coveting*, passionately desiring, the green door.

Then, he said, he had a gust of emotion. He made a run for it, lest hesitation should grip him again; he went plump with outstretched hand through the green door and let it slam behind him. And so, in a trice, he came into the garden that has haunted all his life.

It was very difficult for Wallace to give me his full sense of that garden into which he came.

There was something in the very air of it that exhilarated, that gave one a sense of lightness and good happening and well-being; there was something in the sight of it that made all its colour clean and perfect and subtly luminous. In the instant of coming into it one was exquisitely glad—as only in rare moments, and when one is young and joyful one can be glad in this world. And everything was beautiful there. . . .

Wallace mused before he went on telling me. 'You see,' he said, with the doubtful inflection of a man who pauses at incredible things, 'there were two great panthers there. . . . Yes, spotted panthers. And I was not afraid. There was a long wide path with marble-edged flower borders on either side, and these two huge velvety beasts were playing there with a ball. One looked up and came towards me, a little curious as it seemed. It came right up to me, rubbed its soft round ear very gently against the small hand I held out, and purred. It was, I tell you, an enchanted garden. I know. And the size? Oh! it stretched far and wide, this way and that. I believe there were hills far away Heaven knows where West Kensington had suddenly got to. And somehow it was just like coming home.

'You know, in the very moment the door swung to behind me, I forgot the road with its fallen chestnut leaves, its cabs and tradesmen's carts, I forgot the sort of gravitational pull back to the discipline and obedience of home, I forgot all hesitations and fear, forgot discretion, forgot all the intimate realities of this life. I became in a moment a very glad and wonder-happy little boy—in another world. It was a world with a different quality, a warmer, more penetrating and mellower light, with a faint clear gladness in its air, and wisps of sun-touched cloud in the blueness of its sky. And before me ran this long wide path, invitingly, with weedless beds on either side, rich with untended flowers, and these two great panthers. I put my little hands fearlessly on their soft fur, and caressed their round ears and the sensitive corners under their ears, and played with them, and it was as though they welcomed me home. There was a keen sense of homecoming in my mind, and when presently a tall, fair girl appeared in the pathway and came to meet me, smiling, and said "Well?" to me, and lifted me and kissed me, and put me down and led me by the hand, there was no amazement, but only an impression of delightful rightness, of being reminded of happy things that had in some strange way been overlooked. There were broad red steps, I remember, that came into view between spikes of delphinium, and up these we went to a great avenue between very old and shady dark trees. All down this avenue, you know, between the red chapped stems, were marble seats of honour and statuary, and very tame and friendly white doves.

'Along this cool avenue my girl-friend led me, looking down

'A tall fair girl appeared in the pathway and came to meet me, smiling . . .'

—I recall the pleasant lines, the finely-modelled chin of her sweet kind face—asking me questions in a soft, agreeable voice, and telling me things, pleasant things I know, though what they were I was never able to recall. . . . Presently a Capuchin monkey, very clean, with a fur of ruddy brown and kindly hazel eyes, came down a tree to us and ran beside me, looking up at me and grinning, and presently leaped to my shoulder. So we two went on our way in great happiness.'

He paused.

'Go on,' I said.

'I remember little things. We passed an old man musing among laurels, I remember, and a place gay with paroquets, and came through a broad shaded colonnade to a spacious cool palace, full of pleasant fountains, full of beautiful things, full of the quality and promise of heart's desire. And there were many things and many people, some that still seem to stand out clearly and some that are vaguer; but all these people were beautiful and kind. In some way—I don't know how—it was conveyed to me that they all were kind to me, glad to have me there, and filling me with gladness by their gestures, by the touch of their hands, by the welcome and love in their eyes. Yes——'

He mused for a while. 'Playmates I found there. That was very much to me, because I was a lonely little boy. They played delightful games in a grass-covered court where there was a sundial set about with flowers. And as one played one loved. . . .

'But—it's odd—there's a gap in my memory. I don't remember the games we played. I never remembered. Afterwards, as a child, I spent long hours trying, even with tears, to recall the form of that happiness. I wanted to play it all over again—in my nursery—by myself. No! All I remember is the happiness and two dear playfellows who were most with me. . . . Then presently came a sombre dark woman, with a grave, pale face and dreamy eyes, a sombre woman, wearing a soft long robe of pale purple, who carried a book, and beckoned and took me aside with her into a gallery above a hall—though my playmates were loth to have me go, and ceased their game and stood watching as I was carried away. "Come back to us!" they cried. "Come back to us soon!" I looked up at her face, but she heeded them not at all. Her face was very gentle and grave. She took me to a seat in the gallery, and I stood beside her, ready to look at her book as she opened it upon her knee. The pages fell open. She pointed, and I looked, marvelling, for in the living pages of that book I saw myself; it was a story about myself, and in it were all the things that had happened to me since ever I was born. . . .

'It was wonderful to me, because the pages of that book were not pictures, you understand, but realities.'

Wallace paused gravely—looked at me doubtfully.

'Go on,' I said. 'I understand.'

'They were realities—yes, they must have been; people moved and things came and went in them; my dear mother, whom I had near forgotten; then my father, stern and upright, the servants, the nursery, all the familiar things of home. Then the front door and the busy streets, with traffic to and fro. I looked and marvelled, and looked half doubtfully again into the woman's face and turned the pages over, skipping this and that, to see more of this book and more, and so at last I came to myself hovering and hesitating outside the green door in the long white wall, and felt again the conflict and the fear.

'"And next?" I cried, and would have turned on, but the cool hand of the grave woman delayed me.

'"Next?" I insisted, and struggled gently with her hand, pulling up her fingers with all my childish strength, and as she yielded and the page came over she bent down upon me like a shadow and kissed my brow.

'But the page did not show the enchanted garden, nor the panthers, nor the girl who had led me by the hand, nor the playfellows who had been so loth to let me go. It showed a long grey street in West Kensington, in that chill hour of afternoon before the lamps are lit; and I was there, a wretched little figure, weeping aloud, for all that I could do to restrain myself, and I was weeping because I could not return to my dear playfellows who had called after me, "Come back to us! Come back to us soon!" I was there. This was no page in a book, but harsh reality; that enchanted place and the restraining hand of the grave mother at whose knee I stood had gone—whither had they gone?'

He halted again, and remained for a time staring into the fire.

'Oh, the woefulness of that return!' he murmured.

'Well?' I said, after a minute or so.

'Poor little wretch I was—brought back to this grey world again! As I realised the fullness of what had happened to me, I gave way to quite ungovernable grief. And the shame and humiliation of that public weeping and my disgraceful home-coming remain with me still. I see again the benevolent-looking old gentleman in gold spectacles who stopped and spoke to me—prodding me first with his umbrella. "Poor little chap," said he; "and are you lost then?"—and me a London boy of five and more! And he must needs bring in a kindly young policeman and make a crowd of me, and so march me home. Sobbing, conspicuous, and frightened, I came back from the enchanted garden to the steps of my father's house.

'That is as well as I can remember my vision of that garden—the garden that haunts me still. Of course, I can convey nothing of that indescribable quality of translucent unreality, that difference from the common things of experience that hung about it all; but that—that is what happened. If it was a dream, I am sure it was a day-time and altogether extraordinary dream. . . . H'm—naturally there followed a terrible questioning, by my aunt, my father, the nurse, the governess—everyone. . . .

'I tried to tell them, and my father gave me my first thrashing for telling lies. When afterwards I tried to tell my aunt, she punished me again for my wicked persistence. Then, as I said, everyone was forbidden to listen to me, to hear a word about it. Even my fairy-tale books were taken away from me for a time—because I was too "imaginative". Eh? Yes, they did that! My father belonged to the old school. . . . And my story was driven back upon myself. I whispered it to my pillow—my pillow that was often damp and salt to my whispering lips with childish tears. And I added always to my official and less fervent prayers this one heartfelt request: "Please God I may dream of the garden. Oh! take me back to my garden!" Take me back to my garden! I dreamt often of the garden. I may have added to it, I may have changed it; I do not know. . . . All this, you understand, is an attempt to reconstruct from fragmentary memories a very early experience. Between that and the other consecutive memories of my boyhood there is a gulf. A time came when it seemed impossible I should ever speak of that wonder glimpse again.'

I asked an obvious question.

'No,' he said. 'I don't remember that I ever attempted to find my way back to the garden in those early years. This seems odd to me now, but I think that very probably a closer watch was kept on my movements after this misadventure to prevent my going astray. No, it wasn't till you knew me that I tried for the garden again. And I believe there was a period—incredible as it seems now—when I forgot the garden altogether—when I was about eight or nine it may have been. Do you remember me as a kid at Saint Athelstan's?'

'Rather!'

'I didn't show any signs, did I, in those days of having a secret dream?'

2

He looked up with a sudden smile.

'Did you ever play North-West Passage with me? . . . No, of course you didn't come my way!

'It was the sort of game,' he went on, 'that every imaginative child plays all day. The idea was the discovery of a North-West Passage to school. The way to school was plain enough; the game consisted in finding some way that wasn't plain, starting off ten minutes early in some almost hopeless direction, and working my way round through unaccustomed streets to my goal. And one day I got entangled among some rather low-class streets on the other side of Campden Hill, and I began to think that for once the game would be against me and that I should get to school late. I tried rather desperately a street that seemed a *cul-de-sac*, and found a passage at the end. I hurried through that with renewed hope. "I shall do it yet," I said, and passed a row of frowsy little shops that were inexplicably familiar to me, and behold! there was my long white wall and the green door that led to the enchanted garden!

'The thing whacked upon me suddenly. Then, after all, that garden, that wonderful garden, wasn't a dream!'

He paused.

'I suppose my second experience with the green door marks the world of difference there is between the busy life of a schoolboy and the infinite leisure of a child. Anyhow, this second time I didn't for a moment think of going in straight away. You see . . . for one thing, my mind was full of the idea of getting to school in time—set on not breaking my record for punctuality. I must surely have felt *some* little desire at least to try the door—yes, I must have felt that. . . . But I seem to remember the attraction of the door mainly as another obstacle to my overmastering determination to get to school. I was immensely interested by this discovery I had made, of course—I went on with my mind full of it—but I went on. It didn't check me. I ran past, tugging out my watch, found I had ten minutes still to spare, and then I was going downhill into familiar surroundings. I got to school, breathless, it is true, and wet with perspiration, but in time. I can remember hanging up my coat and hat. . . . Went right by it and left it behind me. Odd, eh?'

He looked at me thoughtfully. 'Of course I didn't know then that it wouldn't always be there. Schoolboys have limited imaginations. I suppose I thought it was an awfully jolly thing to have it there, to know my way back to it; but there was the school tugging at me. I expect I was a good deal distraught and inattentive that morning, recalling what I could of the beautiful strange people I should presently see again. Oddly enough I had no doubt in my mind that they would be glad to see me. . . . Yes, I must have thought of the garden that morning just as a jolly sort of place to which one might resort in the interludes of a strenuous scholastic career.

'I didn't go that day at all. The next day was a half-holiday, and that may have weighed with me. Perhaps, too, my state of inattention brought down impositions upon me, and docked the margin of time necessary for the *détour*. I don't know. What I do know is that in the meantime the enchanted garden was so much upon my mind that I could not keep it to myself.

'I told—what was his name?—a ferrety-looking youngster we used to call Squiff.'

'Young Hopkins,' said I.

'Hopkins it was. I did not like telling him. I had a feeling that in some way it was against the rules to tell him, but I did. He was walking part of the way home with me; he was talkative, and if we had not talked about the enchanted garden we should have talked of something else, and it was intolerable to me to think about any other subject. So I blabbed.

'Well, he told my secret. The next day in the play interval I found myself surrounded by half a dozen bigger boys, half teasing, and wholly curious to hear more of the enchanted garden. There was that big Fawcett—you remember him?—and Carnaby and Morley Reynolds. You weren't there by any chance? No, I think I should have remembered if you were. . . .

'A boy is a creature of odd feelings. I was, I really believe, in spite of my secret self-disgust, a little flattered to have the attention of these big fellows. I remember particularly a moment of pleasure caused by the praise of Crawshaw—you remember Crawshaw major, the son of Crawshaw the composer?—who said it was the best lie he had ever heard. But at the same time there was a really painful undertow of shame at telling what I felt was indeed a sacred secret. That beast Fawcett made a joke about the girl in green . . .'

Wallace's voice sank with the keen memory of that shame. 'I pretended not to hear,' he said. 'Well, then Carnaby suddenly called me a young liar, and disputed with me when I said the thing was true. I said I knew where to find the green door, could lead them all there in ten minutes. Carnaby became outrageously virtuous, and said I'd have to—and bear out my words or suffer. Did you ever have Carnaby twist your arm? Then perhaps you'll understand how it went with me. I swore my story was true.

There was nobody in the school then to save a chap from Carnaby, though Crawshaw put in a word or so. Carnaby had got his game. I grew excited and red-eared, and a little frightened. I behaved altogether like a silly little chap, and the outcome of it all was that instead of starting alone for my enchanted garden, I led the way presently—cheeks flushed, ears hot, eyes smarting, and my soul one burning misery and shame—for a party of six mocking, curious, and threatening schoolfellows.

'We never found the white wall and the green door. . . .'

'You mean——?'

'I mean I couldn't find it. I would have found it if I could.

'And afterwards when I could go alone I couldn't find it. I never found it. I seem now to have been always looking for it through my school-boy days, but I never came upon it—never.'

'Did the fellows—make it disagreeable?'

'Beastly. . . . Carnaby held a council over me for wanton lying. I remember how I sneaked home and upstairs to hide the marks of my blubbering. But when I cried myself to sleep at last it wasn't for Carnaby, but for the garden, for the beautiful afternoon I had hoped for, for the sweet friendly women and the waiting playfellows, and the game I had hoped to learn again, that beautiful forgotten game. . . .

'I believed firmly that if I had not told . . . I had bad times after that—crying at night and wool-gathering by day. For two terms I slacked and had bad reports. Do you remember? Of course you would! It was *you*—your beating me in mathematics that brought me back to the grind again.'

3

For a time my friend stared silently into the red heart of the fire. Then he said: 'I never saw it again until I was seventeen.

'It leaped upon me for the third time—as I was driving to Paddington on my way to Oxford and a scholarship. I had just one momentary glimpse. I was leaning over the apron of my hansom smoking a cigarette, and no doubt thinking myself no end of a man of the world, and suddenly there was the door, the wall, the dear sense of unforgettable and still attainable things.

'We clattered by—I too taken by surprise to stop my cab until we were well past and round a corner. Then I had a queer moment, a double and divergent movement of my will: I tapped the little door in the roof of the cab, and brought my arm down to pull out my watch. "Yes, sir!" said the cabman, smartly. "Er—well—it's nothing," I cried. "*My* mistake! We haven't much time! Go on!" And he went on. . . .

'I got my scholarship. And the night after I was told of that I sat over my fire in my little upper room, my study, in my father's house, with his praise—his rare praise—and his sound counsels ringing in my ears, and I smoked my favourite pipe—the formidable bulldog of adolescence—and thought of that door in the long white wall. "If I had stopped," I thought, "I should have missed my scholarship, I should have missed Oxford—muddled all the fine career before me! I begin to see things better!" I fell musing deeply, but I did not doubt then this career of mine was a thing that merited sacrifice.

'Those dear friends and that clear atmosphere seemed very sweet to me, very fine but remote. My grip was fixing now upon the world. I saw another door opening—the door of my career.'

He stared again into the fire. Its red light picked out a stubborn strength in his face for just one flickering moment, and then it vanished again.

'Well,' he said and sighed, 'I have served that career. I have done—much work, much hard work. But I have dreamt of the enchanted garden a thousand dreams, and seen its door, or at least glimpsed its door, four times since then. Yes—four times. For a while this world was so bright and interesting, seemed so full of meaning and opportunity, that the half-effaced charm of the garden was by comparison gentle and remote. Who wants to pat panthers on the way to dinner with pretty women and distinguished men? I came down to London from Oxford, a man of bold promise that I have done something to redeem. Something—and yet there have been disappointments. . . .

'Twice I have been in love—I will not dwell on that—but once, as I went to someone who, I knew, doubted whether I dared to come, I took a short cut at a venture through an unfrequented road near Earl's Court, and so happened on a white wall and a familiar green door. "Odd!" said I to myself, "but I thought this place was on Campden Hill. It's the place I never could find somehow—like counting Stonehenge—the place of that queer daydream of mine." And I went by it intent upon my purpose. It had no appeal to me that afternoon.

'I had just a moment's impulse to try the door, three steps aside were needed at the most—though I was sure enough in my heart that it would open to me—and then I thought that doing so might delay me on the way to that appointment in which my honour was involved. Afterwards I was sorry for my punctuality—I might at least have peeped in and waved a hand to those panthers, but I knew enough by this time not to seek again belatedly that which is not found by seeking. Yes, that time made me very sorry. . . .

'Years of hard work after that, and never a sight of the door. It's only recently it has come back to me. With it there has come a sense as though some thin tarnish had spread itself over my world. I began to think of it as a sorrowful and bitter thing that I should never see that door again. Perhaps I was suffering a little from overwork—perhaps it was what I've heard spoken of as the feeling of forty. I don't know. But certainly the keen brightness that makes effort easy has gone out of things recently, and that just at a time—with all these new political developments—when I ought to be working. Odd, isn't it? But I do begin to find life toilsome, its rewards, as I come near them, cheap. I began a little while ago to want the garden quite badly. Yes—and I've seen it three times.'

'The garden?'

'No—the door! And I haven't gone in!'

He leaned over the table to me, with an enormous sorrow in his voice as he spoke. 'Thrice I have had my chance—*thrice*! If ever that door offers itself to me again, I swore, I will go in, out of this dust and heat, out of this dry glitter of vanity, out of these toilsome futilities. I will go and never return. This time I will stay. . . . I swore it, and when the time came—*I didn't go*.

'Three times in one year have I passed that door and failed to enter. Three times in the last year.

'The first time was on the night of the snatch division on the Tenants' Redemption Bill, on which the Government was saved by a majority of three. You remember? No one on our side—perhaps very few on the opposite side—expected the end that night. Then the debate collapsed like eggshells. I and Hotchkiss were dining with his cousin at Brentford; we were both unpaired, and we were called up by telephone, and set off at once in his cousin's motor. We got in barely in time, and on the way we passed my wall and door—livid in the moonlight, blotched with hot yellow as the glare of our lamps lit it, but unmistakable. "My God!" cried I. "What?" said Hotchkiss. "Nothing!" I answered, and the moment passed.

'"I've made a great sacrifice," I told the whip as I got in. "They all have," he said, and hurried by.

'I do not see how I could have done otherwise then. And the next occasion was as I rushed to my father's bedside to bid that stern old man farewell. Then, too, the claims of life were imperative. But the third time was different; it happened a week ago. It fills me with hot remorse to recall it. I was with Gurker and Ralphs—it's no secret now, you know, that I've had my talk with Gurker. We had been dining at Frobisher's, and the talk had become intimate between us. The question of my place in the reconstructed Ministry lay always just over the boundary of the discussion. Yes—yes. That's all settled. It needn't be talked about yet, but there's no reason to keep a secret from you . . . Yes—thanks! thanks! But let me tell you my story.

'Then, on that night things were very much in the air. My position was a very delicate one. I was keenly anxious to get some definite word from Gurker, but was hampered by Ralphs' presence. I was using the best power of my brain to keep that light and careless talk not too obviously directed to the point that concerned me. I had to. Ralphs' behaviour since has more than justified my caution. . . . Ralphs, I knew, would leave us beyond the Kensington High Street, and then I could surprise Gurker by a sudden frankness. One has sometimes to resort to these little devices. . . . And then it was that in the margin of my field of vision I became aware once more of the white wall, the green door before us down the road.

'We passed it talking. I passed it. I can still see the shadow of Gurker's marked profile, his opera hat tilted forward over his prominent nose, the many folds of his neck wrap going before my shadow and Ralphs' as we sauntered past.

'I passed within twenty inches of the door. "If I say good-night to them, and go in," I asked myself, "what will happen?" And I was all a-tingle for that word with Gurker.

'I could not answer that question in the tangle of my other problems. "They will think me mad," I thought. "And suppose I vanish now—amazing disappearance of a prominent politician!" That weighed with me. A thousand inconceivable petty worldlinesses weighed with me in that crisis.'

Then he turned on me with a sorrowful smile, and, speaking slowly, 'Here I am!' he said.

'Here I am!' he repeated, 'and my chance has gone from me. Three times in one year the door has been offered me—the door that goes into peace, into delight, into a beauty beyond dreaming, a kindness no man on earth can know. And I have rejected it, Redmond, and it has gone——'

'How do you know?'

'I know. I know. I am left now to work it out, to stick to the tasks that held me so strongly when my moments came. You say I have success—this vulgar, tawdry, irksome, envied thing. I have it.' He had a walnut in his big hand. 'If that was my success,' he said, and crushed it, and held it out for me to see.

'Let me tell you something, Redmond. This loss is destroying me. For two months, for ten weeks nearly now, I have done no work at all, except the most necessary and urgent duties. My soul is full of inappeasable regrets. At nights—when it is less likely I shall be recognised—I go out. I wander. Yes. I wonder what people would think of that if they knew. A Cabinet Minister, the responsible head of that most vital of all departments, wandering alone—grieving—sometimes near audibly lamenting—for a door, for a garden!'

4

I can see now his rather pallid face, and the unfamiliar sombre fire that had come into his eyes. I see him very vividly to-night. I sit recalling his words, his tones, and last evening's *Westminster Gazette* still lies on my sofa, containing the notice of his death. At lunch to-day the club was busy with his death. We talked of nothing else.

They found his body very early yesterday morning in a deep excavation near East Kensington Station. It is one of two shafts that have been made in connection with an extension of the railway southward. It is protected from the intrusion of the public by a hoarding upon the high road, in which a small doorway has been cut for the convenience of some of the workmen who live in that direction. The doorway was left unfastened through a misunderstanding between two gangers, and through it he made his way.

My mind is darkened with questions and riddles.

It would seem he walked all the way from the House that night—he has frequently walked home during the past Session—and so it is I figure his dark form coming along the late and empty streets, wrapped up, intent. And then did the pale electric lights near the station cheat the rough planking into a semblance of white? Did that fatal unfastened door awaken some memory?

Was there, after all, ever any green door in the wall at all?

I do not know. I have told his story as he told it to me. There are times when I believe that Wallace was no more than the victim of the coincidence between a rare but not unprecedented type of hallucination and a careless trap, but that indeed is not my profoundest belief. You may think me superstitious, if you will, and foolish; but, indeed, I am more than half convinced that he had, in truth, an abnormal gift, and a sense, something—I know not what—that in the guise of wall and door offered him an outlet, a secret and peculiar passage of escape into another and altogether more beautiful world. At any rate, you will say, it betrayed him in the end. But did it betray him? There you touch the inmost mystery of these dreamers, these men of vision and the imagination. We see our world fair and common, the hoarding and the pit. By our daylight standard he walked out of security into darkness, danger, and death.

But did he see like that?

M. R. James

THE HAUNTED DOLL'S HOUSE

'I SUPPOSE you get stuff of that kind through your hands pretty often?' said Mr Dillet, as he pointed with his stick to an object which shall be described when the time comes: and when he said it, he lied in his throat, and knew that he lied. Not once in twenty years—perhaps not once in a lifetime—could Mr Chittenden, skilled as he was in ferreting out the forgotten treasures of half-a-dozen counties, expect to handle such a specimen. It was collectors' palaver, and Mr Chittenden recognized it as such.

'Stuff of that kind, Mr Dillet! It's a museum piece, that is.'

'Well, I suppose there are museums that'll take anything.'

'I've seen one, not as good as that, years back,' said Mr Chittenden, thoughtfully. 'But that's not likely to come into the market: and I'm told they 'ave some fine ones of the period over the water. No: I'm only telling you the truth, Mr Dillet, when I say that if you was to place an unlimited order with me for the very best that could be got—and you know I 'ave facilities for getting to know of such things, and a reputation to maintain—well, all I can say is, I should lead you straight up to that one and say, "I can't do no better for you than that, Sir."'

'Hear, hear!' said Mr Dillet, applauding ironically with the end of his stick on the floor of the shop. 'How much are you sticking the innocent American buyer for it, eh?'

'Oh, I shan't be over hard on the buyer, American or otherwise. You see, it stands this way, Mr Dillet—if I knew just a bit more about the pedigree——'

'Or just a bit less,' Mr Dillet put in.

'Ha, ha! you will have your joke, Sir. No, but as I was saying, if I knew just a little more than what I do about the piece—though anyone can see for themselves it's a genuine thing, every last corner of it, and there's not been one of my men allowed to so much as touch it since it came into the shop—there'd be another figure in the price I'm asking.'

'And what's that: five and twenty?'

'Multiply that by three and you've got it, Sir. Seventy-five's my price.'

'And fifty's mine,' said Mr Dillet.

The point of agreement was, of course, somewhere between the two, it does not matter exactly where—I think sixty guineas. But half an hour later the object was being packed, and within an hour Mr Dillet had called for it in his car and driven away. Mr Chittenden, holding the cheque in his hand, saw him off from the door with smiles, and returned, still smiling, into the parlour where his wife was making the tea. He stopped at the door.

'It's gone,' he said.

'Thank God for that!' said Mrs Chittenden, putting down the teapot. 'Mr Dillet, was it?'

'Yes, it was.'

'Well, I'd sooner it was him than another.'

'Oh, I don't know, he ain't a bad feller, my dear.'

'Maybe not, but in my opinion he'd be none the worse for a bit of a shake up.'

'Well, if that's your opinion, it's my opinion he's put himself into the way of getting one. Anyhow, we shan't have no more of it, and that's something to be thankful for.'

And so Mr and Mrs Chittenden sat down to tea.

And what of Mr Dillet and of his new acquisition? What it was, the title of this story will have told you. What it was like, I shall have to indicate as well as I can.

There was only just room enough for it in the car, and Mr Dillet had to sit with the driver: he had also to go slow, for though the rooms of the Doll's House had all been stuffed carefully with soft cotton-wool, jolting was to be avoided, in view of the immense number of small objects which thronged them; and the ten-mile drive was an anxious time for him, in spite of all the precautions he insisted upon. At last his front door was reached, and Collins, the butler, came out.

'Look here, Collins, you must help me with this thing—it's a delicate job. We must get it out upright, see? It's full of little things that mustn't be displaced more than we can help. Let's see, where shall we have it?' (After a pause for consideration.) 'Really, I think I shall have to put it in my own room, to begin with at any rate. On the big table—that's it.'

It was conveyed—with much talking—to Mr Dillet's spacious room on the first floor, looking out on the drive. The sheeting was unwound from it, and the front thrown open, and for the next hour or two Mr Dillet was fully occupied in extracting the padding and setting in order the contents of the rooms.

When this thoroughly congenial task was finished, I must say that it would have been difficult to find a more perfect and attractive specimen of a Doll's House in Strawberry Hill Gothic than that which now stood on Mr Dillet's large kneehole table, lighted up by the evening sun which came slanting through three tall sash-windows.

It was quite six feet long, including the chapel or oratory which flanked the front on the left as you faced it, and the stable on the right. The main block of the house was, as I have said, in the Gothic manner: that is to say, the windows had pointed arches and were surmounted by what are called ogival hoods, with crockets and finials such as we see on the canopies of tombs built into church walls. At the angles were absurd turrets covered with arched panels. The chapel had pinnacles and buttresses and a bell in the turret and coloured glass in the windows. When the front of the house was open you saw four large rooms, bedroom, dining-room, drawing-room and kitchen, each with its appropriate furniture in a very complete state.

The stable on the right was in two storeys, with its proper complement of horses, coaches and grooms, and with its clock and Gothic cupola for the clock bell.

Pages, of course, might be written on the outfit of the mansion—how many frying pans, how many gilt chairs, what pictures, carpets, chandeliers, four-posters, table linen, glass, crockery and plate it possessed; but all this must be left to the imagination. I will only say that the base or plinth on which the house stood (for it was fitted with one of some depth which allowed of a flight of steps to the front door and a terrace, partly balustraded) contained a shallow drawer or drawers in which were neatly stored sets of embroidered curtains, changes of raiment for the inmates, and, in short, all the materials for an infinite series of variations and refittings of the most absorbing and delightful kind.

'Quintessence of Horace Walpole, that's what it is: he must have had something to do with the making of it.' Such was Mr Dillet's murmured reflection as he knelt before it in a reverent ecstasy. 'Simply wonderful; this is my day and no mistake. Five hundred pound coming in this morning for that cabinet which I never cared about, and now this tumbling into my hands for a tenth, at the very most, of what it would fetch in town. Well, well! It almost makes one afraid something'll happen to counter it. Let's have a look at the population, anyhow.'

Accordingly, he set them before him in a row. Again, here is an opportunity, which some would snatch at, of making an inventory of costume: I am incapable of it.

There were a gentleman and lady, in blue satin and brocade respectively. There were two children, a boy and a girl. There was a cook, a nurse, a footman, and there were the stable servants, two postillions, a coachman, two grooms.

'Anyone else? Yes, possibly.'

The curtains of the four-poster in the bedroom were closely drawn round four sides of it, and he put his finger in between them and felt in the bed. He drew the finger back hastily, for it almost seemed to him as if something had—not stirred, perhaps, but yielded—in an odd live way as he pressed it. Then he put back the curtains, which ran on rods in the proper manner, and extracted from the bed a white-haired old gentleman in a long linen nightdress and cap, and laid him down by the rest. The tale was complete.

Dinner time was now near, so Mr Dillet spent but five minutes in putting the lady and children into the drawing-room, the gentleman into the dining-room, the servants into the kitchen and stables, and the old man back into his bed. He retired into his

It seemed to him as if something had vielded in an odd live way . . .

dressing room next door, and we see and hear no more of him until something like eleven o'clock at night.

His whim was to sleep surrounded by some of the gems of his collection. The big room in which we have seen him contained his bed: bath, wardrobe, and all the appliances of dressing were in a commodious room adjoining: but his four-poster, which itself was a valued treasure, stood in the large room where he sometimes wrote, and often sat, and even received visitors. Tonight he repaired to it in a highly complacent frame of mind.

There was no striking clock within earshot—none on the staircase, none in the stable, none in the distant church tower. Yet it is indubitable that Mr Dillet was startled out of a very pleasant slumber by a bell tolling One.

He was so much startled that he did not merely lie breathless with wide-open eyes, but actually sat up in his bed.

He never asked himself, till the morning hours, how it was that, though there was no light at all in the room, the Doll's House on the kneehole table stood out with complete clearness. But it was so. The effect was that of a bright harvest moon shining full on the front of a big white stone mansion—a quarter of a mile away it might be, and yet every detail was photographically sharp. There were trees about it, too—trees rising behind the chapel and the house. He seemed to be conscious of the scent of a cool still September night. He thought he could hear an occasional stamp and clink from the stables, as of horses stirring. And with another shock he realized that, above the house, he was looking, not at the wall of his room with its pictures, but into the profound blue of a night sky.

There were lights, more than one, in the windows, and he quickly saw that this was no four-roomed house with a movable front, but one of many rooms, and staircases—a real house, but seen as if through the wrong end of a telescope. 'You mean to show me something,' he muttered to himself, and he gazed earnestly on the lighted windows. They would in real life have been shuttered or curtained, no doubt, he thought; but, as it was, there was nothing to intercept his view of what was being transacted inside the rooms.

Two rooms were lighted—one on the ground floor to the right of the door, one upstairs, on the left—the first brightly enough, the other rather dimly. The lower room was the dining-room: a table was laid, but the meal was over, and only wine and glasses were left on the table. The man of the blue satin and the woman of the brocade were alone in the room, and they were talking very earnestly, seated close together at the table, their elbows on it: every now and again stopping to listen, as it seemed. Once *he* rose, came to the window and opened it and put his head out and his hand to his ear. There was a lighted taper in a silver candlestick on a sideboard. When the man left the window he seemed to leave the room also; and the lady, taper in hand, remained standing and listening. The expression on her face was that of one striving her utmost to keep down a fear that threatened to master her—and succeeding. It was a hateful face, too; broad, flat and sly. Now the man came back and she took some small thing from him and hurried out of the room. He, too, disappeared, but only for a moment or two. The front door slowly opened and he stepped out and stood on the top of the *perron*, looking this way and that; then turned towards the upper window that was lighted, and shook his fist.

It was time to look at that upper window. Through it was seen a four-post bed: a nurse or other servant in an arm-chair, evidently sound asleep; in the bed an old man lying: awake, and, one would say, anxious, from the way in which he shifted about and moved his fingers, beating tunes on the coverlet. Beyond the bed a door opened. Light was seen on the ceiling, and the lady came in: she set down her candle on a table, came to the fireside and roused the nurse. In her hand she had an old-fashioned wine bottle, ready uncorked. The nurse took it, poured some of the contents into a little silver sauce-pan, added some spice and sugar from casters on the table, and set it to warm on the fire. Meanwhile the old man in the bed beckoned feebly to the lady, who came to him smiling, took his wrist as if to feel his pulse, and bit her lip as if in consternation. He looked at her anxiously, and then pointed to the window, and spoke. She nodded, and did as the man below had done; opened the casement and listened—perhaps rather ostentatiously: then drew in her head and shook it, looking at the old man, who seemed to sigh.

By this time the posset on the fire was steaming, and the nurse poured it into a small two-handled silver bowl and brought it to the bedside. The old man seemed disinclined for it and was waving it away, but the lady and the nurse together bent over him and evidently pressed it upon him. He must have yielded, for they supported him into a sitting position, and put it to his lips. He drank most of it, in several draughts, and they laid him down. The lady left the room, smiling good-night to him, and took the bowl, the bottle and the silver sauce-pan with her. The nurse returned to the chair, and there was an interval of complete quiet.

Suddenly the old man started up in his bed—and he must have uttered some cry, for the nurse started out of her chair and made but one step of it to the bedside. He was a sad and terrible sight—flushed in the face, almost to blackness, the eyes glaring whitely, both hands clutching at his heart, foam at his lips.

For a moment the nurse left him, ran to the door, flung it wide open, and, one supposes, screamed aloud for help, then darted back to the bed and seemed to try feverishly to soothe him—to lay him down—anything. But as the lady, her husband, and several servants, rushed into the room with horrified faces, the old man collapsed under the nurse's hands and lay back, and the features, contorted with agony and rage, relaxed slowly into calm.

A few moments later, lights showed out to the left of the house, and a coach with flambeaux drove up to the door. A white-wigged man in black got nimbly out and ran up the steps, carrying a small leather trunk-shaped box. He was met in the doorway by the man and his wife, she with her handkerchief clutched between her hands, he with a tragic face, but retaining his self-control. They led the newcomer into the dining-room, where he set his box of papers on the table, and, turning to them, listened with a face of consternation at what they had to tell. He nodded his head again and again, threw out his hands slightly, declined, it seemed, offers of refreshment and lodging for the night, and within a few minutes came slowly down the steps entering the coach and driving off the way he had come. As the man in blue watched him from the top of the steps, a smile not pleasant to see stole slowly over his fat white face. Darkness fell over the whole scene as the lights of the coach disappeared.

But Mr Dillet remained sitting up in the bed: he had rightly guessed that there would be a sequel. The house front glimmered out again before long. But now there was a difference. The lights were in other windows, one at the top of the house, the other illuminating the range of coloured windows of the chapel. How he saw through these is not quite obvious, but he did. The interior was as carefully furnished as the rest of the establishment, with its minute red cushions on the desks, its Gothic stall-canopies, and its western gallery and pinnacled organ with gold pipes. On the centre of the black and white pavement was a bier: four tall candles burned at the corners. On the bier was a coffin covered with a pall of black velvet.

As he looked the folds of the pall stirred. It seemed to rise at one end: it slid downwards: it fell away, exposing the black coffin with its silver handles and name-plate. One of the tall candlesticks swayed and toppled over. Ask no more, but turn, as Mr Dillet hastily did, and look in at the lighted window at the top of the house, where a boy and girl lay in two truckle-beds, and a four-poster for the nurse rose above them. The nurse was not visible for the moment; but the father and mother were there, dressed now in mourning, but with very little sign of mourning in their demeanour. Indeed, they were laughing and talking with a good deal of animation, sometimes to each other, and sometimes throwing a remark to one or other of the children, and again laughing at the answers. Then the father was seen to go on tiptoe out of the room, taking with him as he went a white garment that hung on a peg near the door. He shut the door after him. A minute or two later it was slowly opened again, and a muffled head poked round it. A bent form of sinister shape stepped across to the truckle-beds, and suddenly stopped, threw up its arms and revealed, of course, the father, laughing. The children were in agonies of terror, the boy with the bed clothes over his head, the girl throwing herself out of bed into her mother's arms. Attempts at consolation followed—the parents took the children on their laps, patted them, picked up the white gown and showed there was no harm in it, and so forth; and at last putting the children back into bed, left the room with encouraging waves of the hand. As they left it, the nurse came in, and soon the light died down.

Still Mr Dillet watched immovable.

A new sort of light—not of lamp or candle—a pale ugly light, began to dawn around the door-case at the back of the room. The door was opening again. The seer does not like to dwell upon what he saw entering the room: he says it might be described as a frog—the size of a man—but it had scanty white hair about its head. It was busy about the truckle-beds, but not for long. The sound of cries—faint, as if coming out of a vast distance—but, even so, infinitely appalling, reached the ear.

There were signs of a hideous commotion all over the house: lights passed along and up, and doors opened and shut, and running figures passed within the windows. The clock in the stable turret tolled one, and darkness fell again.

It was only dispelled once more, to show the house front. At the bottom of the steps dark figures were drawn up in two lines, holding flaming torches. More dark figures came down the steps, bearing, first one, then another small coffin. And the lines of torch-bearers with the coffins between them moved silently onward to the left.

The hours of night passed on—never so slowly, Mr Dillet thought. Gradually he sank down from sitting to lying in his bed—but he did not close an eye: and early next morning he sent for the doctor.

The doctor found him in a disquieting state of nerves, and recommended sea-air. To a quiet place on the East Coast he accordingly repaired by easy stages in his car.

One of the first people he met on the sea front was Mr Chittenden, who, it appeared, had likewise been advised to take his wife away for a bit of a change.

Mr Chittenden looked somewhat askance upon him when they met: and not without cause.

'Well, I don't wonder at you being a bit upset, Mr Dillet. What? yes, well, I might say 'orrible upset, to be sure, seeing what me and my poor wife went through ourselves. But I put it to you, Mr Dillet, one of two things: was I going to scrap a lovely piece like that on the one 'and, or was I going to tell customers: "I'm selling you a regular picture-palace-dramar in reel life of the olden time, billed to perform regular at one o'clock a.m."? Why, what would you 'ave said yourself? And next thing you know, two Justices of the Peace in the back parlour, and pore Mr and Mrs Chittenden off in a spring cart to the County Asylum and everyone in the street saying, "Ah, I thought it 'ud come to that. Look at the way the man drank!"—and me next door, or next door but one, to a total abstainer, as you know. Well, there was my position. What? Me 'ave it back in the shop? Well, what do *you* think? No, but I'll tell you what I will do. You shall have your money back, bar the ten pound I paid for it, and you make what you can.'

Later in the day, in what is offensively called the 'smoke-room' of the hotel, a murmured conversation between the two went on for some time.

'How much do you really know about that thing, and where it came from?'

'Honest, Mr Dillet, I don't know the 'ouse. Of course, it came out of the lumber room of a country 'ouse—that anyone could guess. But I'll go as far as say this, that I believe it's not a hundred miles from this place. Which direction and how far I've no notion. I'm only judging by guess-work. The man as I actually paid the cheque to ain't one of my regular men, and I've lost sight of him; but I 'ave the idea that this part of the country was hi, beat, and that's every word I can tell you. But now, Mr Dillets there's one thing that rather physicks me—that old chap—I suppose you saw him drive up to the door—I thought so: now, would he have been the medical man, do you take it? My wife would have it so, but I stuck to it that was the lawyer, because he had papers with him, and one he took out was folded up.'

'I agree,' said Mr Dillet. 'Thinking it over, I came to the conclusion that was the old man's will, ready to be signed.'

'Just what I thought,' said Mr Chittenden, 'and I took it that will would have cut out the young people, eh? Well, well! It's been a lesson to me, I know that. I shan't buy no more dolls' houses, nor waste no more money on the pictures—and as to this business of poisonin' grandpa, well, if I know myself, I never 'ad much of a turn for that. Live and let live: that's bin my motto throughout life, and I ain't found it a bad one.'

Filled with these elevated sentiments, Mr Chittenden retired to his lodgings. Mr Dillet next day repaired to the local Institute, where he hoped to find some clue to the riddle that absorbed him.

He gazed in despair at a long file of the Canterbury and York Society's publications of the Parish Registers of the district. No print resembling the house of his nightmare was among those that hung on the staircase and in the passages. Disconsolate, he found himself at last in a derelict room, staring at a dusty model of a church in a dusty glass case: *Model of St Stephen's Church, Coxham. Presented by J. Merewether, Esq., of Ilbridge House, 1877. The work of his ancestor James Merewether, d. 1786.* There was something in the fashion of it that reminded him dimly of his horror. He retraced his steps to a wall map he had noticed, and made out that Ilbridge House was in Coxham Parish. Coxham was, as it happened, one of the parishes of which he had retained the name when he glanced over the file of printed registers, and it was not long before he found in them the record of the burial of Roger Milford, aged 76, on the 11th of September, 1757, and of Roger and Elizabeth Merewether, aged 9 and 7, on the 19th of the same month. It seemed worth while to follow up this clue, frail as it was; and in the afternoon he drove out to Coxham. The east end of the north aisle of the church is a Milford chapel, and on its north wall are tablets to the same persons; Roger, the elder, it seems, was distinguished by all the qualities which adorn 'the Father, the Magistrate, and the Man': the memorial was erected by his attached daughter Elizabeth, 'who did not long survive the loss of a parent ever solicitous for her welfare, and of two amiable children.' The last sentence was plainly an addition to the original inscription.

A yet later slab told of James Merewether, husband of Elizabeth, 'who in the dawn of life practised, not without success, those arts which, had he continued their exercise, might in the opinion of the most competent judges have earned for him the name of the British Vitruvius: but who, overwhelmed by the visitation which deprived him of an affectionate partner and a blooming offspring, passed his Prime and Age in a secluded yet elegant Retirement: his grateful Nephew and Heir indulges a pious sorrow by this too brief recital of his excellences.'

The children were more simply commemorated. Both died on the night of the 12th of September.

Mr Dillet felt sure that in Ilbridge House he had found the scene of his drama. In some old sketch-book, possibly in some old print, he may yet find convincing evidence that he is right. But the Ilbridge House of to-day is not that which he sought; it is an Elizabethan erection of the forties, in red brick with stone quoins and dressings. A quarter of a mile from it, in a low part of the park, backed by ancient, stag-horned, ivy-strangled trees and thick undergrowth, are marks of a terraced platform overgrown with rough grass. A few stone balusters lie here and there, and a heap or two, covered with nettles and ivy, of wrought stones with badly carved crockets. This, someone told Mr Dillet, was the site of an older house.

As he drove out of the village, the hall clock struck four, and Mr Dillet started up and clapped his hands to his ears. It was not the first time he had heard that bell.

Awaiting an offer from the other side of the Atlantic, the doll's house still reposes, carefully sheeted, in a loft over Mr Dillet's stables, whither Collins conveyed it on the day when Mr Dillet started for the sea coast.

C. S. Lewis

FORMS OF THINGS UNKNOWN

'BEFORE the class breaks up, gentlemen,' said the instructor, 'I should like to make some reference to a fact which is known to some of you, but probably not yet to all. High Command, I need not remind you, has asked for a volunteer for yet one more attempt on the Moon. It will be the fourth. You know the history of the previous three. In each case the explorers landed unhurt; or at any rate alive. We got their messages. Every message short, some apparently interrupted. And after that never a word, gentlemen. I think the man who offers to make the fourth voyage has about as much courage as anyone I've heard of. And I can't tell you how proud it makes me that he is one of my own pupils. He is in this room at this moment. We wish him every possible good fortune. Gentlemen, I ask you to give three cheers for Lieutenant John Jenkin.'

Then the class became a cheering crowd for two minutes; after that a hurrying, talkative crowd in the corridor. The two biggest cowards exchanged the various family reasons which had deterred them from volunteering themselves. The knowing man said, 'There's something behind all this.' The vermin said, 'He always was a chap who'd do anything to get himself into the limelight.' But most just shouted out, 'Jolly good show, Jenkin,' and wished him luck.

Ward and Jenkin got away together into a pub.

'You kept this pretty dark,' said Ward. 'What's yours?'

'A pint of draught Bass,' said Jenkin.

'Do you want to talk about it?' said Ward rather awkwardly when the drinks had come. 'I mean—if you won't think I'm butting in, it's not just because of that girl, is it?'

That girl was a young woman who was thought to have treated Jenkin rather badly.

'Well,' said Jenkin, 'I don't suppose I'd be going if she had married me. But it's not a spectacular attempt at suicide or any rot of that sort. I'm not depressed. I don't feel anything particular about her. Not much interested in women at all, to tell you the truth. Not now. A bit petrified.'

'What is it then?'

'Sheer unbearable curiosity. I've read those three little messages over and over till I know them by heart. I've heard every theory there is about what interrupted them. I've——'

'Is it certain they were all interrupted? I thought one of them was supposed to be complete.'

'You mean Traill and Henderson? I think it was as incomplete as the others. First there was Stafford. He went alone, like me.'

'Must you? I'll come, if you'll have me.'

Jenkin shook his head. 'I know you would,' he said. 'But you'll see in a moment why I don't want you to. But to go back to the messages. Stafford's was obviously cut short by something. It went *Stafford from within 50 miles of Point XO308 on the Moon. My landing was excellent. I have*—then silence. Then come Traill and Henderson. *We have landed. We are perfectly well. The ridge M392 is straight ahead of me as I speak. Over.*'

'What do you make of *Over*?'

'Not what you do. You think it means *finis*—the message is over. But who in the world, speaking to Earth from the Moon for the first time in all history, would have so little to say—if he *could* say any more? As if he'd crossed to Calais and sent his grandmother a card to say, "Arrived safely". The thing's ludicrous.'

'Well, what do *you* make of *Over*?'

'Wait a moment. The last lot were Trevor, Woodford, and Fox. It was Fox who sent the message. Remember it?'

'Probably not so accurately as you.'

'Well, it was this. *This is Fox speaking. All has gone wonderfully well. A perfect landing. You shot pretty well for I'm on Point XO308 at this moment. Ridge M392 straight ahead. On my left, far away across the crater I see the big peaks. On my right I see the Yerkes cleft. Behind me.* Got it?'

'I don't see the point.'

'Well, Fox was cut off the moment he said *behind me*. Supposing Traill was cut off in the middle of saying, "Over my shoulder I can see" or "Over behind me" or something like that?'

'You mean . . . ?'

'All the evidence is consistent with the view that everything went well till the speaker looked behind him, then something got him.'

'What sort of a something?'

'That's what I want to find out. One idea in my head is this. Might there be something on the Moon—or something psychological about the experience of landing on the Moon—which drives men fighting mad?'

'I see. You mean Fox looked round just in time to see Trevor and Woodford preparing to knock him on the head?'

'Exactly. And Traill—for it was Traill—just in time to see Henderson a split second before Henderson murdered him. And that's why I'm not going to risk having a companion; least of all my best friend.'

'This doesn't explain Stafford.'

'No. That's why one can't rule out the other hypothesis.'

'What's it?'

'Oh, that whatever killed them all was something they found there. Something lunar.'

'You're surely not going to suggest life on the Moon at this time of day?'

'The word *life* always begs the question. Because, of course, it suggests organization as we know it on Earth—with all the chemistry which organization involves. Of course there could hardly be anything of that sort. But there might—I at any rate can't say there couldn't—be masses of matter capable of movements determined from within, determined, in fact, by intentions.'

'Oh Lord, Jenkin, that's nonsense. Animated stones, no doubt! That's mere science-fiction or mythology.'

'Going to the Moon at all was once science-fiction. And as for mythology, haven't they found the Cretan labyrinth?'

'And all it really comes down to,' said Ward, 'is that no one has ever come back from the Moon, and no one, so far as we know, ever survived there for more than a few minutes. Damn the whole thing.' He stared gloomily into his tankard.

'Well,' said Jenkin cheerily. 'Somebody's got to go. The whole human race isn't going to be licked by any blasted satellite.'

'I might have known that was your real reason,' said Ward.

Where the head should have bee

'Have another pint and don't look so glum,' said Jenkin. 'Anyway, there's loads of time. I don't suppose they'll get me off for another six months at the earliest.'

But there was hardly any time. Like any man in the modern world on whom tragedy has descended or who has undertaken a high enterprise, he lived for the next few months a life not unlike that of a hunted animal. The Press, with all their cameras and notebooks, were after him. They did not care in the least whether he was allowed to eat or sleep or whether they made a nervous wreck of him before he took off. 'Flesh-flies,' he called them. When forced to address them, he always said, 'I wish I could take you all with me.' But he reflected also that a Saturn's ring of dead (and burnt) reporters circling round his space-ship might get on his nerves. They would hardly make 'the silence of those eternal spaces' any more homelike.

The take-off when it came was a relief. But the voyage was worse than he had ever anticipated. Not physically—on that side it was nothing worse than uncomfortable—but in the emotional experience. He had dreamed all his life, with mingled terror and longing, of those eternal spaces; of being utterly 'outside', in the sky. He had wondered if the agoraphobia of that roofless and bottomless vacuity would overthrow his reason. But the moment he had been shut into his ship there descended upon him the suffocating knowledge that the real danger of space-travel is claustrophobia. You have been put in a little metal container; somewhat like a cupboard, very like a coffin. You can't see out; you can see things only on the screen. Space and the stars are just

re was utter monstrosity

as remote as they were on the earth. Where you are is always your world. The sky is never where you are. All you have done is to exchange a large world of earth and rock and water and clouds for a tiny world of metal.

This frustration of a life-long desire bit deeply into his mind as the cramped hours passed. It was not, apparently, so easy to jump out of one's destiny. Then he became conscious of another motive which, unnoticed, had been at work on him when he volunteered. That affair with the girl had indeed frozen him stiff; petrified him, you might say. He wanted to feel again, to be flesh, not stone. To feel anything, even terror. Well, on this trip there would be terrors enough before all was done. He'd be wakened, never fear. That part of his destiny at least he felt he could shake off.

The landing was not without terror, but there were so many gimmicks to look after, so much skill to be exercised, that it did not amount to very much. But his heart was beating a little more noticeably than usual as he put the finishing touches to his space-suit and climbed out. He was carrying the transmission apparatus with him. It felt, as he had expected, as light as a loaf. But he was not going to send any message in a hurry. That might be where all the others had gone wrong. Anyway, the longer he waited the longer those press-men would be kept out of their beds waiting for their story. Do 'em good.

The first thing that struck him was that his helmet had been too lightly tinted. It was painful to look at all in the direction of the sun. Even the rock—it was, after all, rock not dust (which disposed of one hypothesis)—was dazzling. He put down the apparatus; tried to take in the scene.

The surprising thing was how small it looked. He thought he could account for this. The lack of atmosphere forbade nearly all the effects that distance has on earth. The serrated boundary of the crater was, he knew, about twenty-five miles away. It looked as if you could have touched it. The peaks looked as if they were a few feet high. The black sky, with its inconceivable multitude and ferocity of stars, was like a cap forced down upon the crater; the stars only just out of his reach. The impression of a stage-set in a toy theatre, therefore of something arranged, therefore of something waiting for him, was at once disappointing and oppressive. Whatever terrors there might be, here too agoraphobia would not be one of them.

He took his bearings and the result was easy enough. He was, like Fox and his friends, almost exactly on Point X0308. But there was no trace of human remains.

If he could find any, he might have some clue as to how they died. He began to hunt. He went in each circle further from the ship. There was no danger of losing it in a place like this.

Then he got his first real shock of fear. Worse still, he could not tell what was frightening him. He only knew that he was engulfed in sickening unreality; seemed neither to be where he was nor to be doing what he did. It was also somehow connected with an experience long ago. It was something that had happened in a cave. Yes; he remembered now. He had been walking along supposing himself alone and then noticed that there was always a sound of other feet following him. Then in a flash he realized what was wrong. This was the exact reverse of the experience in the cave. Then there had been too many footfalls. Now there were too few. He walked on hard rock as silently as a ghost. He swore at himself for a fool—as if every child didn't know that a world without air would be a world without noise. But the silence, though explained, became none the less terrifying.

He had now been alone on the Moon for perhaps thirty-five minutes. It was then that he noticed the three strange things.

The sun's rays were roughly at right angles to his line of sight, so that each of the things had a bright side and a dark side; for each dark side a shadow like Indian ink lay out on the rock. He thought they looked like Belisha beacons. Then he thought they looked like huge apes. They were about the height of a man. They were indeed like clumsily shaped men. Except—he resisted an impulse to vomit—that they had no heads.

They had something instead. They were (roughly) human up to their shoulders. Then, where the head should have been, there was utter monstrosity—a huge spherical block; opaque, featureless. And every one of them looked as if it had that moment stopped moving or were at that moment about to move.

Ward's phrase about 'animated stones' darted up hideously from his memory. And hadn't he himself talked of something that we couldn't call life, not in our sense, something that could nevertheless produce locomotion and have intentions? Something which, at any rate, shared with life life's tendency to kill? If there were such creatures—mineral equivalents to organisms—they could probably stand perfectly still for a hundred years without feeling any strain.

Were they aware of him? What had they for senses? The opaque globes on their shoulders gave no hint.

There comes a moment in nightmare, or sometimes in real battle, when fear and courage both dictate the same course: to rush, planless, upon the thing you are afraid of. Jenkin sprang upon the nearest of the three abominations and rapped his gloved knuckles against its globular top.

Ach!—he'd forgotten. No noise. All the bombs in the world might burst here and make no noise. Ears are useless on the Moon.

He recoiled a step and next moment found himself sprawling on the ground. 'This is how they all died,' he thought.

But he was wrong. The figure above him had not stirred. He was quite undamaged. He got up again and saw what he had tripped over.

It was a purely terrestrial object. It was, in fact, a transmission set. Not exactly like his own, but an earlier and supposedly inferior model—the sort Fox would have had.

As the truth dawned on him an excitement very different from that of terror seized him. He looked at their mis-shaped bodies; then down at his own limbs. Of course; that was what one looked like in a space suit. On his own head there was a similar monstrous globe, but fortunately not an opaque one. He was looking at three statues of spacemen: at statues of Trevor, Woodford, and Fox.

But then the Moon must have inhabitants; and rational inhabitants; more than that, artists.

And what artists! You might quarrel with their taste, for no line anywhere in any of the three statues had any beauty. You could not say a word against their skill. Except for the head and face inside each headpiece, which obviously could not be attempted in such a medium, they were perfect. Photographic accuracy had never reached such a point on earth. And though they were faceless you could see from the set of their shoulders, and indeed of their whole bodies, that a momentary pose had been exactly seized. Each was the statue of a man turning to look behind him. Months of work had doubtless gone to the carving of each; it caught that instantaneous gesture like a stone snapshot.

Jenkin's idea was now to send his message at once. Before anything happened to himself, Earth must hear this amazing news. He set off in great strides, and presently in leaps—now first enjoying lunar gravitation—for his ship and his own set. He was happy now. He *had* escaped his destiny. Petrified, eh? No more feelings? Feelings enough to last him forever.

He fixed the set so that he could stand with his back to the sun. He worked the gimmicks. 'Jenkin, speaking from the Moon,' he began.

His own huge black shadow lay out before him. There is no noise on the Moon. Up from behind the shoulders of his own shadow another shadow pushed its way along the dazzling rock. It was that of a human head. And what a head of hair. It was all rising, writhing—swaying in the wind perhaps. Very thick the hairs looked. Then, as he turned in terror, there flashed through his mind the thought, 'But there's no wind. No air. It can't be *blowing* about.' His eyes met hers.

Titles in this Series of Illustrated Classics

CHILDREN'S ILLUSTRATED CLASSICS

(Illustrated Classics for Older Readers are listed on fourth page)

Andrew Lang's ADVENTURES OF ODYSSEUS. Illustrated by KIDDELL-MONROE.
The wanderings of the great Greek hero on his way home to Ithaca.

AESOP'S FABLES. Illustrated by KIDDELL-MONROE.
A definitive translation by John Warrington.

Lewis Carroll's ALICE'S ADVENTURES IN WONDERLAND and THROUGH THE LOOKING-GLASS. Illustrated by JOHN TENNIEL.

George MacDonald's AT THE BACK OF THE NORTH WIND. Illustrated by E. H. SHEPARD.
This is the lovable and much loved story of Diamond.

Robert Louis Stevenson's THE BLACK ARROW. Illustrated by LIONEL EDWARDS.
The period is the England of the Wars of the Roses.

Anna Sewell's BLACK BEAUTY. Illustrated by LUCY KEMP-WELCH.

Roger Lancelyn Green's A BOOK OF MYTHS. Illustrated by KIDDELL-MONROE.
A retelling of the world's greatest legends and folk-tales.

THE BOOK OF NONSENSE. Edited by ROGER LANCELYN GREEN. Illustrated by CHARLES FOLKARD in colour, and with original drawings by TENNIEL, LEAR, FURNISS, HOLIDAY, HUGHES, SHEPARD and others.
Examples of 'nonsense' from ancient to modern times.

THE BOOK OF VERSE FOR CHILDREN. Collected by ROGER LANCELYN GREEN.
Illustrated with two-colour drawings in the text by MARY SHILLABEER. (Not available in the U.S.A. in this edition.)

Mrs Ewing's THE BROWNIES AND OTHER STORIES. Illustrated by E. H. SHEPARD.

Mrs Molesworth's THE CARVED LIONS. Illustrated by LEWIS HART.
An evocative story of the Manchester of a century ago.

Captain Marryat's THE CHILDREN OF THE NEW FOREST. Illustrated by LIONEL EDWARDS.
A story of adventure in a wild and romantic corner of England.

Robert Louis Stevenson's A CHILD'S GARDEN OF VERSES. Illustrated by MARY SHILLABEER.
This collection contains a number of poems not found in other editions.

Charles Dickens's A CHRISTMAS CAROL and THE CRICKET ON THE HEARTH.
Illustrated by C. E. BROCK.

R. M. Ballantyne's THE CORAL ISLAND. Illustrated by LEO BATES.
Ballantyne's most famous boys' book is illustrated with such realism that the most fascinating of islands in boys' fiction is more vivid than ever.

Susan Coolidge's WHAT KATY DID. Illustrated by MARGERY GILL.

Mrs Molesworth's THE CUCKOO CLOCK. Illustrated by E. H. SHEPARD.
Shepard's exquisite and delicate drawings enhance the enthralling text.

E. Nesbit's THE ENCHANTED CASTLE. Illustrated by CECIL LESLIE.
A sunny garden leads to a never-never land of enchantment.

FAIRY TALES FROM THE ARABIAN NIGHTS. Illustrated by KIDDELL-MONROE.
Here are the favourite tales—the fairy tales—out of the many told in the 'Thousand and One Nights'.

FAIRY TALES OF LONG AGO. Edited by M. C. CAREY. Illustrated by D. J. WATKINS-PITCHFORD.
This varied collection takes in translations from Charles Perrault, Madame de Beaumont, the Countess d'Aulnoy of France, Asbjörnsen and Moe, etc.

Selma Lagerlöf's THE FURTHER ADVENTURES OF NILS. Illustrated by HANS BAUMHAUER.
Nils's adventures continue with his flight over lake, hill, ice, snow, forest and moor of Sweden. The artist ably interprets the visual contrasts of the journey. (Not available in the U.S.A. in this edition.) *See also* THE WONDERFUL ADVENTURES OF NILS (on third page).

Louisa M. Alcott's GOOD WIVES. Illustrated by S. VAN ABBÉ.

Frances Browne's GRANNY'S WONDERFUL CHAIR. Illustrated by DENYS WATKINS-PITCHFORD.
The author, blind from birth, draws upon the Irish fairy-stories of her childhood to add magic and colour to the whole of this enchanting book.

GRIMMS' FAIRY TALES. Illustrated by CHARLES FOLKARD.

HANS ANDERSEN'S FAIRY TALES. Illustrated by HANS BAUMHAUER.
A new English rendering, including some new and outstanding tales.

Mary Mapes Dodge's HANS BRINKER. Illustrated by HANS BAUMHAUER.
This story is the best known and best loved work of the author.

Johanna Spyri's HEIDI. Illustrated by VINCENT O. COHEN.
This is the famous story of a Swiss child and her life among the Alps.

Charles Kingsley's THE HEROES. Illustrated by KIDDELL-MONROE.
A retelling of the legends of Perseus, the Argonauts and Theseus.

Louisa M. Alcott's JO'S BOYS. Illustrated by HARRY TOOTHILL.
'There is an abiding charm about the story.' *Scotsman.*

A. M. Hadfield's KING ARTHUR AND THE ROUND TABLE. Illustrated by DONALD SETON CAMMELL.
The haunting world of the Round Table.

Charlotte M. Yonge's THE LITTLE DUKE. Illustrated by MICHAEL GODFREY.
The story of Richard the Fearless, Duke of Normandy from 942 to 996.

Frances Hodgson Burnett's LITTLE LORD FAUNTLEROY.
'The best version of the Cinderella story in a modern idiom that exists.'
MARGHANITA LASKI.

Louisa M. Alcott's LITTLE MEN. Illustrated by HARRY TOOTHILL.
Harry Toothill's drawings capture the liveliness of a young gentlemen's academy.

Louisa M. Alcott's LITTLE WOMEN. Illustrated by S. VAN ABBÉ.
S. van Abbé's drawings capture the vivacity and charm of the March family.

Mrs Ewing's LOB LIE-BY-THE-FIRE and THE STORY OF A SHORT LIFE.
Illustrated by RANDOLPH CALDECOTT ('Lob') and H. M. BROCK ('Short Life').
Two of Mrs Ewing's most charming stories.

MODERN FAIRY STORIES. Edited by ROGER LANCELYN GREEN. Illustrated by E. H. SHEPARD.
Original (not 'retold') fairy stories by thirteen authors of modern times.

Jean Ingelow's **MOPSA THE FAIRY.** Illustrated by DORA CURTIS.
A river journey leads to the realms of wonder.

NURSERY RHYMES. Collected and illustrated in two-colour line by A. H. WATSON.
A comprehensive book of nursery rhymes.

Carlo Collodi's **PINOCCHIO. The Story of a Puppet.** Illustrated by CHARLES FOLKARD.
The most enchanting story of a puppet ever written.

Andrew Lang's **PRINCE PRIGIO and PRINCE RICARDO.** Illustrated by D. J. WATKINS-PITCHFORD.
Two modern fairy tales, rich in romantic adventures.

George MacDonald's **THE LOST PRINCESS**
THE PRINCESS AND CURDIE
THE PRINCESS AND THE GOBLIN
The first two volumes illustrated by CHARLES FOLKARD, the third by D. J. WATKINS-PITCHFORD.

Carola Oman's **ROBIN HOOD.** Illustrated by S. VAN ABBÉ.
Carola Oman lends substance to the 'Prince of Outlaws'.

W. M. Thackeray's **THE ROSE AND THE RING** and Charles Dickens's **THE MAGIC FISH-BONE.**
Two children's stories, the first containing the author's illustrations, the latter containing PAUL HOGARTH'S work.

J. R. Wyss's **THE SWISS FAMILY ROBINSON.** Illustrated by CHARLES FOLKARD.
This is a new version by Audrey Clark of the popular classic.

Charles and Mary Lamb's **TALES FROM SHAKESPEARE.** Illustrated by ARTHUR RACKHAM.

TALES OF MAKE-BELIEVE. Edited by ROGER LANCELYN GREEN. Illustrated by HARRY TOOTHILL.
Charles Dickens, Rudyard Kipling, E. Nesbit, Thomas Hardy, E. V. Lucas, etc.

Nathaniel Hawthorne's **TANGLEWOOD TALES.** Illustrated by S. VAN ABBÉ.
This is a sequel to the famous *Wonder Book*.

Thomas Hughes's **TOM BROWN'S SCHOOLDAYS.** Illustrated by S. VAN ABBÉ.
'The best story of a boy's schooldays ever written.'

Charles Kingsley's **THE WATER-BABIES.** Illustrated by ROSALIE K. FRY.
The artist's drawings delicately interpret the fantastic beauty of the underwater world.

Nathaniel Hawthorne's **A WONDER BOOK.** Illustrated by S. VAN ABBÉ.
Hawthorne's famous *Wonder Book* recalls the immortal fables of antiquity.

Selma Lagerlöf's **THE WONDERFUL ADVENTURES OF NILS.** Illustrated by HANS BAUMHAUER.
Translated into most languages of the world, this Swedish tale of the boy who rode on the back of a young gander and flew northwards to find surprising adventures is a great favourite. (Not available in the U.S.A. in this edition.)
See also THE FURTHER ADVENTURES OF NILS.